PENGUIN BOOKS

CARRY THE ONE

Praise for Carry the One *from the USA:*

'You'll love this compelling book' *Entertainm...*

'Carol Anshaw is one of those authors who should be a household name . . . . eloquent novel' *USA Today*

'Moving and engaging . . . Anshaw has written not only a funny, smart and closely observed story, but also one that explores the way tragedy can follow hard on celebration, binding people together even more lastingly than passion' *The New York Times Book Review*

'Provocative . . . dead-on' *Dallas Morning News*

'Beautifully observed . . . intimately dissects how one event or choice can alter the trajectory of a life, how a fork in the road can lead to wholly unexpected and divergent outcomes' Michiko Kakutani, *The New York Times*

'Graceful and compassionate . . . writing with rueful wit and a subtle understanding of the currents and passions that rule us, Anshaw demonstrates that struggling to do one's best, whatever the circumstances, makes for a life of consequence' *People*

'Anshaw is that rare, brilliant, witty writer whose prose is rich and buttery, and whose plotting is as well-conceived and seamlessly executed as that of the most intricate thriller' *Chicago Tribune*

'Here's passion and addiction, guilt and damage, all the beautiful mess of family life. *Carry the One* will lift readers off their feet and bear them along on its eloquent tide' Emma Donoghue

'Superb . . . Anshaw has a knack for capturing a personality in a single phrase' *Financial Times*

'A brilliant feat of storytelling . . . one of the most intensely vibrant novels I've ever read' *Boston Globe*

ABOUT THE AUTHOR

Carol Anshaw is the author of *Aquamarine, Seven Moves* and *Lucky in the Corner*. She has received the Ferro-Grumley Award, the Carl Sandburg Literary Arts Award for Fiction and a National Book Critics Circle Citation for Excellence in Reviewing. She lives in Chicago. You can visit her website at www.carolanshaw.com.

carry the one

carol anshaw

PENGUIN BOOKS

PENGUIN BOOKS

Published by the Penguin Group
Penguin Books Ltd, 80 Strand, London WC2R 0RL, England
Penguin Group (USA) Inc., 375 Hudson Street, New York, New York 10014, USA
Penguin Group (Canada), 90 Eglinton Avenue East, Suite 700, Toronto, Ontario, Canada M4P 2Y3
(a division of Pearson Penguin Canada Inc.)
Penguin Ireland, 25 St Stephen's Green, Dublin 2, Ireland (a division of Penguin Books Ltd)
Penguin Group (Australia), 707 Collins Street, Melbourne, Victoria 3008, Australia
(a division of Pearson Australia Group Pty Ltd)
Penguin Books India Pvt Ltd, 11 Community Centre, Panchsheel Park, New Delhi – 110 017, India
Penguin Group (NZ), 67 Apollo Drive, Rosedale, Auckland 0632, New Zealand
(a division of Pearson New Zealand Ltd)
Penguin Books (South Africa) (Pty) Ltd, Block D, Rosebank Office Park,
181 Jan Smuts Avenue, Parktown North, Gauteng 2193, South Africa

Penguin Books Ltd, Registered Offices: 80 Strand, London WC2R 0RL, England

www.penguin.com

First published in the United States of America by Simon & Schuster 2012
First published in Great Britain by Penguin Books 2012
001

Two sections of this book were originally published in slightly different versions as stories – 'Hammam' in *Story*, then in *Best American Short Stories*; 'Touch and Go' in *Tin House*

Printed in England by Clays Ltd, St Ives plc

ISBN: 978–0–241–96396–8

www.greenpenguin.co.uk

Penguin Books is committed to a sustainable future for our business, our readers and our planet. This book is made from Forest Stewardship Council™ certified paper.

ALWAYS LEARNING PEARSON

in memory of my brother, doug

oh the night came undone like a party dress

and fell at her feet in a beautiful mess.

—*"barroom girls"*
gillian welch/david rawlings

carry the one

hat dance

So Carmen was married, just. She sat under a huge butter moon, on a windless night in the summer of 1983, at a table, in front of the remains of some chicken cordon bleu. She looked toward the improvised dance floor where her very new husband was doing the Mexican hat dance with several other large men, three of them his brothers, other Sloans. Matt was a plodding hat-dancer; his kicks threw the others off the beat. In spite of this lack of aptitude, he was waving her over, beckoning her to join in. She waved back as though she thought he was just saying hi. She was hoping to sit out this early phase of her marriage, the mortifying dances segment.

"Don't be discouraged. Everything will get better from here."

This was Jean Arbuthnot, who sat next to Carmen, tapping the ash off her cigarette, onto her rice pilaf. Jean and Alice, Carmen's sister, were among the artists who had taken over this old farm in the middle of Wisconsin. Jean played and recorded traditional folk music in a workshop on the edge of the property. Alice painted in a studio that occupied half the barn.

"Bad dancer doesn't mean anything else, does it?" Carmen said. Matt was now doing a white-guy boogie to a bad cover of "Let's Get

Physical," shooting his hands out in an incoherent semaphore. "Like being bad at parallel parking means you're bad in bed?" She pushed back her chair. "I've got to pee. This is apparently a big part of being pregnant. I didn't know that before."

"Just use the outhouse."

"I did that. Once."

"You looked in. You can't look in," Jean said.

"I am going up to the house, where looking in is not a problem."

Jean took Carmen's hand for a moment, then let go. They were old friends, which made this brief touch a little slip of regular in the middle of these unfamiliar, celebratory events. Seated on Jean's other side was Tom Ferris, a minor Chicago folksinger. At the moment he was banging his forehead softly on the table, to indicate he couldn't abide the terrible cover band. Even though it was now definitely night, he was still wearing his signature accessory—Wayfarer shades. Today he sang while Carmen and Matt exchanged rings. Some Scottish ballad about a pirate and a bonny bride, a ship on stormy seas. Jean backed him up on a dulcimer. The two of them were fiercely committed to preserving traditional music. Superficially, that was their whole connection. Their covert connection was being tragic lovers, the tragedy being that Tom was married, with small kids. Carmen thought Tom was a total waste of Jean's time, but of course didn't express this opinion to Jean.

"I wonder where our backup bride has gone off to?" Carmen looked around as she stood up. Her brother, Nick, had shown up for the occasion in a thrift-shop wedding dress. His new girlfriend, Olivia, was wearing a Vegas-y, powder-blue tux. Some nose-thumbing at gender roles, or one of Nick's elaborate, obscure jokes. Neither of them was in evidence among the crowd.

"Or your bridesmaids for that matter?" Jean observed, meaning Carmen's sister Alice, Matt's sister Maude. "Many lost siblings tonight."

Carmen entered the farmhouse by the back door into the kitchen, which at the moment was vacant of humans, going about a life of its own. An ancient refrigerator emitted a low, steady buzz. The pump spigot dripped into a sink whose original porcelain was, in a circle around the drain, worn down to the iron beneath. A fat fly idled around the open window amid dangling pieces of stained glass. The room sighed out its own smell—a blend of burnt wood and wet clay. Trace elements of blackstrap molasses, tahini, apples, and dirty socks were also in the mix.

She passed through the living room with its brick-and-board bookshelves, walls filled with paintings by Alice and the other painters who lived here. In the corner, a giant wood stove hulked (the house had no central heating). The only undisguised piece of furniture was a ruby red velvet sofa from the 1930s, left by some distant, previous tenants. Everything else had been brought up from city apartments—cheap, rickety furniture draped with feed-sack quilts. A coffee table littered with seeds and rolling papers and a stagnant bong.

She headed up the stairs.

Alice was going to have to pull herself together, get herself outside, get her feet back on solid ground, she knew that. Instead she was lingering in surprising circumstances, having been dragged out of the ordinary progress of life into a hurtling, and (of course) sexual, detour. Which accounted for her not properly participating in her sister's wedding reception. Not living up to her duties as maid of honor. Particularly, currently, not doing the Mexican hat dance, whose ridiculously peppy melody drifted up from the dance floor, through the screen of her bedroom window, audible in spite of the giant box fan wobbling on the floor. Rather she found herself naked, face down on her bed, pinned beneath the groom's sister.

So far, this was the best moment of her life.

Draped over the edge of the bed, she looked down at their abandoned clothes. The parachute pants and slinky silk tops she and Maude bought together a couple of weeks ago—the day they met as bridesmaids—lay in a shimmery clutter on the plank floor. They hadn't seen each other again until this afternoon when they walked together down the petal path, then stood side by side witnessing the ceremony. When Maude's bare arm brushed against Alice's for the third time, Alice decided not to take it as an accident.

And now, with a few intermediate steps, they had arrived exactly here. The evening was nearly as hot as the day it had come out of. The box fan had been running on high and was angled toward the bed, but still both of them were slick with sweat, also a little surprised to find themselves in their current situation. Still neither blamed it on the stunning weed they smoked just before the ceremony. Something had happened, they just weren't sure what.

"We should probably get back out there." Maude said this, but in an unconvincing voice, and without making a move to go anywhere.

"I don't know what to say about this," Alice said.

Maude was cupping Alice's buttocks and had worked her fingertips lightly between Alice's legs, teasing. "It could just be a one-wedding stand."

While the fingers slid in, then out, Alice asked, "Could you stay over tonight?"

"I have a shoot tomorrow afternoon in the city." Maude was in nursing school, but was also a model, for Field's. Carmen had shown Alice a brochure. In it Maude's hair was puffed and sprayed into a housewife helmet. The problem, according to Carmen, was that Maude was too gorgeous for a department store. They had to suppress her wild looks, tamp her down to pleasant and purchase-inducing. Then they could prop her next to coffee makers and bathroom vanities, in small-print dresses, quilted robes.

In this particular moment, Alice didn't think she could ever get enough of her. She lay very still, listening for rejection in Maude's excuse, but all she could hear were the soundless fingers. Then Maude said, "Maybe you could come back to the city with me? Stay overnight?" And Alice flooded with a goofy euphoria.

As they passed a cigarette back and forth while they shimmied back into their wedding gear, Alice was a slightly different person than she had been an hour earlier, more alive. Medical tests, she was sure, would show her pulse elevated, her blood thicker with platelets.

"We could maybe get a ride with my brother and his girlfriend," Alice said. "I mean I don't particularly want to spend the next three hours in your parents' backseat with the Blessed Virgin statue. When they came up the drive, I thought she was some elderly relative."

"They didn't like the outdoor wedding concept. They wanted it to seem more like a church. What can I say? They're religious maniacs."

Above Alice and Maude, in the attic of the farmhouse, far enough up and away that the music and crowd noise outside was filtered through several parts rural nighttime, Alice and Carmen's brother, Nick, stretched luxuriantly, aroused for a moment by the slippery sensation of satin between his legs. He felt sexy in his gown. Sexy and majestic. His arms, in the low light from a single bulb hanging within a Japanese paper shade, looked black. He had been working construction all summer; everything about him was either tanned or bleached white.

"I'm glad you found your way up here, into our small parallel universe," he said. "To pay respect to the shadow bride."

"And his groom," Olivia said, tugging her lavender cummerbund down.

Their audience—temporary acquaintances, teenage cousins from the groom's side—nodded. They were beached against huge floor cushions patterned with Warhol's Mao and Marilyn Monroe. Neither kid had done mushrooms before. Nick had brought these back from a trip to Holland last year for an astrophysics conference in The Hague. He gave a paper on dark energy. He loved mushrooms.

One of the cousins had discovered that the shag carpet in the attic was tonal. "Listen," he tried to make the rest of them understand, "if you press it here. Then here."

Nick smiled and gave the kid a thumbs-up. Nothing he enjoyed more than turning people on. He'd skipped about half the grades along his academic way and so, although only nineteen, he was now a graduate student at the University of Chicago, studying astronomy. On his off nights he explored—through doors opened by hallucinogens and opiates—an inner universe. On drugs, he experienced no anxiety in the company of other humans, and did great with women. Olivia was new. At the moment, she was curled against him like a cat. They had only been seeing each other a few weeks. He had met her at a party. She was a mail lady. It was a job she said she could do better if she was high. Until Nick met her, he hadn't thought of mail carriers going around stoned, but now he wondered if they all did. He could imagine them sorting *so* carefully, this letter here, that bill exactly there. Then walking their routes with deliberation, attuned to everything—the subtly changing colors of the leaves, the light rustle of the wind.

Olivia grew up in Wisconsin. "I know this stretch of road like the back of my hand," she told him on the way up. So she drove while he just stared out at the wide fields edging the road, high with corn, low with soybeans. The sun-bleached sky, the tape deck whining out Willie Nelson, a hash pipe passing back and forth between them, angel flying too close to the ground. Could life get any better?

Now Nick looked down at her satin shirt spilling from the front of her tux jacket like Reddi-wip. He dipped a finger into the folds to test whether it was cloth or cream. He suspected Olivia would be new to him for a little while, then gone. Okay by him. He wasn't looking for anything long term. He enjoyed moving through experiences, traveling without having to go anywhere. Other people and their lives were countries he visited. So far, Olivia's main attraction, her local color, was the way she was always subtly touching him. The other excellent thing about her, of course, was her easy access to drugs.

The upstairs was a maze of narrow hallways. The only sounds were the heavy whir of a fan in one of the bedrooms, and a thumping bass coming down through the ceiling. Carmen found the bathroom, and used the toilet, which was painted to make it appear melted in a Daliesque way. She washed her hands in a paint-splattered sink with a large, misshapen bar of soap the color of glue. She inspected her makeup in the mirror, decided against using any of the extremely funky hairbrushes in a basketful on the windowsill, and made do with running wet fingers through her hair. She closed the toilet lid and sat sideways so she could press her forehead to the chilled porcelain of the sink. She suddenly found herself wobbly in the middle of all this tradition rigged up around something she wasn't all that sure about. Child brides in India came to mind, kidnapped brides in tribal cultures, and mail-order brides for pioneer farmers. The vulnerable nature of bridehood in general. Still, there was nothing to be done about it now. Forward was the only available direction.

"We cut with the knife upside-down, then we feed a piece to each other." Matt told Carmen this as if she was a foreign exchange student just off the plane. His mother had given him this information. She was the boss of this wedding, the commandant. The only thing Carmen got was the location—behind the farmhouse in the dreamy flower garden, a relic from some earlier incarnation of the farm. Wood and wire fences submerged beneath waves of climbing roses, Boston ivy, clematis. Stone paths mossed over, the surface of the small pond at the back burnished ochre with algae, paved with water lilies. Throughout the wedding, in the late hours of this afternoon, the scent rolled off the flowers in sheets that nearly rippled the air. A small threat of rain was held to a smudge at the horizon. Just this once, Carmen got perfection. Now though, things seemed to be slipping off that peak.

"Maybe we could just skip the cake-feeding thing?" she said to Matt, trying to gauge how drunk he was. A little, maybe.

"Oh, my aunts really want it," he said. "I couldn't say no to them." Carmen could see these women gathering, clutching their Instamatics, tears already pooling in the corners of their eyes, tourists on an emotional safari, eager to bag a bride.

It suddenly occurred to her that Matt was a stranger. This was not some nervous, paranoid overreaction. The truth was she had known him only a few months, as yet had only his general outlines. He was a volunteer on the suicide hotline she ran. She trained him through nights drinking burnt coffee while talking down or bringing in or referring out kids on bad drug trips, guys who'd gambled away the family savings, women despairing in abusive marriages, gay guys and lesbians running the gauntlet of coming out—all of these callers sitting in motel rooms with some stash of pills they hoped would do the job, or looking out a high window they planned to use as a door.

Like Carmen, Matt believed in the social contract, in reaching out to those in need. He wanted to do his part; he was a good guy. Also she was pregnant, which was an accident, but they were both going with it. She was optimistic about heading into the future with him, but still, he was basically a stranger.

Now his aunts were clamoring—waving stragglers left and right—to gather a lineup of the bride and groom and his parents. Carmen's parents were hipsters and atheists, way too cool for weddings. They were not present today.

Fatigue hit Carmen like a medicine ball; she was a bride, but also a woman in the middle months of pregnancy, and even ordinary days tired her out. Everyone had had their fun, and now she just wanted them all to go home. She wanted to be teleported to the squeaky bed in the room at a Bates sort of motel Alice had found for them nearby; it was slim pickings for tourist lodgings this far from a main highway. It was okay that it wasn't a romantic setting. This was more of a symbolic wedding night. They'd been living together since February, sleeping together since about three weeks after they met. Tomorrow they were going fishing. Matt loved to fish and had brought rods and a metal box of lures. Carmen tried to imagine herself fishing. It was a whole new world she was walking into. Everything important was just beginning. Her earlier fears gave way to little slips of the giddiness that comes with potential.

◆ ◆ ◆

Setting everyone off in the right direction, getting cars out of the yard by the barn, washing casserole dishes and ladles, and making sure they went off with their proper owners was a huge project, like getting the Conestogas out of Maryland, setting the wagon train off toward Missouri. Although it was nearly three a.m., the moonlight in the cloudless summer sky set up a weak, alternate version of day. Olivia's cavernous old Dodge had room for a few stragglers, refugees from already-departed carloads. Tom Ferris stowed his guitar in the trunk—filled, Carmen noticed, with a high tide of what appeared to be undelivered mail—and got into the backseat along with Maude and—a little surprise—Alice, who Carmen wouldn't have thought needed a ride anywhere, as she was already home. Carmen tried to make eye contact with her sister, but Alice ducked. She and Maude looked softened by sleepiness and lust; they were holding hands as they tumbled into the car one after the other, like bear cubs. Carmen was clearly way out of the loop on this.

She thanked Tom for singing at the ceremony. He stretched himself a little ways out the car window to bless Carmen with a sign of the cross. "I only perform at weddings of people I think were made for each other. My blessing on you both." Almost everything Tom said came off as pompous.

She walked around to see how her brother was doing—still pie-eyed on something. He had twisted himself so the back of his head rested on the frame of the open passenger window. The sky was alive with stars and he was lost in them, like when he was a kid. Carmen pinched his ear, but he didn't so much as blink. She couldn't get a read on Olivia, who was starting up the engine, which faltered a couple of times before kicking in and required a bit of accelerator-tapping to keep it going.

"You okay?" Carmen asked her, peering past her brother so she could get a better look.

"Oh yes," Olivia said brightly, maybe a little too brightly, but then Carmen didn't know her well enough to know how she usually was at three in the morning. "Everything's copacetic." She flipped Carmen a little salute of confidence, and shifted into drive.

Carmen watched them weave down the long dirt road that led to the highway. They were the last of the guests to go. Billy Joel was on the car's tape deck, "Uptown Girl" getting smaller and tinnier as the car drifted away, Nick's head still poking out the open window. Carmen could see only the vague yellow of the car's fog lamps ahead of it. "Hey!" she shouted. "Your lights!"

When the car disappeared from view, Matt said, "She'll figure it out eventually." And then he picked Carmen up.

"To the cave, woman!" he said, carrying her to his car, where he set her gently on the hood. He kissed her and said, "Don't get me wrong. This whole thing was great. But I am so glad it's over."

"Oh, me too," Carmen said. "All I want is a good-looking husband and a bed and about fifty hours' sleep." Some of the time when she talked to Matt, she felt as if she was in a movie scripted by lazy screenwriters. The two of them were still generic characters in each other's stories. Girlfriend/boyfriend. Bride/groom. Wife/husband. But maybe that's all marriage was—you fell into a groove already worn for you. You had a place now. The music had stopped and you'd gotten a chair.

By the time the car reached the end of the dirt road, everyone had grown quiet. Alice looked around at her fellow passengers. Maude was sleepy against her, within the circle of her arm. Nick was zoned out in the front, watching a mosquito flit up and down his forearm. Tom Ferris, on the other side of Maude, was staring out the side window, tapping down, pulling up, tapping down the door lock. Olivia turned left onto the two-lane—Route 14—and let it rip. Alice stuck her head a little ways out the window thinking there was nothing like traveling a country road at night. The sky was so clear, the moon so high and luscious.

A few miles on, the road dipped a little, then cut through a stand of trees. The leaves shimmered in the high moonlight, and now Billy Joel was singing "You're Always a Woman to Me." The first Alice saw of the girl was not her standing on the side of the road, or even running across it, but already thudding onto the hood of the car. A jumble of knees and elbows, and then her face, frozen in surprise, eyes wide open, huge on the other side of the windshield.

route 14

No owls hooted, no nocturnal animals skittered, no wind shivered through the leaves heavy on branches. It was as though, for an instant, everything had been stunned. The moon, a few slivers shy of fullness, hung ghostly white, referring out a pale, insubstantial light that made the surrounding sky appear navy blue.

The Dodge, in attempting to occupy the same space as a massive oak, had been thwarted by the laws of physics. It now rested on its side, front bumper embedded in the trunk of the tree. Its tires had stopped spinning, the passengers inside were as still as sacks of flour. This was a small inhalation, a bracing for the immediate future, which was racing in.

Alice both came into consciousness and wasn't sure she had even been knocked out. She wiggled her fingers and flexed her feet and concluded she was not seriously hurt, just banged up a little. She could feel bruises purpling. The back of her head ached, her elbows, her butt. She craned her head out the window, which was now above rather than beside her. She found she was the top human in a pancake stack of three. Maude was beneath her; her hand—in a leftover gesture—was stuck inside Alice's bra, still palming a nipple as if it was a coin in a magic trick. Any world where sleepy sex play might have occurred now seemed very far off, part of another epoch or universe.

She suddenly remembered the kid. She was out there somewhere in the surrounding darkness.

"You okay?" Maude said in a pinched voice beneath Alice's shoulder.

"I think so." Alice turned as much to her left as she could. "You?"

"Something's wrong with my ankle. It's jammed under the front seat. The guy, the singer, he's underneath me, knocked out. Breathing, but there's blood coming from his head. I'm going to try—"

"I'm awake," Tom said. "I might be dying, though. Really."

"Head wounds just bleed like crazy," Maude said, wiping the blood away with her hand. "I don't think this is deep." She pulled her silver scarf from around her neck and tied it tight around his head. "There. Just keep pressing your hand against the cut."

Alice said, "The big problem is there's a kid, a girl, I think. We hit her. She's outside somewhere." Then to Maude, "I know this isn't great, but I'm going to have to step on you a little to pull myself through the window."

"S'okay," Maude said, but groaned as Alice stood on her arm.

Once she hoisted herself out, Alice reached in and slipped her hands under Maude's arms, pulled her to where she could boost herself up the rest of the way. In the front seat, the satin and polyester of Nick's and Olivia's costumes shushed against each other. Alice looked inside, and tried to rally them.

"What about you guys? Can you get yourselves out? There's a little kid out here somewhere."

"I didn't see her, and then she was just hitting the car. I thought maybe she was an angel." Olivia's voice was coy and whispery. Like Marilyn Monroe's. Given the circumstances, this voice was extremely annoying.

Nick turned from where he had settled, nearly behind the steering wheel, crushing Olivia, and looked up at Alice, smiling sheepishly, reaching a hand up toward her in a sort of semi-wave. She saw he was trying to approximate sociability. As though that was what was being asked of him.

"They're useless," Alice turned to tell Maude, then looked at Maude's ankle, which was only minorly cut, but quite swollen. "Can you walk on that?"

Maude took a few test steps, inhaling sharply with each one, but said, "Let's go. Let's find her."

This wasn't difficult. The girl lay maybe thirty feet behind the car, in the ditch that bordered the gravel shoulder of the road. She looked to be about nine or ten, although she had the adult features of kids from rougher places. She was quite beautiful, with a mop of hair bleached white by half a summer, green eyes staring at absolutely nothing. She was wearing denim cutoffs and a plaid madras shirt, a crosshatch of pinks and greens. Indian moccasins patterned with colored beads. Her clothes were blackened by the earth she had fallen onto, skidded through. There was very little blood, just scrapes here and there. She could be napping but for the position of her body, which looked something like an extremely advanced yoga pose, limbs bent in unlikely ways. Also, beneath the skin of her forearm, a bone poked out midway between her elbow and her wrist.

When she noticed this, Alice turned aside quickly to throw up.

Maude knelt and pressed her ear to the girl's chest. She listened for a heartbeat, held her fingers to the girl's neck.

"I don't know," she said to Alice, who was still doubled over. "I'm feeling something, but it's so faint, like an echo. I'll try CPR; you go for help. Do you know where we are?"

Alice straightened, wiped her sour mouth with the back of her hand. She looked up and down the sign-less road into the woods lining a summer night mild and still as some interior place, a vast, darkened room without walls. The trees seemed to end a ways off toward the east, replaced by fields. But whose fields? Did they already pass the turnoff to the town? What bend in the road was this? Which of the many ancient oaks that were as common out here as pennies in a jar? Making out in the backseat with Maude had obscured both time and distance. They might be quite far from the farm by now. She shook her head. "I wasn't paying attention. Of course I wasn't. So now I don't know. We're between somewhere and somewhere else. But either way I walk, I'll come across a house eventually." Maude was already at work, pressing the girl's chest, listening for returning breath.

Tom Ferris lurched toward them like a zombie, still holding the side of his head, bound up with Maude's scarf, soaked with blood, which appeared black in the sharp moonlight.

"Tom," Alice said, looking up from the girl, "it's bad."

But he was already folding onto his knees next to her. He was crying, sobbing really. His shoulders heaved. But although this was the saddest moment imaginable, something about his tears, the ease with which he accessed them, seemed false. Alice was brought up short by this, but had no time to think it through. When she stood to go for help, Tom said, "I'd better come along."

Nick understood something had gone wrong. He had seen the girl dancing onto the road. He thought she was magical, but now it was definitely beginning to appear she was real. He looked over at Olivia. Maybe she could offer some clue, a prompt about what happened, what to do. But she was only staring up at him with curiosity, as if he was the one with the answer. She had a dark, serious bulge on her forehead.

With some effort, she wrestled her tapestry bag from between them, pulled out a Baggie, plucked from it a couple of pills, and extended her hand toward him. "Take one of these. We're probably going to need something for whatever happens next."

Despite the late hour, when Tom and Alice finally came to a house, all the lights were on inside. Bad Company poured out through screenless windows.

"This must be the Hell's Angels place," Alice said. The front yard was full of choppers. Before she could go farther, Tom put a hand on her shoulder to make her stop and turn around. "The thing is, I was wondering if you'd mind me sort of disappearing here. I'm just going to hitch a ride back to the city."

For the first time, she noticed that his guitar case was slung over his shoulder. He'd had the presence of mind to get it out of the car.

"It's just a professional consideration. The negative publicity. You know. And really, you guys don't need me from here on. I was asleep. I basically missed the whole thing."

"Hey. You need to stop. You're not leaving now. Nobody's leaving now." What she held back from saying was that his celebrity was too small to worry about ruining. All she could do in this moment was try to summon up her sister's voice. Carmen was very good at keeping people from their worst behavior.

The bikers turned out to be tequila drinkers, bandana wearers, snake keepers. The whole place smelled like the inside of a very bad shoe, a shoe with a piece of cheese in it. In the clutch, though, these guys proved to be surprisingly model citizens. One of them offered up his bandana to replace Tom's blood-caked scarf-bandage. Alice used their phone to call the cops. The Angels offered to go out to the accident scene, but they only had their bikes, no way to transport the girl. And so they hid their hookah and then everyone just waited. Alice and Tom sat, sunk in papasan chairs, watching the snakes writhe around on the coffee table. Eventually, an ambulance sped by, siren wailing, followed by a highway patrol car. Another pulled up the dirt drive to the house, and picked up Tom and Alice. They sat in the backseat in silence, looking out in opposite directions.

When they got back to the accident, the scene had gone static. Maude appeared to have run out to the end of her nursing skills. Now she just sat next to the girl, holding one of her hands flat between her own. She had rearranged the girl's limbs into more reasonable positions, as though there was some element of modesty to consider.

Alice glanced over at Nick and Olivia, who sat on the other side of the road, silent and serious, a little too serious. High as kites, kites impersonating heavy stones. They nodded at her, solemn as judges. She wanted to bang their heads together, like coconuts.

The cops and the medics took over and began dismantling the tragedy. The girl went off in the ambulance, no siren. Maude stood in the sharp moonlight and the waving beams of flashlights, watching the ambulance go. Her bad ankle was swollen and dark.

"Hey," Alice said, putting a hand to her arm to establish contact. "You did everything you could."

Maude didn't reply, didn't even turn to acknowledge that Alice had said anything. She shrugged a little, maybe to shake off Alice's hand.

One of the cops peered into the open trunk of the Dodge.

"We've got a little mail problem here," he said.

The other cop had found Olivia's tapestry bag on the ground, and was fishing out various Baggies filled with grass and hash and pills; also cellophane envelopes, amber prescription bottles.

Olivia hiked herself onto her wounded car, then sat smoking on the upended fender, white patent leather boots planted on the side of the tire. Graciously, she told the cops, "Please. Help yourself."

"Looks like you'll be riding with us," one of the troopers said. He pressed the back of her head down and folded her into the backseat of one of the cruisers. As the car pulled away, she turned so she could look out the rear window. She appeared confused, unclear why she was being singled out.

The girl's name was Casey Redman. She was ten years old. One of the ER nurses identified her immediately; her son was in the girl's fifth-grade class. Her family lived very near where she had been hit, on the stretch of highway between Black Earth and Cross Plains. The parents were stunned, of course, that she had been killed, but also just that she had been outside at night by herself. No one knew what she might have been doing there. She'd been sleeping over at a friend's. She was on her way home for some ten-year-old's reason. Her father was headed to the station now.

They got this information piecemeal from one side of phone calls taken and made by the young deputy who typed their statements very slowly, with two fingers. They had little to offer him in the way of details. They were all sorry, of course. Their sorrow was huge. But they were, variously, asleep, distracted, to be honest, a little drunk. No one offered anything to lift any of the blame from Olivia, who had been taken into custody—a place that existed somewhere beyond a pale-green metal door inset with a small, thick, wire-meshed window. Except for Nick, they didn't even know her. She was driving; she was stoned. Laying the accident at her feet turned out to be a small, nearly synchronized motion.

The girl's father—Terry Redman—came through the front door of the police station. He did this by kicking it open. He was small, but wiry, as if he had been forged, sparks flying off him, rather than born. The first thing he did was yank Nick off the plastic chair where he had nodded off. He pulled him up by the lace front of his wedding dress and proceeded to smash Nick's nose with a single punch to the center of his face.

They all watched him go down. Everyone was tacitly deferring to some universal law that, while his daughter lay in the hospital morgue, a father was allowed to punch out the guy lounging around in the wedding dress.

When all the statements had been taken, all the forms filled in, then whited-out here and there, then filled in again, the cops took Maude and Tom and Nick off to the hospital to get their injuries looked after. Alice asked Maude if she wanted her to come along, a suggestion that elicited a stare as blank as paper.

It was morning by now. Alice stepped out the front door of the police station and started down the road alone.

titanium white

Alice walked the last block home to cool down. She was quickly chilled, having worn only shorts and a T-shirt. The morning she had just run through would turn into a warm spring day. The air was still sharp, but the bottom had fallen out of winter. Inside the loft, she went looking for cigarettes. She was a smoking runner these days. She hoped these activities canceled out each other, leaving her about even in terms of health.

She had been back living in Chicago a couple of years, since right after the accident. She had needed to get back to the real world, provide herself with urban distractions. She'd found a huge, moldering loft, half of one floor in what used to be an industrial laundry. Nick put in a shower and sink and toilet, helped her sand the floors, scrub the walls, then paint them titanium white, like gesso on a fresh canvas.

She painted here every day she could afford. To support herself, she pushed out illustrations for low-end newspaper ads. Flank steaks and buckets of tripe for Moo & Oink, the South Side grocery. Mattresses and recliner chairs for Goldblatt's, a budget department store. She also had a volunteer gig through the park district—two workshops at a senior center. One in crafts, another in painting. The most popular project was laminating grandchild photos onto vinyl tote bags. Two women were becoming adept at making stuffed terrycloth picture frames. In the painting class, although some of the students had a deft hand, their subject matter veered into a kind of contemporary religious area. Angels working as school crossing guards. Jesus mediating peace with world leaders. Helping her students make art that was hideous but meaningful to them was a small torment Alice had devised for herself.

She was left with a couple of days a week to work on her own paintings. She inhabited a hardscrabble world with friends who, like her, rose and fell on the inhale/exhale of reviews and group shows and sales to collectors. Some had MFAs and adjunct teaching positions, but no one made a decent living. All of Alice's friends struggled along in musty lofts like hers, or in apartments that smelled sour with roach spray and still had tons of roaches. They worked as costumed waitresses in theme restaurants, night doormen in Gold Coast buildings, bike messengers in the Loop. They belonged to food co-ops and had refrigerators filled with many heads of lettuce and industrial blocks of cheddar. They drank Louis Glunz wine ($3 a bottle), Red White & Blue beer ($1.49 a six-pack).

Today she painted all the way through into night, then cleaned brushes and sorted out the studio, made a cheese sandwich and fell into bed around one in her painting clothes. The buzzer woke her. She looked at the clock; the numbers were flipping from 3:23 to 3:24. This happened occasionally; there were two rowdy bars on her block. She didn't answer, but the buzzing continued. She got up and went to the window, pushed her shoulders through the frame so she could look down. Standing in the shadows between streetlights was a tall blonde who, as she looked up, revealed herself to be Maude.

Alice got stuck for a moment, then went to buzz her in. This was a completely surprising event. Since the accident Alice had only seen her once, at the baptism of Carmen and Matt's baby, Gabriel. They gave each other a wide berth. Now here she was in some agitated state, in jeans and a sweatshirt turned inside out. Ten feet tall. Hair a tangle, expression feverish, smelling like lilac and biscuits. If Alice believed in a God she would have asked him: Please give me this.

"I don't know anything about how to do this," Maude said. It was the first thing she said.

"Shhh," Alice said, kissing her, biting her lower lip.

"Here it is, so much later and—"

"Yes," Alice said.

And then Maude was crying all over Alice's neck, but at the same time pushing Alice's hair back, snagging her fingers on a few small snarls, making Alice wince. Then dragging her big, stupid model's lips down the side of Alice's neck, stopping when she ran into the hollow at the very beginning of shoulder, where she sucked hard, drawing skin between teeth and tongue.

Something dumb and profound stirred inside Alice, like sound running over the tiny filaments of the inner ear, tendrils of coral rustled by a tropical sea. As a lover, Maude was not artful, only blunt. Before they even made it to the bed, her hand was so far in that Alice could feel the chunky silver links of Maude's bracelet clicking against her where she opened up. "Can you hear me?" Maude said. "I'm trying to tell you something." And suddenly Alice was so wet she was embarrassed. She was the hostage in the darkened cellar, or in the forest clearing, a gun pressed into the small of her back.

This was how it began again.

She was awakened the next morning by the smell of butter sizzling. She pulled on some jeans, a T-shirt. Maude was at the stove, fixing an omelet.

"In college I worked at the Happy Pan," she said, and her moves did appear assured. She whisked the eggs into froth, then slid them into the buttered pan. She was a study in motion efficiency and body English—a shove then a quick flip and the omelet folded onto itself. This seemed to Alice not just an inconsequential set of assembly-line skills, rather another sparkly aspect of an overwhelming whole. All through the night Alice had tried to break down the elements of Maude, then add her up, but she kept getting lost in the higher math, the exponential blur.

Like now. Maude, turning quickly, pulled an about-to-be-lit Marlboro from between Alice's lips, slid her hands under Alice's arms to lift her onto her feet, then pressed her against a blank stretch of wall.

"Your choice," she said at Alice's ear, already unbuttoning Alice's jeans, "omelets or smoke or sex."

Alice experienced Maude like a drug—an element facilitating sensory change.

What happened from there was all the same thing, just in different locations. In the studio. Also at Maude's apartment. At the movies. At Chez Josie, a cheap French restaurant down on Lincoln where, while feeding each other crème brûlée, they were asked to leave. On the third beach down from Fullerton. Maude laid claim to Alice and Alice, in turn, surrendered the territory of herself. She made herself utterly vulnerable, and not just sexually. By two weeks in, she had told Maude so much of her darkest stuff—unsavory fantasies, of course, but also low moments of pettiness and envy, descriptions of various embarrassments. She could make herself thrillingly ill imagining the betrayal and treachery ahead. Still, all this exposure seemed necessary to set their course.

They broke only for work and Maude's classes. She was finishing up her nursing degree. (She put Alice's limbs into splints, made the bed with Alice still in it, listened to Alice's heart, checked the pressure of the blood in her veins.) She said there wouldn't be enough years in front of the camera to make a career of modeling; she would need a backup.

Maude wasn't out as a dyke; this was not the whole problem, but it was the largest piece. She was the daughter of a mother who ran a tight ship. Marie's children were expected to get married, to someone Marie approved of. Someone Catholic. Then it was time for a baby, a bun in the oven. And then, they didn't want little Timmy or Lucy to grow up an only child, did they? The family was already on Carmen to get knocked up again. Family was what mattered, and got celebrated at every possible occasion. Weddings of course, baptisms, first communions, confirmations, anniversaries. Maude had not yet found a way to let her mother know how far she had veered off this program. Marie already thought Maude's friendship with Alice was unhealthy. Alice couldn't really blame Maude for ducking, but she still didn't like being forced back into the closet herself. This was, she supposed, one of the pitfalls of bringing someone out.

That she wouldn't be able to bring Maude all the way over wasn't her biggest fear. In a deep recess, an inchoate space where thoughts tumble around, smoky and unformed, Alice's biggest fear was that she and Maude and the accident were tied in an elaborate knot—that her true punishment for what happened that night would be God, or the gods, or the cosmos giving her Maude, then taking her away. But this had not happened yet.

Maude told Alice the worst medical story. She had been working at the hospital long enough that by now there *was* a worst. It was a degloving, a man brought in from a factory accident. He'd been caught in a machine, his skin peeled off in one piece down the bottom half of his body. Maude had degloved Alice's soul. If Maude left, Alice supposed she would never get over her, that the application of time—even in great quantities—would not be up to the job of getting over Maude.

This, of course, put Alice in a very bad position. She could never quite be relaxed and normal around Maude. A haze of supplication, she knew, hovered over her like incense at an altar. This was another part of the problem. Maude would have had to be a better person not to use this advantage, and she was not; she was merely an ordinarily good person. Maybe, Maude would speculate, when she'd finished school she should move to New York for a while, to wring as much as she could out of modeling. Or she should move to L.A. to see if she could break into movies. Her fascination with hypothetical versions of herself was bottomless.

When she was attentive to Alice, though, it was with such ferocity and ardor that Alice was stunned, went around for days at a time exhausted and exhilarated, bleary, bumping into things, her spatial sense way out of whack, her mouth bruised, her joints aching, hollows under her eyes, her appetite engaged only by strong lures. M&Ms. Fries with mayonnaise.

Alice saw this disorientation as a good thing, maybe the best thing, but Maude was ambivalent. She would suddenly get claustrophobic. Alice was too close for comfort, or too intense, or too complex; Maude would need to get away to sort things out, or breathe some uncomplicated air. For Alice, unfortunately, the air was always uncomplicated. She only ever loved Maude. That was where she was every day. And so she could only stand still and breathe shallowly and brace herself through Maude's tremors and vacillations. Bad weather that would pass.

Today, a Saturday, Maude was sleeping in, dozing on her stomach and Alice lazily traced the edges of her shoulder blades, thinking what she knew was a fatuous lover's thought—that they look like the place where wings would be attached on angels. And then suddenly this moment was zapped by the door buzzer.

"Oh shit. I forgot," Alice said, looking at the clock. "Carmen and Gabe." It was one p.m. on the dot. Carmen was always on time.

"Did we interrupt anything?" Carmen said coming out of the elevator, probably sniffing sex in the air. Carmen didn't much care for Maude. Alice wasn't sure why, but was certain this would smooth out with time.

"Hey big guy," she said to Gabe, and set him up with paper and finger paints, then got Carmen and Maude moving. "Let's hang some paintings."

"Over a little more," Alice gestured at Maude and Carmen with a freshly lit cigarette. They were each holding on to a side of the painting's stretcher, and made an odd pair of helpers. Maude in threadbare cords and a Superman T-shirt, yellow leather Moroccan slippers; Carmen coordinated in burgundy wool slacks and a peach sweater. She was wearing makeup. Her hair was, as always, perfect—heavy and dark, spilling lustrously (but in an organized way) over her shoulders.

Everything about Carmen was organized. She kept an appointment book and a little wipe-off marker board on her refrigerator door to keep track of her days on at the shelter, her pickup times for Gabe at day care. She was in possession of a schedule, a child, and a husband. Carbon steel kitchen knives and a new sofa—as opposed to Alice's sprung red velvet junker brought down from the co-op. She had a serious approach to every aspect of life—motherhood, her job, her political work. Still a ways shy of thirty, Carmen had Alice beat hands-down in the race to adulthood. Coming at life as Alice did, from a more oblique angle—a lack of any real plan at all, a tenuous relationship, a line of work that yielded no security of any kind—it would be easy for her to ridicule Carmen as a tight-ass, but she didn't, ever. Their alliance was deep, formed in the trenches of childhood where they were each other's landsmen, comrades in strategy and survival, in warding off the contempt of their parents, and in protecting their brother. These positions had been set up early and were not subject to realignment. So she and Carmen always approached each other carefully, with respect—minor diplomats, one from an arctic, the other from an equatorial nation, attempting to understand each other's customs, participate in each other's holidays.

◆ ◆ ◆

Crushing out her cigarette, Alice headed over with pencil, hammer, and nails. This was the last and largest canvas for the show, which was to start Friday—a group project of the artists who had studios in this old laundry. They were getting write-ups in the *Reader* and *Newcity*. They might get some real traffic through here.

"I see hordes descending," Maude said. "I hear hoof beats." She was always encouraging about Alice's work.

Alice said, "There might be people, but they could just be cheese-seekers. There. Perfect. Don't move."

"It doesn't matter if they come for the cheese," Carmen said, leaning against the wall a little dreamily, filling in the blank of Alice's future for her while Alice pounded in a nail. "The more people, the larger presence you have on the scene. You're entering the marketplace."

"Maybe," Alice said, but really she was happy for her sister's belief in her, to hear her use words like "presence" and "marketplace," which until now they'd only used in reference to their father, a painter whose presence in the marketplace of art was fairly large. He encouraged Alice's aspirations until she started being taken seriously. Now he was subtly dismissive. Horace saw every other painter as a threat, now even (or maybe especially) Alice.

"Finish," Gabe said from the floor, but didn't look up. Then, he found he was mistaken, that something wasn't quite finished, and so he just kept painting.

"Man." Alice hunkered down behind him. He had painted, from memory, his backyard and, in the corner, Carmen's garden-in-progress. It was all there, wobbly and from about four different perspectives, but there. The beat-up garage, a doghouse left behind by the previous owners, a trellis draped in clematis, his father asleep in the hammock. It wasn't really a child's painting.

"All here," he said. Each of his fingers was dabbed with its own color. He was a tidy little guy.

"Yeah, well, this is—" Alice didn't say it was incredible, that at two and a half he should only be up to green and brown trees, round yellow sun, stick-figure humans. He hated being told he was too young to do things. "Next time we're moving you up to a brush." He wore a striped jersey tucked into the elastic waist of his pants. His bottom was padded out with trainer pants. Despite being an artistic genius, he was not yet 100 percent potty trained. His hair fell over his eyes as he painted. He looked like a kid from an earlier era, or a smaller place, heading into the rougher neighborhood of real life.

Maude came over and added her own flourish of praise. Sometimes Alice got a little rush around all of them being related. Siblings paired off with siblings and now a new generation extending their presence in the universe. Sometimes this seemed so cutting edge, as though they were creating a new, hip version of family. Other times it was as if they were all from the same holler and didn't get out enough.

It was a family tree that looked better in the abstract than in real life where, truthfully, Alice found Matt dull and Carmen was wary of Maude. Or rather what Maude turned Alice into. Carmen didn't think love should be about casting a spell over someone. She thought it should be a more balanced constellation of emotion, about mutual support and prospering. She had made all this clear to Alice, which put a hard brace on further conversation on the subject.

Alice and Maude fetched Cokes for everyone. Carmen scanned the room. "These are just wonderful paintings, Alice."

Alice wished she shared her sister's assurance. She understood that she was a good painter, but she wanted to make important paintings, and that was loamy ground—importance—difficult to gain footing there. In her better moments, she could get euphoric with the potential for making these paintings that were pushing around inside her, like the ghostly pains in her legs through the nights of her adolescence when she was doing the last of her growing.

In an interview that hadn't yet taken place, Alice would say her work was most influenced by Gerhard Richter, Lucian Freud, and Balthus.

She wanted to paint humans in ways that set up a disturbance between the painting and the viewer, ways that disrupted the conventional notions of portraiture. Her current subjects were women wrestlers from the forties and fifties. She painted them as they were in their heyday, drawing from posters and photos of their matches. She also painted them now, from life, in their various retirements. These were amazing women, having made themselves up out of spit and bravado. A few months back she had a small show in a storefront gallery—the first of these portraits—and it nearly sold out. Alice attributed the small success of these paintings to their subjects as much as to her rendering of them.

"Oh, did we miss some—" Carmen started toward the canvases propped on the wide windowsills at the back of the studio. Midway across the room, she stopped, saw what these paintings were, understood they would not be part of the show.

Alice never talked about these portraits. She never brought them out, but neither did she hide them. She had completed one so far, had two more in progress. They were all of the girl, in different poses, at successive ages. When Casey Redman hit the windshield, all Alice could register were her stunned eyes. The first time she really saw her face was when she was already on the ground, expression no longer present. So, although the girl in the paintings was going through the motions of growing up—floating on a raft on an indigo lake, sitting inside a snow fort, dancing awkwardly at a birthday party—she was always wearing cutoffs and a thin pink and green madras shirt, the only clothes Alice ever saw her wear. And her face was as dead as a saint preserved inside a glass altar.

Alice didn't talk about these paintings because everyone seemed to be done talking about the accident. For Alice, a low, yellow-gray cloud had formed, obscuring the movement of responsibility being pushed around, sorted into amorphous parcels. Her parcel: Why had she even gotten into the car in the first place, and once there, seeing how fucked-up Nick and Olivia were, why had she stayed in the backseat, not for a moment thinking to offer herself up as a more reasonable driver? Just because she wanted to keep making out with Maude? Now when she dragged out the scales of conscience, her desire, she could see, was a feather; Casey Redman's life a rock. A rock as big as a mountain. A mountain made of lead.

Alice never had a day she didn't think about the girl. Everybody, she figured, had to coat the grain of sand in his or her own way. Making these paintings was hers. How the others managed their own unwieldy burdens she didn't know. How the girl's parents bore the loss of her, she couldn't even get close to thinking about.

She knew Carmen tortured herself for letting them all leave the farm that night in a car running with just fog lamps. She knew it was too late, and that they were too tired, too stoned, too goofed-up on sex, a perfect confluence of weak elements that only needed the addition of a stray child to coalesce into tragedy. And so Alice was certain that once Carmen understood the nature of the paintings, she would pause for a moment inside her hesitation, then turn and come back and they would all be released back into the present, into the slow forward motion of their lives.

Carmen checked her watch.

"We've got to get going. I need to get some dinner together. Then I'm meeting Jean at Broadway and Belmont." She pulled from her carryall a handful of buttons printed with TAKE BACK THE NIGHT. There was a march tonight, which Alice had totally forgotten. Carmen was on the board of this group, which promoted a safer urban environment for women, and taught heightened awareness in risky situations along with self-defense tactics. Another of Carmen's undeniably worthy missions. Almost everyone Alice knew had a story of being squeezed into a dangerous or just too-weird situation at the hands of the creep in the shadowy parking garage, the cab driver who suddenly veered off the expected route, or (this from her straight friends) the guy who seemed okay in the bar, then, once in his apartment, set about chaining you to his radiator.

Carmen came to this cause already burdened with a close-up view of the dark side of male/female—and some times female/female—interaction. Her job at the women's shelter had exposed her to all the soft spots where the fist or belt had landed. The stories dragged in by these women were harrowing. She told them to Alice; sometimes Alice could hardly listen. One woman walked in with a number of her recently dislodged teeth rattling around in her pocket. Another had a face that, when looked at straight on was okay, but from the side, had no profile; it had been punched flat. From close contact with these women, Carmen herself had acquired a bleaker gaze, a twitchy pulse at the hinge of her jaw.

Her presence at marches and demos worried Alice a little, but there was really nothing she could say. Getting in the way of what was wrong or wicked or unjust in the world was pretty much Carmen's main point. She was in firm solidarity with the oppressed and downtrodden. She still hoped America was on its way to becoming a socialist state with homes and health care and higher education for everyone. She saw Communism as a flawed but fascinating social experiment. In college she went on cultural visas to Cuba and Russia. She made a game try at learning Russian out of an old textbook that primarily gave her a stockpile of useless phrases like "I love to smoke cigarettes at the factory."

Carmen was Clark Kent, traveling incognito as a social worker and middle-class mother, but always with cheese crackers and a bail card in her purse, ready to spring into action. Because of all this, Carmen was the most important person Alice knew.

A riptide of guilt tugged Alice down. She should take one of the buttons and go along with Carmen and Jean. Although Carmen wasn't pressing (she wouldn't), Alice knew her presence would be appreciated to fill out the ranks. But she also knew from a flickering look Maude gave her a few minutes earlier, and a quick glance of knuckles across nipple (Maude's knuckles, Alice's nipple) in the kitchen earlier when they were getting the Cokes, that if she backgrounded the issue of women's safety, and stayed here after Carmen and Gabe left, she could spend the stretched end of this Saturday naked with Maude. And the thing was, she didn't know how many of these Saturdays they had left.

That night Maude pushed Alice home in a grocery cart full of still-warm, clean clothes. Although Alice lived in a former laundry, she nonetheless had to take her clothes to a laundromat. Maude would bring her stuff over and they'd make a night of it. They found the cart in their alley months ago. One would push the other on the way over to the laundromat, the other pushed on the way home. There was a terrible bar next door. A windowless den sour with old beer, sweet with urine and disinfectant, its clientele mainly retirees with hospital hair, pressed flat to the backs of their heads from lying down through the hours they weren't in the bar. Alice and Maude grabbed a booth near the front in case a stumbly fight broke out, which happened often enough. They had a couple of beers interrupted by runs to add fabric softener and throw the clothes in the dryer. They talked about everything and nothing, questioned each other with a casual invasiveness, assassins trying to learn everything essential about their victim before the kill.

And then they headed home. This particular night, sunk in clean clothes that smelled like synthetic flowers, the night air whooshing lightly over her face, a low buzz inside her head from the beers, Alice understood that what they had—this amalgam of passion and chatter and tearing their way inside each other—was defined by its transience. This was the thing that wouldn't last. Losing Maude would be Alice's punishment. All of her present with Maude was made excruciatingly valuable in this way, for being tinted with the sure sorrow held by the future. The pure, acidic penance she had earned.

As they passed the old guy bar, the pay phone in its doorway began to ring, and Alice had a brief, illogical moment of certainty that the call was for her.

general relativity

The phone had been ringing for maybe five minutes. No one but Nick appeared to hear it. No one made a move to answer. Incoming calls were tricky for the Lisowskis. Most likely the caller was a dunning bill collector. Olivia's family was an epicenter of credit card frivolity. They were also, at the moment, distracted by a Packers game on the TV in the paneled den. Olivia's brothers—both of them sanitation workers for the township, single and still living at home as they glided through their twenties—were perched on the front edges of, respectively, the sofa and the BarcaLounger. They had bright yellow dishtowels in their back pockets; whenever they spotted bad behavior on the part of the opposing team, they leapt up to throw down penalty flags on the play.

"Fun in Wisconsin" was the category Nick had come up with to cover this sort of activity. Fun in Wisconsin was also the old car the towns-people parked out on the ice of the lake in winter, then took bets on the date in spring when it would fall through. There was even more fun to be had in Wisconsin, activities Nick had so far successfully avoided—Friday fish fries, a card game called Sheepshead. Nick liked to say—but not to Olivia or her family, of course—that Wisconsin was an argument for Einstein's general relativity theory, for there being masses so dense they caused depressions in the space-time fabric, places where the fabric warped. He knew he was being a snob, but it was a private snobbery—his fun in Wisconsin. He realized some people had fun in Illinois.

He spent more time with Olivia's family than he would have expected. This time he came up to spend last night at Yerkes, the University of Chicago's crumbling observatory near Lake Geneva. He and his old professor, Bernie Cato, sometimes got together to talk shop—their shop being all of creation. Then, if the sky was clear, as it was last night, they got on the platform and raised it, opened the roof and spent some time searching for supernovas, puzzling out the gorgeous, operatic deaths of stars.

This morning, he had headed over to the Lisowskis'. He could have just driven straight to the prison, but he usually stopped here first, then rode the rest of the way up with them. He had never known the family under ordinary circumstances. The first time he met them was at Olivia's sentencing.

"Time to go, boys," Olivia's mother said, clicking off the TV. The brothers went sullen, but rose and hovered out to find their jackets.

In the visitors' room, the brothers whiled away the dead time doing Travis Bickle impersonations at each other. They loved *Taxi Driver*. They had the collector's edition of the tape, with special features and outtakes.

"You talkin' to me?"

"You talkin' to me?"

And then Olivia entered from beyond a heavily painted metal door. She had changed in prison, but it wasn't really prison that had changed her. She was whittling herself out of hardwood, remaking herself with only planes and edges. She looked more severe, more adult. She had lost that breathy way of speaking he used to think was sexy; that was gone. She had used her time inside to reformulate herself in opposition to the person she used to be—that is, someone who would smoke a day's worth of hash, then eat some mushrooms, then do a little coke to balance off, then get behind the wheel of a car and kill a kid. She took a dim view of this person. Nick envied her. Prison was forcing her to atone. And eventually she would be released.

She'd been in almost two years now, and was going to be in for a while longer. She most likely would have been out by now if the matter had gone to trial. But she went down for the whole mess, pleaded guilty to all of it. She wanted to pay, not just for her crimes, but also for her sins. At this point, she was not in for the reckless driving or the drugs; she was in for the undelivered mail in the trunk, a federal offense.

The extreme order of prison life seemed to calm her. She worked breakfast and lunch in the cafeteria. She mixed vats of powdered eggs and water; ladled canned peach halves into tiny, battered, plastic dishes; slapped slices of bologna between slices of white bread. There were nearly three hundred inmates, so there was a lot of mixing and ladling and slapping to be done every day.

She shared a cell with a huge woman named Freddi, told Nick, "You definitely want her in the bottom bunk." Freddi was nearing the end of a stiff sentence for armed robbery; she had been inside prison walls more than half her life. The two of them were enrolled in the prison's cosmetology program. When she got out, though, Freddi said she would probably bypass the beauty service industry and just go back into armed robbery, which was more rewarding financially and didn't involve toxic substances, unless you counted guns. Olivia, on the other hand, had surprised herself by taking to the business of hair, and hoped to have her license by the time she got out. The cosmetology instructor said Olivia had real talent technically, but a terrible chair-side manner. She told her nobody wants her hair done by some broody, glowering vulture.

"We'll see about that," Olivia said to Nick.

Her own hair, which used to spill down her back, she now wore in a crew cut. Nick understood this was a statement, but he wasn't sure what the statement was. It was weird; this revised version of Olivia wasn't anyone he would stop to talk to on the street and yet she was the person he most wanted to be with. This had to do with confinement. She would circumscribe him. She would be his soft, gray prison. In return he would take care of her. He owed her that.

He could not bring himself to tell her he saw the girl before she did. He could have shouted, or pulled the steering wheel around to get the car out of her way. But the thing was he thought the girl was magical, a talisman of something, maybe. One of the small surprises that come your way when you're high.

He could have changed everything. How could he tell her that? So he just sat with this sickening piece of information, replayed it on an endless loop. Then he imagined another version where he reached for the wheel just in time and took the car over the shoulder, into the ditch. Everyone in the car was banged up a little, Maude had a sprained ankle, Tom got a good-sized gash on his head. But the girl kept running into the long rest of her life.

Olivia did not share his vision of the two of them together. Not yet anyway. She accepted these visits, but that was about as far as it went. He didn't take this personally; she didn't show much interest in her family either. She had made a retreat from the world outside, and prison was her monastery. She had, of course, found religion, a jailhouse brand that was all about scripture quotes and photocopied screeds and a God generous with forgiveness and second chances.

She had given Nick a few of these tracts, also a picture of herself, taken by Freddi. He kept this in his wallet. The inmates here wore denim shirts, so there was no uniform to give away her location. She might be relaxing at home, if her home had cement block walls. In the photo she is not smiling. Nick would say her expression in this picture was "reflective." Like she was thinking about something important and still needed to think about it a little more.

"You have such dark circles under your eyes, it worries me," Olivia's mother told her. She was a worn-down woman. Her shoulders were like a wire hanger off which her dress hung. Her face was the face of someone a few hundred miles west of here, and fifty years back. Her daughter's imprisonment, you got the feeling, was only her latest bridge to cross.

The goofy brothers were silent. They almost never came up with anything to say to their sister on these visits. At first Nick thought they were ashamed of her, but over time he had come to see it was exactly the reverse. Her father was long gone, wherever. No one even mentioned him; her brothers underachieved in a reliable way. By doing something dramatic enough to land herself in prison, Olivia had earned the top spot. She was the most important person in the family.

They sat on old wooden office chairs across a scarred metal table from her. It was not a situation conducive to relaxed conversation. The family locked into a somber mood for these visits. For her part, Olivia never seemed particularly happy to see them, only relieved that they had come, that she hadn't been forsaken. Once they were here, she could relax and give them desultory attention during their visit.

"A decent night's sleep is hard to come by in here," she said. "Half these women are crazy in addition to being criminals. They need to tell everybody about whatever's pissing them off. Even if you can get to sleep in the middle of all the crap that goes on in here, you only have until three or four before the maniacs start babbling and the depressives start moaning. And well, by four, it's all over for me anyway because I have to go down and start mixing up the egg powder. Breakfast is at five. Meals in here are basically just another punishment thing."

Near the end of the visiting hour, the family always left Nick and Olivia alone, to give them a little privacy, although neither of them had ever asked for this.

"You don't have to keep coming up here," she said.

"I was in the neighborhood."

"We don't have any real connection. Not really."

"I'm almost done stripping the dining room set. When I'm finished, I'm just going to oil it. No varnish."

"I forgot to ask Mama for more paper." This was for her book on what Jesus really meant to communicate to the world. Nick didn't want to talk about this. She didn't want to talk about the apartment he was fixing up for them. She wasn't interested. That was okay. In here, he figured she could go ahead and be bored with him and his plans. When she got out—with luck, next year—she would have a clearer picture of her options. And by then he would have something solid to offer. What he was doing now was feathering the nest. The apartment was in a six-flat in Rogers Park; he got reduced rent for serving as the building handyman. He was buying up old furniture and refinishing it. He was trying to pull his lifestyle more in line with hers. He moderated his drug use. He wanted to keep his habits manageable, small quiet vices he would be able to shed when she got out.

"And Bic pens. They get stolen. They're a big deal in here. Everybody has something they want to write down about why they don't belong in here." She took a closer look at him. "You should wear a hat in the sun. Your face is starting to look like a dried apple."

"Thanks," Nick said, and laughed. He took this criticism as a sign of affection. "I'll get myself a flowered sun hat. That'll go down real well with the guys on the job. I won't take any shit about that."

This pushed Olivia to a weak smile, and she reached across the table to pat his hand before getting up to leave. Her touch unfurled inside Nick's head, and immediately seemed cause for a small celebration.

He waited in his car in the parking lot by the lake, eating Raisinets, tapping them out of the box one at a time. He clicked an Earth, Wind & Fire cassette into the tape deck. Most of the music he liked had happened during his adolescence. Great stuff and he was sticking with it.

He opened a folder of radio images someone sent Bernie from the dish at Arecibo. An event horizon, signaling a black hole beyond it. Nick and Bernie had been looking at this data for a while. He pulled an equation up in his head:

```
z(r)=sqrt(R3 / 2M) [sqrt(1 - (1 - (2Mr2 / R3)))] for r <= R
```

then,

```
z(r)=sqrt(R3 / 2M) [sqrt(1 - (1 - (2M / R)))] +
sqrt(8M (r - 2M)) - sqrt(8m (R - 2M)) for r >= R
```

He and Bernie collaborated even though Nick was no longer enrolled as a student. The whole school gestalt had gotten to be problematic. There was a casual quality to his attendance that burned the administration. In general, Nick was not terribly interested in showing up anywhere on a regular basis. He and the academic establishment differed on the importance of this.

The daytime population of the parking lot included apprentice drivers practicing three-point turns or parallel parking, or old men waxing their cars, but for the most part the lot at night was a bustling marketplace of sex and drugs. Every now and then some guy mistook the point of Nick's presence and pulled up next to him and looked over with an insolent expression that Nick now understood was supposed to be provocative. At first, he tried to look uninterested, but sometimes this was only interpreted as coyness, so now he would say straight out, "Hey. I'm just here for drugs. You know."

Specifically, he was here to meet up with one of two dealers. Angelo or Don. If one didn't have something for him, the other would. They both offered a good line of product and always showed up; if you had the money, they had the drugs. In the world of addicts, who were pretty much totally unreliable, good dealers were almost parental figures. Pillars of the transient community that cruised this lot. They were reassuring to him; their presence implied a population still interested in the clarifying experience of drugs. Used to be everyone was into getting high, or could be persuaded. More and more, though, people seemed to have left partying behind for a creeping, phony "adult" culture that was all about jobs you had to wear suits to, and success. Whatever that was.

Waiting in the lot was part of the whole experience; it built a little tension around scoring. While he waited, he closed his eyes and lit up an equation behind his lids.

Mb=Co3 / 2(pi)GPo2

The sound of a large engine idling interrupted this thought. It was Don in his black Mercedes. Nick turned off the dome light in his car.

"Really nice night," Don said once he had pulled next to Nick and rolled down his window. He was looking up at the sky where a full moon hung low and fat. But he wasn't talking about the clear sky or the mild fall temperatures. "I've got some excellent morphine drops," he said, clicking a small, brown bottle against the window opening. "Undiluted. Straight from hospice."

The price tag on these was too steep, though, so Nick just picked up a dozen Percodan.

"Hey. You can probably help me with this. My living room is the coldest room in my house. There's an old fireplace, but I've never tried it." Dealers always liked to talk to you as though you were a real person, or as though they were. Little conversations like this lubricated a transaction.

Nick told him, "Get someone over. Make sure the flue is working. Get it cleaned, get the chimney lined. You can build a fire in it then. Nice and cozy." He had told Don that he worked in construction, which was true on the mornings he could get it together to show up at this or that job. Telling people you are an astronomer, he found, was not usually a conversation starter. Or, worse, it started a conversation with the other person telling you his sign.

As he pulled onto the Drive, Nick popped three percs to get the party rolling, then headed over to Alice's. Something was wrong with her toilet; it ran on unless you did some complicated jiggling with the handle. He had promised to take care of this a week ago then lost track of time. He had a wrench and a new ball stopper on the passenger seat next to him. He took pride in Alice's loft; he'd done a lot of work on it, helped turn it from a gray space with a strong bleachy odor into an apartment she could live in.

According to her lease, Alice was only supposed to use the loft as a place to paint, but she lived there too, sort of openly on the sly. She had made a kitchen in one corner with counters that were planks across sawhorses, a two-burner hot plate, a giant sixties refrigerator in harvest gold—an artifact from an earlier American epoch. Nick rigged up a metal stall shower off the pipes on the big wash sink. Next to this was a toilet—the one now running on—that he had enclosed with drywall.

By the time he parked down the block from her, the pills were pushing through his blood, spreading their grace, casting a tint over Alice's neighborhood that was not a color so much as a mood. Even with the dog-boarding kennel and the dry cleaning plant, the atmosphere was definitely homey. He opened the plastic bag and took one more pill—a shooter to put him in a visitation groove.

"Boocs," Alice greeted him, opening the door. The nickname was ironic. All three siblings were named after operatic characters. Horace, their father, was a huge buff. Naming his kids was a little opportunity to show off his erudition. Alice was really Lucia. Nick was Nabucco. Only Carmen had hung with the deal.

Alice was surprised to see him, he could tell. People, he noticed, seemed less and less into the idea of dropping by. Now you were supposed to call first. The dropping-by era was, apparently, over.

"Are you high?" she asked him once he was inside. The question caught him off guard and in pondering it, he forgot what it was.

"High?" she tried again, pointing upward as a visual aid.

"Oh. No. No way." He didn't want to disappoint. She was so earnest. He adored Alice. At this exact moment, he was overwhelmed by how much he loved his sister. A lot of people loved her, many at first sight. They wanted to be her friend, or lover. They wanted to hire her or get her on their team. This was all due to something she put out, into the atmosphere around her. She was not beautiful in any conventional sense. The elements of her face were too severe, her eyes brown edging toward black, the whole effect weaving between mysterious and tragic. Something about this blend made people want it, want her. She had been hit on by gay guys, also by women in straight bars.

Right now she just continued to stare the truth out of him.

"Well, maybe a little," he admitted. "Just a little feel-good thing. A top-off. Today was visiting day."

"Oh," Alice said. "Right."

"You know, Olivia is really a very fascinating person." He pulled out his wallet, but Alice stopped him with a hand pressed on his arm. "I've seen the picture. Listen, we have to be quiet. Is toilet repair quiet? The thing is Maude's asleep already. She has to be downtown at five a.m. tomorrow so they can get her into makeup and out on the Michigan Avenue Bridge in some evening gown before the morning rush hour."

"Evening *pants,*" Maude said from the bed at the far end of the loft, around the corner so she was only a ghostly voice. The voice sounded wide-awake, though. "Who can sleep at eight-thirty at night?" she said as she came out in a T-shirt and men's striped pajama bottoms.

"Toddlers," Alice said as Maude pulled her into a headlock. She was way taller than Alice, so it was an easy move. "Toddlers are definitely asleep by now. Don't bother calling any of them."

Maude was great looking, but also a pain in the ass. She had disappeared after the accident, and now she was back again. Sort of. She wasn't sure she wanted to be a dyke. In Nick's opinion, Alice was too vulnerable to her. But just now, as he looked at them standing there so perfectly together, he got a whole other view. He could see how Alice, with Maude's arm draped over her shoulder, was taken care of. He saw now the way the two of them occupied a space that extended into the future. The image filled him with hope. The wide, flat plane of hope it lifted you onto—this was what he loved best about Percodan.

"I'm starving," Maude said.

"We could order some gyros from the Greek place," Alice said.

"Oh honey," Maude said. "You know my stupid job, my stupid life. We could order a grape, maybe."

Alice turned to Nick. "Are you hungry?"

He shook his head. He was trying to follow what they were saying, but the words kept clicking right and left, like a Ping-Pong ball being volleyed across the table. Clickety-clack. Clackety-click.

"I hate when he shows up like this," he heard Maude saying, but from a great distance, like an animated character on a cartoon show being played on a TV in another room. When he was straight, she scared him with her arrogance, that and her low opinion of him. She hated him for bringing Olivia to the wedding, for taking some stupefying amount of drugs with her, then letting her drive. He could tell she had also written him off as a loser. She thought he was blowing off a big career on account of the drugs.

He couldn't explain to her, to anyone, the whirl astronomy sets up inside a person's head, the vertigo that comes with trying to understand what's going on way out there. He might be the first person to understand a significant piece of missing information. People didn't see that pursuing information on this scale can be agitating. He needed something to help him chill out. Drugs were just extremely helpful. Also manual labor, which let him back off from the abstract into the concrete, finite, orderly nature of carpentry and plumbing. Tools and measures. Something, in the end, he could put his hand on.

"I can't let him back out on the street to drive around like a bumper car," Alice was telling Maude when he tuned back in. Then Alice guided him to the sofa. "Good thing you brought that wrench, Mr. Handy. You're going to be doing a lot of work tonight."

He saw the sofa coming into view. Lying down was so right. You couldn't argue with lying down. A perfectly simple equation appeared before him, linking black holes to dark energy. It shimmered for just a second, then dissolved.

small breeze

A few thousand kisses, maybe a hundred fights into their relationship, Maude leaned over the back of the sofa to kiss Alice, who was in the throes of a bad summer cold.

"I don't think you have a fever," she said. "Just take some Contac and you'll be fine.

"Stay and play doctor with me," Alice said.

"Can't. I've got a shoot at ten." But even as she said this, Maude was getting undressed, letting Alice pull her on top of her. "Okay. You win. Give me your cold. Come on. Really try."

This moment, taken out of context, would be misleading, making it appear their relationship had moved along to some further place where Alice could feel secure. What Alice wanted was for Maude to love her and they could go on from there to wherever people go when they have paved the road they'll be traveling together. That was not happening. They were still in the place where Maude was deciding which fork in the road to take. Maybe further back than that even. Maybe they were still waiting for the asphalt truck.

The problem was not between Alice and Maude. Their time together, their conversations, their shared jokes, the sex, even though they were three years in, was all still dense with color, everything so amazingly vibrant. The problem lay in the connection between Maude and her mother, Marie, who had by now figured out what was going on between Maude and Alice, and had persuaded her daughter to move back into her own apartment. She referred to Alice's loft as an occasion of sin. Alice was resigned to this move. What worried her more was that Maude had taken on some of her mother's crazy queer hating herself. She saw her attraction to Alice as something inside her, but not exactly who she was. Alice feared Maude saw it as something she should be able to kill.

"This won't really change anything," Maude said, now deeply late for the shoot, rushing back into her clothes and clattering handfuls of tape cassettes into a duffel. "I'll call to see how you are tonight. And I'll see you this weekend."

Alone, Alice sat at the kitchen table while her coffee went cold, then finally went into the studio and sanded a gessoed canvas to begin a fresh portrait of Casey Redman. This would be the fifth. The early ones came to Alice set in places of Casey's childhood—inside a snow fort in a field by the toboggan hill, on a raft in what was clearly Sullivan Lake. Like that. As these were also places familiar to Alice from her time at the co-op, she was remembering as much as imagining. But the next one—Casey awkwardly slow-dancing with a boy at a party—came to Alice already articulated, though she had no familiarity with the specific setting, what seemed to be a paneled family room. In this new painting—which she already saw complete although she had yet to touch brush to canvas—Casey is about fourteen, as she would have been if she were still living. She still has white-blond hair although Alice realized that, had the girl lived, it might well have darkened by now. In this picture, she is leaning inside a shadow, against a pole, which supports the high, blue-white light pouring across the edge of a football field.

Alice was beginning to see the terms of these paintings. She would wait for them to arrive and then paint them, like clicking a shutter, making snapshots out of oil and canvas. This was the central point of her art now, to record the girl's unlived life. Also, these would be her best paintings. She knew this already. She could see a whole world of paintings ahead of her that she wanted to make, and she would make them, but none would be as good as the Casey Redman paintings. She wasn't sure if this was a gift, or a sentence.

Around noon, she looked out the window next to her easel. Across the street, there was a vestigial patch of the neighborhood as it used to be—a short row with a wholesale butcher, a fishmonger, a greengrocer. On the sidewalk directly below Alice's windows, there was a cart that sold sno-cones with breathtakingly lurid syrups. Chartreuse and ultraviolet and blood orange. The scents, which in a weird way matched the colors, drifted sweetly up through the gray, slightly industrial air.

She broke for lunch at the *taqueria* downstairs. Coming back in, she could feel Maude's absence as a small breeze whipping through the place. She sat down by the phone, but didn't know who to call. None of her friends wanted to hear about Maude anymore—her comings and goings, her waffling about her sexuality. They had said what they could say, put an arm around Alice's shoulders, bought her a drink, took a few weepy calls graciously, and now they were done. Alice was on her own with this now. Then she thought, Jean. Jean might have a few drops of sympathy left in her. Alice biked up Halsted to her studio. Jean was at a soundboard pushing small levers up and down. She had headphones on and didn't see Alice until she looked up.

"What're you working on?" Alice said.

"Oh. Finishing up the Sylvie album."

A year ago, Jean's uncle dropped dead at a Cubs game, cheering then dead. Suddenly she was in possession of a small windfall. She moved back to the city, bought herself some state-of-the-art recording equipment and a real studio—a two-story brick building on Halsted with a storefront at street level, an apartment above. Free of financial constraints, she was now able to make a significant contribution to music preservation. She had already signed a few neglected artists she considered truly important, even though almost no one knew their work. She intended to change that.

One was Sylvie Artaud, an elderly *chanteuse réaliste* Jean discovered in a tourist trap in Montmartre, playing piano, backed by a Mr. Drum, singing "C'est si bon" and "Hi-Lili, Hi-Lo" for Americans killing time waiting for showtime at the Moulin Rouge.

"I think Sylvie's problem—in terms of commercial success—is that she's too good at what she does. Her songs, you know, about the crippled streetwalker. Or that one about the woman whose lover is killed as he's bringing her flowers and doesn't see the falling safe from behind his bouquet. Who could bear to listen to that? I think her records are bought by the same handful of fans. Women with a few divorces behind them. Older gay guys. People who live in some far reach of romantic nihilism. For them, Sylvie's songs are kind of a liturgy. Which is great. All that intense devotion. Still, I'd like to see her reach a wider audience."

Alice couldn't listen to Jean talk about Sylvie at the moment. She told her that Maude might have left her.

"You don't know for sure?"

"What can I say? She's here, then not here. She won't stay put. I am either with her or waiting for her. I'm so used to the pattern I'm imprinted with it by now. Like T. E. Lawrence. He was beaten and maybe buggered by Turkish guards in a prison cell, and then for the rest of his life, to get aroused he had to hire someone to give him a good whipping."

"Yes," Jean said. "Just like you. A little more exotic than your case, maybe, what with the Turks and the prison cell and all."

"There's something else," Alice said. She needed to tell someone who knew Carmen, to test the waters. "Matt is having an affair with the babysitter. I saw them in his car in a 7-Eleven lot."

"Maybe they were getting milk."

"They were not getting milk. They were having a big serious conversation. It's worse than if they were making out. It means they're already up to the serious conversation stage."

"What's Carmen going to do?"

"I haven't told her. I'm still thinking about that. I'm thinking maybe I shouldn't. Maybe it's better she doesn't know. Maybe it'll blow over."

Long blank of dead silence from Jean. One eyebrow went up and didn't come down.

"Okay, I know. But shut up about it now. Shut up that silence. And especially shut up that eyebrow."

On the way back into her building, Alice pulled a handful of mail out of the box. Here was something good. She had won a fellowship. A few thousand dollars. She had applied for this, among many others, so many months back she recalled its specifics only vaguely. Coming off the elevator into her loft, another small surprise awaited her. The small breeze of Maude's absence was no longer present. The space was filled with vague energy. Maude was on the sofa, reading a script. She was making tentative moves out of modeling, into acting.

"I missed you," she said, then took Alice's hand, pulling her down on top of her. "I just fucking missed you."

At the bank the next day, Alice hummed along to the jaunty instrumental piping ludicrously from the speaker in the ceiling above her. "He blew his mind out in a car," she hummed as she filled out a deposit slip, and saw that she had misread the amount of the fellowship check, that there was another zero at the end, ten times what she thought she was getting. About twice what she made in a year. She went over and sat down on a long leather-covered bench near the entrance. Alice had wondered in the past what this padded bench was for, who would need to sit down at the bank. Now she knew. People who needed a moment or two to accommodate the news that their life was about to change.

saints and martyrs

Carmen was frosting a cake in a kitchen electrically bright, and cozy—twice warmed by the furnace and the oven, an atmosphere antidotal to the damp chill pressing against the windows. "Imagine" was playing on the radio. Today marked ten years since John Lennon's death and the airwaves were thick with Beatles songs.

She was so exhausted she could almost fall asleep right here, standing up. Her nights lately passed with a tumble of fatiguing dreams, wet socks in a dryer.

Abruptly, a work crew—husband, son, dog—barged in through the side door. They dragged big smells—adrenaline and chilled sweat, damp fur—with them from the alley, where they'd been shoveling last night's snow to clear a patch in front of the garage door. The blast of cold air, the noisy explosion of arrival, filled the kitchen and jostled the delicate balance of elements Carmen had assembled around her.

Matt was big when she met him, but a couple of years ago he started working out at the Y, and his mass had taken on architecture. He had turned himself from a Paul Bunyan kind of guy, into a hunk. Now any room he entered strained to contain his physicality. He hadn't reinvented himself for Carmen; she thought he was fine the way he already was.

Gabe followed Matt with an exaggerated, slouchy walk, trying to imitate his father, trying to figure out what being a man felt like. So far, he was a mild disappointment to Matt, who was extremely sports-minded. Gabe hadn't shown any interest in catching or throwing or hitting any sort of ball. Neither was he interested in watching professionals throw or catch or hit balls. Of course, Matt tried not to let his disappointment show, but still, somehow, Gabe knew.

Since they'd come inside, their dog, Walter Payton—an unsortable jumble of breeds, they'd had him almost a year now—skittered back and forth among them, trying to translate for Carmen the excitement of their hard work. *All done!* Gabe caught him and knelt to kiss the dog's head, to show him he had been a big help.

At six, Gabe was tall for his age, but with a fragile air. He wanted to make paintings, like his aunt, his grandfather. He wore glasses and his complexion was pale, his cheeks freckled. Skinny and often distracted, he looked beat-upable, snatchable. This pressed on Carmen's heart and made her fearful every time he stepped out of her view, into the wider world.

"It's chain-gang work out there," Matt said, pumping up Gabe's pride in the job. "Warming up. Everything's turning into ten-ton slush." He dragged a passing finger through the frosting bowl, the sort of invasive gesture Carmen hated when they first got together, then became inured to, and now hated in a fresh way. She didn't say anything, though, just kept spreading the cream cheese frosting over the cake, like a patient in a mental institution performing a calming, repetitive task. The cake was for her father's birthday dinner tonight, an old-fashioned prune cake recipe from his childhood.

Gabe had shrugged off his parka and was going through the *Tribune* on the table to find the comics. Walter had opportunistically wedged himself between Carmen's legs and the cabinets under the counter where she was working, just in case any frosting might drip his way. This warm family tableau was deceptive. It only existed because Carmen stood here in this kitchen, determined to keep things small and regular.

"What about we just get some takeout for supper? Chinese maybe," Matt said to Gabe. "Give your mom a break?"

Carmen's response to this innocuous suggestion was to start crying—because Matt was being kind to her, because she hadn't had any good sleep in days, also because he had completely forgotten her father's birthday, an occasion they used to have fun dreading together. She kept standing at the counter and braced up her voice. "We can't," she said. "We have to go see Horace."

"Oh boy, I totally forgot," Matt said. "The thing is, I've got someplace I have to be later." As he said this he moved to put a hand on her shoulder, to touch her, but stopped shy. This was worse even than his telling her the other day that she had been such an important person in his life. These were the sort of terrible, quiet things that had been happening in the weeks since Matt told Carmen about him and Paula.

That Paula was only nineteen and Gabe's babysitter made the whole situation look like a giant lurid cliché, like some sort of early midlife crisis for Matt, or some delayed oat-sowing. But it wasn't any of this. Matt was not an oat-sower, and he was too sane and organized for an inner crisis. And "nineteen" and "babysitter," while both true, gave no picture at all of Paula. She was not a naughty nympho teenage babysitter. She was a studious, willowy, plain girl with late braces she had been paying for herself. The affair had been going on for several months and had yet to be consummated. Matt was Catholic, and Paula was very Catholic, and so they were waiting until he got out of his marriage.

The reason Matt had given Carmen for discarding his marriage was that Paula was "more traditional, more religious." She went to daily Mass and wore her hair long and straight, parted down the center. She wore a lot of clothes patterned with small flower prints; she sewed a lot of these out-of-date garments herself. She told Carmen she loved helping her mother at home, both with the housekeeping and with the younger kids. When Carmen tried to make conversation with her beyond what Gabe ate for lunch or did the guy come to service the furnace, she quickly found herself drowning in long anecdotes about Paula's large, ailment-ridden family and their miraculous cures as the result of prayers, particularly the family rosary. Or an installment of Paula's school life, or her latest failure with one or another of her complicated knitting projects. How could she be the person Carmen was being left for?

Now Matt was waiting for their divorce to come through, also for an annulment so he could remarry within the Church. This was apparently a tricky business and Carmen had no idea how long all this would take. She was letting him stay so they could have Christmas as a family. If all the legal rigmarole lingered past January, she would ask him to move out. But for the time being, she just stood in the kitchen at the back storm door at night, watching Matt sit on the steps hunched inside his pea coat, his exhalations creating small clouds of condensation, his heart sunk with the gravity of his love.

Gabe would probably be fine with the rearrangement. Paula had been part of his life for half its length, and if his father moved in with her, it might not be all that disruptive. His people would still be in place for him. In reality, Carmen was the only one being left.

She was beginning to see the depth and breadth of her misunderstanding. She thought, in spite of their differences, that their partnership was complicated and interesting. Marriage and parenthood seemed so fascinating to her right from the start. Matt had come into the picture already assembled, a full complement of personality aspects with which she had to acquaint herself. Gabe was a total surprise. Until his arrival she had only considered him hypothetically, as someone small who would need to be fed and changed and kept from harm and illness. One or another of the generic babies on the covers of the books she read in preparation. From the moment of his birth, though, he had been such a specific person. So particularly kind, and reflective. As soon as he discovered that meat came from animals, he would no longer eat it. So she and Matt became vegetarians by default and sympathy. Once everyone wore out on grilled cheese sandwiches and scrambled eggs, Carmen tapped into cookbooks from nostalgic non-places like Greenwood Hollow, or volumes like *The Bountiful Bean* that came at the challenge from a particular angle. All of this minutiae was so interesting, life spilling into the blanks without her having much to do with it. And she thought that this was what family comprised, the creation of little dilemmas and challenges, which then had to be figured out, or met, and that both she and Matt were equally engaged in this enterprise. She let herself be lulled by a companionship that seemed to blossom and prosper, a day-to-day built on small conversations, endless amazement at their child, hilariously awful camping trips, messages left on a kitchen marker board for ingredients that needed to be picked up for dinner. The only problem with this calm assessment was that she was, as it turned out, completely wrong.

When Matt took Carmen to dinner one night last week at her favorite restaurant, the Paradise Café (while Paula stayed home with Gabe; that was the truly noxious part), to talk about "something important," she thought he was going to say he'd found a way they could move into a bigger house. Their current one was too far west, and too small. They were on Ravenswood, facing the tracks. The urgent rush of the commuter trains heading north to the suburbs and south to the Loop was a large component of their immediate surroundings. They would have both preferred a less locomotive setting.

So she thought the "something important" was "new house." All of Matt's surprises up to that point had been pleasant ones. But this time the surprise was Paula. Now Carmen could see, with heated humiliation, that the peaceful atmosphere in the room of their marriage was, for Matt, only a muted backdrop to a large, loudly ticking clock. While she had been going on, pretending their union was a rough but working organism, he had been quietly waiting for something to get him out of a marriage he had always seen as tainted. Carmen saw the stain, too. She could still, anytime, look back and see herself standing there in her ironic red wedding dress, just wanting her guests to leave, sleepily watching the splayed fins of Olivia's old Dodge sashay with her good wishes down the dirt road, off the farm, navigating by its fog lamps, on its short, murderous course. At first they talked a lot about their culpability. They even went a few times to a couples' counselor. After that, Carmen didn't think the problem had gone away, or would ever go away, but that it was something they shared, as opposed to something that divided them. But now she could see the whole of the marriage played out under a long stretch of shadow it couldn't outrun.

Carmen and Gabe dressed up a little for Horace's party. For Gabe this meant fresh pants, shined shoes, and a dress shirt. An outfit to which he added a cheesy red satin magician's cape.

"Peeeuuw!" He climbed into their car, following Walter, who liked to come along, anywhere. He didn't mind the sour mildew aroma at all, and settled with a wheeze into the pile of old clothes in the back.

"Just hold your nose," Carmen told Gabe. "We don't have very far to go." Yesterday she spent the afternoon combing the racks at AMVETS and Salvation Army for large-size dresses and pants suits for women at Hearth/Home, the shelter where she worked—women who were going on job interviews, or back to school. Except for the really old women, who could be small and gnarly, clients at the shelter tended to be large gals. They lived on McDonald's and sweet wine. Plus, they hadn't been putting in much of an effort to keep themselves up.

Coming up the stairs to her parents' apartment, Carmen could hear the overlapping ebb and spike of party conviviality. Walter had rushed ahead and was already standing with his nose touching the apartment door.

"Pay attention to your grandfather," Carmen told Gabe, her hand on the doorknob. "It's his birthday."

"Okay. But inside me, I don't like him. He's too loud, and he's always mad at everybody."

✦ ✦ ✦

The apartment, which occupied the floor above her father's studio, was pure sixties bohemian, beatnik through and through. Danish modern furniture, blond and webbed; sagging brick-and-board bookcases; a set of bongos gathering dust in the corner, primitive African art on the walls along, of course, with Horace's paintings. The apartments of all her parents' Old Town crowd bore a similar stamp. These were the lairs of old artists and their younger trophy muses, women who were themselves now creeping through late middle age, variously thinning down or plumping up dramatically. These apartments were historic sites of landmark parties filled with artistic proclamations, the ignition of feuds, the birth of signature cocktails. Also of false teeth lost in toilets, tatami mats puked on, friendships bitterly ended, chops busted, cross-pollination among couples transacted in bathrooms and broom closets, and usually someone naked found passed out between the layers of coats on the bed.

This apartment had also—between the parties—been Alice and Carmen and Nick's home. There was little of the empty nest to it now, though. The girls' room had been refurbished into Loretta's office when she got her realtor's license. Nick's was now home to a giant ornate wood console television Alice called the Credenza Cordoba, and a low-slung, U-shaped sofa. Loretta referred to the room as the "entertainment center." Everything else was much the same as it had always been. The whole apartment had its own distinct, static smell.

Gabe zipped through the crowd in the living room and headed for Nick's old reflector telescope, which had, over time, washed up against the far wall of windows. Carmen set her cake at the end of the buffet and told Walter, "Nothing on this table is for dogs." At the center of the buffet was Loretta's infamous Texas jailhouse chili. Carmen got a cautionary aura of heartburn as she stared it down.

She checked out the crowd, mostly old friends of her parents, the people who represented adulthood to her when she was a child. Paco and Cindy Beecham. Larry and Giselle Zorn. Phaedra Carlson, who was now widowed and on her own.

She found her brother sitting by himself against the wall beyond the buffet table, a little too upright on a frayed sofa, holding a can of ginger ale as though it were a grenade on which he had just pulled the pin.

"Hey," he said, and shifted over a little to make room for her.

She was by now used to the thinner, more aquiline nose that emerged from the reconstruction after it had been broken by Casey Redman's father. It made him look maybe British, like someone who collected butterflies and had read all of Trollope. She also noticed that his hair was meticulously cut, the tips blonder than the rest.

"Has Olivia been doing something bleachy here?" She pulled at a piece for inspection.

"Ouch. Come on, you think that doesn't hurt? What can I say? When you live with a hairdresser, shit happens." His breath, as usual, was deeply wintergreen. It was like talking to someone in a Norwegian forest. He used tiny squeeze bottles of concentrated freshener he picked up at truck stops. He had used this stuff since the days when he needed to show up for work, but was dead drunk.

"Where is she anyway?"

"She's supposed to be parking, but my guess is she's just sitting in the car, building enough critical mass to come in here."

Carmen was grateful—everyone was—for Olivia's presence in Nick's life, for the constraining effect she had on him. She was the one thing he seemed to value more than getting high. Carmen no longer thought of Olivia as a murderer. By now she was stern and focused, a new person who seemed to have been designed in opposition to the stoner who casually got behind the wheel and killed a girl. Plus she had paid, paid a little for each of them. They were all aware of this.

"Well, sure. I can see that." And she could. She could picture Olivia in sharp detail, sitting in her car down the block, drumming her fingers on the steering wheel. "So what's up? How is it being back at school?"

"It's weird. You drop out for even just a couple of years and you come back and you're already the old guy."

"But you're finishing the thesis," Carmen prompted.

"Sort of. The thing is, I have way too much stuff. I've got to start pruning. Tons of new information is rolling in. By the time you find something and pin it down, something more has been discovered. Not just theoretical stuff, but stuff we can actually see. We have better scopes, and more ways of looking. Radio scopes, of course. Also X-ray scopes. They're getting ready to send a big reflector scope into space, to get clear views from outside our atmosphere. The bang put a lot into motion and now we have more ways to watch the action."

"I love the big bang," Carmen said.

"Yeah." He exhaled wearily. "Everyone loves it. It's very lovable."

From Nick, she knew that the bigness started very, very, very small. But extremely compressed. In the moments before the bang happened, the whole universe was the size of a dime. And Nick didn't really let you say "happened"; there wasn't any space or time for it to happen in. Back then—although he didn't let you say "then" either—space-time and matter and energy were all just rolled into something incredibly dense and hot.

Carmen had to flex her mind to accommodate stuff like this. Astronomy was not her strong suit. It took Nick three demonstrations with a tilted apple Earth circling a peach Sun to get her to understand the seasons.

"Probably lots happening on the alien front." Space aliens and astrology were his least favorite subjects. Really, he didn't even consider them subjects.

So he didn't say anything.

So she didn't say anything either.

Finally he said, "If they come for a visit, it probably won't be with friendly intentions. And they won't be little green men. The distances are too great for any sort of humanoid creatures to make it all the way here. Even traveling at the speed of light—and you know what's faster than the speed of light?"

"Something," she guessed.

"Nothing. To get here they will have to be more advanced than us. Which probably means they'll have evolved into artificial intelligence." He stopped and looked at Carmen with well-founded suspicion.

"But I just read somewhere another farm wife said she was taken onboard a saucer by very smooth creatures with short horns. And, of course, she was measured and anally probed."

"It would take so long for images of Earth to reach those green guys that they'd be watching dinosaurs. Based on their information, when they came for a visit, they'd bring very large anal probes. Which would be useless on us."

"You're so much fun," Carmen said.

He pulled her toward him to kiss her hair at the temple. Aside from his irresponsibility, he was a very sweet person. You just couldn't count on him for anything. Anything. Nor could you believe anything he said about himself or his life. Ultimately, this made him a tiresome person to talk with. Carmen had scaled back her expectations. She was just thankful that he was sitting next to her on this sofa, to all appearances sober. Before Olivia came out of prison and he straightened up to get her back, there was a scary stretch. Detox, then rehab, then retox, then back through the cycle again. Two days after they put him on a plane to a boot camp rehab in Minnesota, the baggage claim in Minneapolis called to say he had never picked up his suitcase. He hadn't been able to make it past a bar in the Twin Cities airport. Then a month later, on his way out, back at the airport, he got snagged by the same bar.

"Airports are hard for him" was Alice's analysis.

"Right," Carmen said, "Airports are the problem."

Olivia came through the door in a pea coat and a Mongolian hat with earflaps. She looked great in a flinty, soviet way. Whatever blandness there was to her before, prison had cut away. Horace seemed to be giving her a big welcome, putting an arm around her shoulder. Out of her presence and Nick's, he referred to her as Butch. As she disappeared into the back of the apartment to get rid of her jacket, Horace glanced in Nick and Carmen's direction. He bowed like a butler, then lumbered across the room toward them. Nick started humming the theme from *Jaws*. Horace still projected a hearty image, although some of his former, evenly distributed bulk had slipped off his shoulders to form a gut that hung over his belt. His craggy features had lumped up a little. Carmen hadn't figured on this, that age would make him more sympathetic. As he approached them, he opened his arms in a giant air hug.

"Glad you could make it," he said, then to Nick, "I just ran into your lovely bride at the door." There was something off about the way he said this, but nothing to respond to directly. Something about Olivia, maybe her indifference to his charms, bugged Horace.

"You know, I think I might go look for her," Nick said. "She doesn't know many people here." Nick pinched Carmen's arm to signal that he was leaving Horace all to her, then got up and slipped off sideways through the crowd.

"I hate this party," Horace said. "Every year I hate it. I just go along with it to please your mother." He was lying. He loved this party. He adored it. So Carmen called his bluff.

"Join the club. Really, we could have a party for all the people who hate this party."

Eventually Horace was given his due with a falling-apart rendition of "Happy Birthday," then a moment to blow out the candles on Carmen's prune cake, then an opportunity to hold forth about the length and breadth of life, the importance of work, and of course, the compulsory jokes about getting older—like how he needed the prunes now more than the cake.

Gabe, fresh from a headlong run across the room, screeched to a halt in front of his grandfather.

"Hey, boy." Horace ran a hand through Gabe's hair, then tugged on his cape. "How's the magic business these days? How's tricks?"

Horace was fascinated by Gabe, or more accurately had found in him someone he'd like to be a little fascinating for. Maybe he was looking for a kid with whom he could do it better. Maybe. Carmen tried to be optimistic, but at the same time she kept an eye out for so much as the first sign of sabotage, the first discouraging word. She would yank Gabe out of Horace's reach before the old man could blink.

"I brought you something." Gabe handed Horace a cardboard tube purporting to hold

Candy Mints

Horace opened it gamely and laughed in an explosive, bogus way when a cloth-and-coil snake leapt out. Although Gabe was older than his years in many ways, his sense of humor was squarely that of a six-year-old—although perhaps a six-year-old from an earlier generation—and for the past year or so he had been fascinated by practical jokes. He was abetted by Alice and Nick, and now had a collection of mischief that also included a little pad of plastic vomit, a rubber spiral of dog poop, an ink bottle with its accompanying spill, a whoopee cushion, a tube of blackening toothpaste and a squirting lapel flower. Everyone braced a little when greeting him.

Now Horace folded his free arm around Alice's narrow shoulders. Alice currently had a drastic look to her. Her hair was short and gelled straight back off her face.

"Sharon Stone wore her hair like this when I painted her," Horace informed anyone listening. A while back he had a stretch of painting celebrity portraits. Carmen noticed that lately he was more than ever into puffing himself up. She supposed this must be a hard time for him. Alice had had a solo show in October. A new Kenney was stepping into the art world. Of course he came to the opening, full of praise and paternal pride. But then Alice got terrific notices, particularly in the *New York Times* and *Artforum*. Horace would have read these, also would have noticed that only the local reviews mentioned that she was his daughter. He bided his time until she had some new paintings. Then praised them to her as "technically interesting."

Alice stood inside the circle of his arm, not bothering to listen. She was extremely adept at dealing with him, taking neither his charms nor his malice very seriously. Carmen admired this self-protection. She couldn't quite muster it herself. She could still (and hated herself when she did) fall for her father's faint praise, and be stung by his withheld approval. But Alice hadn't gotten off scot-free. She came to the party to please Loretta, to whom she would always be in thrall. Basically, she was still bouncing up and down, waiting for her mother to watch her jump off the diving board. But Loretta was and always would be too distracted to turn her head to see.

For a few years after she came out, Alice essentially got dumped by Loretta, who couldn't see the point of being a lesbian. In her scheme of things where men were everything, if you weren't one, or attached to one, what was your value? Alice took the rejection on the chin. She stayed away. It was Horace who mended the break. He put pressure on Loretta, invited Alice home for dinner. Although he could be vicious—a sniper, a setter of hidden traps—he did reach out to Alice. Carmen had to give him that. Her Jungian analyst had helped Carmen look at people as holograms, see through and around to all their sides. Horace and Loretta were fairly terrible, narcissistic parents, there was no arguing that, but they weren't Pol Pot, they weren't Idi Amin. Or at least they were confined to a smaller stage.

"Come with me for a smoke," Carmen said to Alice, tugging her out of the circle of Horace's well-wishers.

Alice went for their coats while Carmen made sure Gabe was happy enough in the company of the two other kids at the party—somebody's grandchildren—a fat girl and a boy who looked as if he was going to teach the other two how to play doctor. She found Walter curled up, sacked out on the Indian-print pillows on her parents' bed, enjoying a lull in his socializing.

"Come on," she said, scratching his head. "Let's go outside. Have a pee."

The day had warmed up unseasonably in the afternoon, but now that the sun was down, it was too cold to be sitting outdoors. Even swaddled in sweaters and wool coats, Carmen and Alice sat with their feet up, arms wrapped around their calves. The building's backyard garden was still in a state of abandonment from the fall—oilcloth cushions on the wrought iron furniture puddled with damp, matted leaves, the limp arteries of Loretta's tuberous begonias draped over the edges of painted clay pots. Walter lifted a leg to pee on one of them, then went off to sniff the perimeter of the patio an inch at a time.

On one of the low tables, Alice found an ashtray half-filled with soaked and shredded cigarette stubs.

"Butts of yesteryear," she said, then gave them a closer look. "They might even be ours." She dumped them onto the soil surrounding a small, extremely dead bush, then lit up fresh smokes for them both.

"Technically, I'm eight minutes early for this one." She was on a quitting program. She could have cigarettes, but only at precise intervals. This was supposed to break down links between smoking and certain daily activities like being on the phone, or having a cup of coffee. Or conversations like this one, where smoking seemed integral to the discourse. The program also involved movies of lung cancer surgeries and gasping cowboys. She had to keep a jam jar with her, filled with water and the butts of all the cigarettes she had smoked that day.

"It's supposed to repulse me."

"How's that going?"

"Actually, it's more just embarrassing. I mean, when I'm out I either have to explain the jar, or worse, look like I'm someone who saves my wet butts."

Carmen, who was in no place to quit just now, inhaled deeply, then exhaled and said, "I'll bet some cigarettes are harder to resist than others."

"Oh yes. I think about that—how it'll be after I've totally quit. Like, say, after years and years of being a heterosexual, Sigourney Weaver suddenly decides she needs to have a queer experience, or maybe she needs to practice for some movie role, and anyway she decides to do it with me. And it's great of course, and afterward she lights up and offers me one."

"Yeah," Carmen said, mulling this over. "That cigarette Sigourney passes across the bed would be a tough one to say no to."

They smoked in silence a while.

"Well, I guess we've done the Sloans," Alice said. Carmen had told her about the breakup with Matt. This, of course, was no surprise to Alice, who'd seen him and the babysitter months ago in the 7-Eleven lot. Maude, the other absent Sloan, had moved from Chicago to L.A., from modeling to acting. Based on what little Carmen had seen of Maude on TV—in a miniseries in which she played a bored housewife who was secretly a drug-addicted call girl, and a movie about a troop of alien girl scouts—she was a terrible actress, wooden. Often she appeared stunned by the other actor's line. Really, it was a testament to how great looking she was that she got any parts at all. She was living with a cameraman, although in the *People* article, he looked pretty gay to Carmen, so what was that about?

"Why do I feel she's not really, truly gone?" Carmen said. "Why do I feel her hovering above this conversation?" Carmen considered Maude an addiction—a boring one like an addiction to Afrin, or bingo, but one that had nonetheless arrested Alice's emotional development.

"Who cares where she is, whether she's coming or going? It doesn't matter. I'm done," Alice said.

Carmen liked this firm tone, although, of course, she didn't trust it at all.

"She'll try to come back," Alice said. "She can try all the men she wants. She'll come back to women. She's a bloodhound who's been given the scent on the glove."

Carmen was always a little startled (and titillated) when Alice said things like this. She wasn't sure if this was her sister's way of being shocking, or if lesbians all talked this way among themselves. It always tripped her up. She used to imagine love between women as a languid extension of friendship. Something Virginia Woolf-ish involving tea and conversation and sofas and afternoon eliding into evening, a small lamp needing to be turned on, but left unlit. And so she was brought up short by Alice's exhausting—even just to witness—passion for Maude, her desolation since Maude walked out of her life. This cynicism was a new element, maybe a further phase.

"Fuck," Alice said, as though Carmen had been interrogating her and her story had been shattered. She took Carmen's cigarette and from it lit a fresh one for herself—way off the schedule; the butt jar sat far away on one of the lawn chairs. "I'm just a blockhead. I'll get over her; I just need a little more time."

Carmen watched Walter suddenly digging furiously in a corner of the yard. He probably smelled a critter.

"You and Matt," Alice said, "your thing was so much weirder. He didn't seem like an affair type and you guys seemed to really like each other. It's like somebody misheard something. Like meet me under the big clock at noon on Wednesday, but the other person heard one p.m. on Thursday."

"I know. But what could I do once Paula was in place, when they were already off and running? They have common goals, he told me. They want to become missionaries. Basically all I could do was step aside and let them get on with their plans."

"That would be way too civilized for me. Too saints and martyrs. I'd be ready for some hair pulling about now. Some driving my pickup broadside into her trailer."

Carmen had heard—from Jean—that Alice was pretty dramatic around her "final" breakup with Maude. Bad phone calls. Public scenes. A car was keyed.

Carmen said, "I guess I was looking at everything from the wrong angle. I didn't think we were breaking up. I thought he and I were just having this interesting conversation about how to be married in the late twentieth century. And how to go forward, together. It was kind of like when I had all those parking tickets I was contesting with the city. I thought that was a lively back-and-forth, too, and then I came out of the house one day and my car was booted."

Alice tried to help, but all she had to offer was a pageant of less-than-helpful suggestions. She made divorce sound like a breeze, like enrolling in a night school class in Portuguese, or organizing a closet. Some minor reassignment of Carmen's time and interest. She didn't understand that, beyond the humiliation and sorrow, Carmen would be left with no credit in her name, and a skimpy salary from Hearth/Home. These were the sorts of details that bored Alice.

"Let's go prowl around a little," Carmen said, meaning in Horace's studio. She made a little chich-chich sound to call Walter over. "Let's see what the old guy has percolating in there."

They would have attracted attention by turning on the lights, so they poked around in semidarkness, silent except for Walter's slight wheeze, the small clink of his tags. Their father was present even in his absence. This was his territory. Here he could be the center of his universe, lathering up his overscaled paintings. Long days with Puccini blaring over the huge speakers and Loretta slipping in and out with lunch or tea on a tray as though Horace was the "Van Gogh of the Prairie," as some fawning exhibition catalog described him some years ago, and not just a lucky, self-inflated hack.

Tonight they hit pay dirt—two huge new paintings tilted against the wall, ready to be packed up and shipped off to the corporate client that had commissioned them. They were titled on small brass plates nailed at the bottom of their frames. Both were on a racing theme. *Sunrise at Santa Anita* and *Dusk in the Paddock*. Everything was muted, colors subdued, action suspended, a benevolent dusting of sunshine brought to bear on the equine subjects.

"We probably shouldn't make fun of him anymore," Carmen said, "now that he's started getting old with the hip surgery and the pasty, skinny-chest thing."

"The skinny-chest thing and the white-hair-creeping-out thing," Alice said.

"Yes, creeping out because he still leaves his shirt unbuttoned. His velour shirt. He looks like someone who hung out with Frank Sinatra. Someone who kept Frank amused in the limo."

When Horace was still making his own gestural paintings, he could hang on to the illusion that he ranked somewhere in the world of artists. Now all his work was subdued, representational, and commissioned, the subject matter and canvas sizes specified in advance, color schemes suggested. He was a dancing bear now, a bear in a hat and frilly skirt. This, Carmen suspected, had given him a deeper, more covert sort of meanness, as opposed to the light, capricious version he used to practice.

"It's sad," she said now.

"It's so fucking sad," Alice said.

The dark of the airless hallway held perfectly still. And then Alice whinnied. Carmen pawed at the ground with a hoof.

"We're rotten," Carmen said.

"No. We've earned our lousy jokes. They're prepaid."

They came up the stairs and into the apartment. Carmen went down the hall to check on Gabe, who was doing card tricks for his own small audience in the entertainment center. She came back into the living room and was beckoned over by her father, who was talking with Nick and Olivia, who had their coats on, but were being detained.

"They bought a little trailer," Horace told her. "They're going to see America."

"The Teardrop," Nick said. He was nervous, like an animal sensing the coming tsunami. He was never wrong about Horace, and so Carmen got nervous herself. As Olivia moved toward the door, Horace plucked the sleeve of her jacket.

"I'm coming down this week to collect my birthday present." He turned to Carmen. "She's going to give me a haircut and a blowjob." And then he looked sideways just a little, to show the mistake was not innocent, not a confusion of blowjob and blow-dry. He got away with this sort of thing all the time. They all let him. Not this time, though. Olivia was not in on this policy. She hauled back and brought her hand forward with enough velocity that when her palm met the side of his smirk, it made a sound like a cap gun, and Horace tipped sideways and before he could right himself, fell into the bar table, knocking over several bottles and a few glasses. His expression—pure bewilderment—was so satisfying to see that Carmen didn't make any move to help. A few partygoers rushed into this gap. Olivia took off, Nick behind her.

Alice said in a low voice to Carmen as she tugged her by the elbow, "Here's the good news. I think the party might be over."

On the drive home, Carmen and Gabe stopped at the Golden Nugget on Lincoln. One of the best things about not eating meat was that they were exempt from Loretta's jailhouse chili. But this left them, at the moment, in need of some vegetarian junk food. Pancakes. They ate silently, steeped in their own separate thoughts. Gabe wrapped up a pancake in a paper napkin for Walter, who waited in the van. They could see him through the restaurant window; he was in the driver's seat, looking back at them.

Carmen put the nightmare of Horace to the side for the moment. She had her own situation to take care of. She was going to have to get in gear soon; she'd have to talk with Nola Flanders, the lawyer connected to the shelter. She'd have to find a financial planner and go back to her old Jungian analyst. She was determined she would never be so unprepared again, for anything; she would keep a much sharper eye on the horizon from now on, and a suspicious nature approaching every corner, now that the future had turned out to be a perilous topography.

"Do you mind . . ." she asked Gabe while they stood at the cash register waiting to pay. He was still wearing the furry black glue-on eyebrows and a matching bushy wig Alice gave him earlier tonight. "Do you mind if you live some of the time with me and some with your dad and Paula?"

"I think it'll be okay." He pinched his nose shut as he climbed back into the passenger seat and turned to unwrap the pancake and give it to Walter.

"I do, too." She gave this an upbeat inflection.

"An adventure," Gabe said.

They were trying to help each other out.

sous les pavés, la plage

"How come it smells fruity in here?" Jean asked, getting into the backseat of the van. "As opposed to hideous?"

"I did a giant cleaning on it. Gabe helped. We hosed out the back, used some spray foam stuff on the seats, then got some cherry air freshener at the car wash." Carmen was driving, Alice riding shotgun.

"I don't think they use real cherries," Alice said.

Carmen did a lot of her political work on Saturdays while Gabe was over at Matt and Paula's apartment. This would be one of his last nights over there. Matt and Paula were leaving soon for Nigeria. They would be Catholic missionaries for a year in a remote, barren, sun-parched village where, from the photos in the ministry's brochure that Gabe had shown Carmen, everything—food, animals, eyes—was covered in bustling patches of flies. She enjoyed thinking of Matt and Paula swatting away a year's worth of large African flies.

Carmen said, "Did you get to watch the hearings yesterday? I could only listen in bits on NPR." They were all three caught up in the Anita Hill–Clarence Thomas drama.

"I dragged the little TV into my studio," Alice said. "There are so many creepy details coming out."

"The pubic hair on the Coke can," Jean said.

"The porn movies? The Long Dong Silver thing. That much I heard." Carmen tapped the horn to encourage the spaced-out driver in the car ahead to move forward through the newly changed light. "Ain't gonna get any greener."

"Worse than him, though," Jean said, "was the Wall of Guys, the supposedly impartial senators but all they're really doing is preserving their old boys' club. And in the end, Anita Hill is probably going to be stoned in the town square while Thomas will get put on the Supreme Court. Where he's going to be showing up for work every fucking day for the rest of our lives."

Jean had some discouraging personal news, discouraging to her anyway.

"Tom's wife is pregnant again."

Alice, who made it no secret that she thought Tom was a waste of Jean's time, said, "I wonder how that happened?"

"I thought he was trying to get out of his marriage?" Carmen said. "That it was a political thing, to get her citizenship and now he was working on getting out of it? Did that plan get lost along the way?"

Jean was silent for a while, then said, "Conversations about this are hard. I think maybe the problem is that I don't know how to have the right conversations with him."

They took the corner and suddenly they were in nearly stalled traffic and some guy just outside the window was holding up a glass jar of viscous red liquid with a naked rubber doll curled up inside.

"Well," Carmen said. "Here we go."

The action started out like all the others; the forces were assembling, getting louder. By now the rhythms were predictable. By now, they knew that what looked like total chaos was really only two oppositional, well-rehearsed pieces of political theater.

The three of them, in black pants, turtlenecks, and pea coats, like cat burglars, were on the side of women's right to control their own lives. The particular women they helped on these mornings were pregnant women wanting to be unpregnant women. The other side showed up to represent God, who they were certain wanted these women to have their babies, no matter what.

Over the past few years, Carmen and Jean had become old hands at this sort of thing. Their histories were dense with demos and actions and protests—for voting rights and in support of striking unions, against nuclear armament and poor treatment of women in prison. They figured they had nice, thick FBI files by now. They had linked arms in human chains surrounding military bases, at army recruiting offices, in front of the White House, on the National Mall. They were practiced at keeping their cool in the face of being called commies and Antichrists. Baby killers. Sisters of Satan. And dykes. They were always called dykes. Recently, Alice, the only actual dyke, started to join them on some of these excursions. Having painted through the night, Alice would rather have been in bed this morning, on her way to sleeping through the afternoon. Instead she was pushing against a wall of insults. She hadn't been quick enough with an excuse to get out of this intervention. She should have been prepared with something ironclad. No prior engagement would have been enough. Surgery maybe, but nothing elective. Her sister was not someone on whom to try out a flimsy story.

Carmen saw the world in clear moral terms, held herself to high standards and expected the same of everyone else. Which on occasion made her a pain in the neck. But a tricky one. Never openly self-righteous, she traveled with an air of self-effacement (which subversively exuded self-righteousness). She never told anyone else what to do, but she would look a little too long at your honey, which was in a non-biodegradable plastic bottle instead of an old, endlessly reusable glass jar you could take down to the Bread Shop and fill from the honey vat. Or she might helpfully suggest you turn off the pilot light on your stove and save who-knew-how-much gas, by instead lighting the burner each time with a match.

"Sous les pavés, la plage," Carmen said now, as they surveyed the

scene. "You have to keep thinking everything is going to be a little better because we were here." She could say stuff like this and not seem fatuous. The strength of Carmen's belief in what could be accomplished on the streets had tugged Alice onto some pavement she would have otherwise avoided.

"I'm already beat just going into this," Jean said. "I was up all night with the chain gang. Just getting them all to show up is exhausting." She was recording an album of prison and chain-gang songs. This was turning out to be a difficult project. The old guys who had made up and sang these songs to pass hard time realized in principle that they held historical value. But emotions ran high in performing them. Singing them harked back to a past on which they had shut the door. Too often one or another of them didn't show up for the session and Jean had to drive to the West Side to persuade him into her car and up to the studio.

This women's clinic was in Rogers Park. The crowd they were pushing through was armed with placards—bad drawings of bloody fetuses, coat hangers dripping blood. They looked tired, worn out maybe from the hard work of interfering with other people's lives. Most of the sign bearers were women, but the bullhorn shouters were guys. Guys with apocalyptic gazes, staring straight past Armageddon, through to the Rapture.

"I can get really afraid for the women whose lives are run by these lunatics," Alice said.

"Did you ever notice how religions all have the same timeline?" Carmen said as they wove through the crowd to find their cohort. "First the people feel the need to worship something. The sun or the giant corn ear. That's the first thing. Then the guys say okay, now that we've got the giant corn thing going, how can we use it to oppress women?"

Carmen had become scathing in her criticism of religion since the crumbling of her marriage. What she had thought was a common interest she and Matt shared in the social contract had turned out to be two very different impulses.

"Everything Matt's doing now is through the Church. The missionary thing. And he coaches in a CYO basketball league on the South Side. He works with some young priest who's supposedly great with kids. Charismatic priests make me queasy, how they're always making you aware that they should be wearing a cassock instead of a rugby shirt, that you probably should be calling them Father Whoever, but that you're an insider who gets to call them Joe or Bob."

Alice didn't think Matt was a jerk, exactly, but he did come out of the same hidebound family as Maude. Daddy owned the business, brought home the bacon. Marie stayed home with the kids, then with more kids, now with a couple of the grandkids. Carmen had shown her the file of recipes Marie had copied, organized in a decorative binder, and given to each of her daughters-in-law (although not, of course, to Alice). Marie liked to put herself out there as with-it, and so the cover design was Wonder Woman graphics, and there were goofy recipes for "Dishwasher Fish" and "Car Engine Meatloaf," but that was just a gloss. The subtext was deep respect for the domestic.

Carmen had writhed within these strictures. Sharing a single credit card—in Matt's name. Carmen had to call him before making any purchases on the card. Even for a sweater, she had to call. He also didn't like Carmen going out at night on her own. Sometimes he pushed too hard and she balked. Early on, he told her he didn't like leftovers and expected a fresh, home-cooked dinner every night. In that case, she told him, some of those dinners cooked in their home would have to be cooked by him. But the whole thing was an uphill battle. Now—as Alice saw it—Carmen was back on flat ground. From here, she could be who she actually was, instead of playing a role in an ill-fitting costume. But Alice also knew her sister thought the breakup was at least partly about Matt's wanting to get away from the accident, to erase that blot on his permanent record. Maybe. But whatever it was that pulled him out of the marriage, Jean and Alice both thought Carmen was lucky he was gone, even if it would take her a little longer to see that.

* * *

The pregnant woman they were helping today was in her twenties. She looked very nervous. The protesters were hassling her, pleading for the life of her unborn child. Sometimes they managed to scare off the patient. They knew the pressure points.

"Let's get this going!" Lenore Charles from the local NARAL chapter hustled the volunteers into a circle around the woman. Alice could see that Jean was getting antsy. Her presence at these actions was in part due to her social concerns, in part a way of letting off steam. She was basically a hooligan with a conscience. If she didn't have a cause, she'd be out robbing banks.

"What I'd like to see right about now is some police presence." Alice looked around for uniforms. "This goon squad is a little too fired up." The pro-life women, as always, had distant gazes and wore pale-print dresses like farm wives. They chanted "Baby-killers. Baby-killers." And "God loves the little children."

"He might not be all that crazy about you, though," Jean clipped the woman. "Just last night, Jesus came to me in a dream and he said, 'Like I want to spend all eternity with these morons.'"

Lenore got in the way of a brawl starting up. "Ladies? Let's move *now*."

The volunteers—they were ten in number this morning, a good-size crew—locked arms in a scrum around the skittish woman and made a slow, rolling charge toward the clinic door. They'd done this dozens of times. By now they were very efficient. Jean led the way as they approached the door of the clinic.

Alice said to Carmen, "Actually—"

The flare came in from the right, whistling and then, when it was just grazing Carmen's right ear, it blossomed with a crackling report into a cloud of liquid, orange-red smoke. Carmen slapped a hand against the side of her head, and bent forward, then folded to the ground. What came out of her was not a human cry, just pure wounded animal. And it kept on going. Alice went down next to her and pried Carmen's hand off the ear, which was blackened and in great part missing; what was left was smoking like a piece of bacon, also releasing a fast stream of blood.

"Oh God. Oh Jesus, come on," Alice said as she lifted her up and started pushing their way back out of the crowd. Using a counterintuitive circuit of logic, she got Carmen as fast as possible away from the medical clinic and toward the first police car she saw. What was going through her head as she ran with Carmen's arm over her shoulder, her own hand now holding in place what was left of Carmen's ear, was fear for her of course, but also shock that her sister had turned out to be vulnerable after all.

teardrop

Nick pulled Olivia's arm over his shoulder as she stood. She had stubbed her toe on an unambitious hike they took that morning. He set her into the side opening of the Teardrop.

"I know it's a little early to hit the hay, but the outdoors wears me out." She took the mug of cowboy coffee he handed her. Her nightcap. Caffeine was nothing to her. After learning to sleep through prison nights, nothing could keep her awake. She gave him a pinch under his ribs. Olivia dispensed affection in athletic gestures—arm punches, noogies, little flicks of a damp towel in the bathroom—as though they were teammates rather than husband and wife.

"I'm just going to hang out up here," he said as he hoisted himself past her, up onto the roof of the trailer. "Like Snoopy." He loved this—lying on top of the camper, looking through his very old Nikon binoculars, the ridges on the focus wheel nearly worn away from a million rubs of his forefinger. He could watch the lazy way he did when he first noticed stars, before he saw them up close through a Newtonian reflector, or read them by their radio waves, before he knew their chemical composition, the weight and age of their gases, the rate at which they were burning themselves up—back when they still held a blinky mystery.

He read the heavens like a worn page of a favorite book. He picked out constellations of the summer northern sky—Scorpius, Hercules with its brilliant star Vega, the harder-to-find Corona Borealis. Arcturus, a showman star, burning its heart out. And even though he knew better, knew that what he saw was still roiling and burning and exploding and being born, also dying an icy death, he could still calm himself by doing this sort of casual, Boy Scout survey, finding everything superficially in place.

His early stargazing had evolved into a narrowed vision that was his strong suit in the groves of astronomy. Although he could construct a decent equation, map out the Doppler shift of a star's spectra to calculate its mass, that sort of thing, his real talent lay in being an astronomer rather than a physicist. He could look through a telescope, or read a radio image and see something others had missed, particularly what hid within the shadows of stars. This had put him on the receiving end of a lot of material, stuff that had stumped someone and someone else, who then, as a last-ditch gesture, fielded it off to Nick. This ability allowed him, in spite of a spotty attendance record and a few unfortunate incidents at school social occasions, to still occupy a place in the scientific academy. He would never get tenure. He'd run off the rails of that track. He had his doctorate now, but his recommendation letters overflowed with faint praise, and held between their lines invisible-ink warnings about his unreliability, his unpredictable behavior. He wouldn't get an important job anywhere, ever. They kept him on part time down at the U of C. He might turn out to be a credit to them. In the meantime, they let him teach a basic astronomy course every semester, kept an eye on his student evaluations.

Nobody else wanted him. He was too much trouble. But a lot of people wanted his findings, that was what kept him on the game board. Recently he had scored a succession of grants to go down to Arecibo, the big dish radio scope in Puerto Rico. At the moment he could find what he needed through radio waves. But optical astronomy was still a big player, and poised for huge discoveries. This was its time. NASA had already launched its big telescope—Hubble. A repair was necessary; a camera had to be replaced, to overcome the spherical aberration of the primary mirror. Once that mission was accomplished, the scope would linger in space, clicking away, capturing pictures not blurred by the earth's atmosphere, and then the whole of cosmology would probably break wide open. It was a great time to be looking around, but also—for Nick—a little spooky. Like being the first people to stick their toes in a deep and unknown lake of water that was purple, or peach.

And now he didn't have drugs to buffer this anxiety. Now he had to fall back on carpentry and Olivia as his calming forces. He was a married man now, half of a two-income couple. He worked construction four days a week, taught one day. She cut hair at a neighborhood beauty shop and had a good base of clients. She made decent money. They owned a condo on Addison, near the lake. He drove an Impala that was only two years old. He was getting extremely close to respectability. He had Olivia to thank for this.

Even though the incident was a couple of years back now, Nick was still thinking about how to deal with Horace's grotesque behavior at the birthday party. Nick had gone back to his parents' place later that night, but just sat out front in the car. A few days later he bought a gun. He didn't have a plan, didn't even have an image of himself being able to use it. When Olivia came across it in the back of his underwear drawer, she said, "This is for your old man? Oh, please. Who is he really? Someone you're connected to by sperm."

He was so grateful to be let off the hook. And of course by now, so much time had passed. The longer he thought about how to deal with Horace, the more complicated it became and he had to further refine his message. He thought he'd be ready by the time they got home from this trip. Ready, or nearly ready.

He knew Olivia thought he was weak, but she didn't seem to care.

"If I wanted tough, I would have married Freddi. Don't think that wasn't an option."

* * *

He rolled over, hopped off the roof and climbed into the Teardrop. The little trailer's sleeping cabin held a double mattress, but just barely; its sides rolled up the walls a little. He loved the trailer. He bought it from a guy in Ohio, then took the better part of a year to restore it. The outside he spray-painted a high-gloss robin's egg blue, seven coats. Inside, he covered the walls with white paneling. He and Olivia hooked the Teardrop to the Chevy and spent long weekends driving around the Midwest to cat shows, camping along the way. They were their own traveling circus.

Inside, Olivia slept soundly, snoring. She had a deviated septum that she periodically considered having straightened out. Every now and then, she saw another specialist to get a tenth or eleventh opinion. She was not one to jump into anything. Nick shimmied out of his jeans, slid under the jumble of old bedspreads and army blankets, sheets soft with use and a dash of grime—they were, neither of them, big on housekeeping—then pushed his butt against her, and put a pillow over his head to shut out the noise. Sleeping with Olivia, touching her in some way, any way, especially inside the tiny trailer, kept him from hurtling into the special void he had created for himself.

When he woke up, the cats were meowing and walking over the pillows, also all over his head. It was five in the morning according to the small clock dangling from a string above them. One of the cats was standing on her hind legs, batting the clock around with a paw.

"I'll get up and feed them," Olivia said, leaving behind a ruffle of breath sour from sleep. She plucked a cat off his face, pushed open the door, and dropped it gently outside.

When he woke again, it was six-thirty. No Olivia, no cats. He stepped out into an air heavy with dew steaming off the surrounding pines.

"It's so early. What can anyone do this early in the morning?" he said to Olivia, who sat cross-legged on a webbed chaise, eating a bowl of Frosted Flakes. The cats peered out from inside their carriers, even though the doors were open. They were total cowards when faced with the wilderness.

"I know," she said. "That's the thing about the outdoors. It does get started a little sooner than you'd like." They were rookie campers. This was a whole new thing to them. They were still getting the hang of it, and often gave up on whatever dinner they'd managed to scorch on the little gas stove, and drove out of this or that campsite to see if there was a McDonald's by the highway. They defaulted to motel mode more often than they'd admit to anybody.

"How's that doing?" Meaning her toe, which still looked like a red lightbulb, but a smaller one of a lower wattage.

"Nothing like yesterday. And all we have to do today is drive, so it'll be fine."

The cats emerged tentatively from their crates and circled his ankles; their purring made them seem motorized. They smelled shrimpy, from the special food Olivia gave them. They were not regular cats, not ordinary pets. They were Himalayans, white with puckered faces and long, ornate names on their pedigree papers. In their regular life around the house, Olivia called them Eggdrop and Chop Suey. Nick hated both the pretentious pedigree stuff and these over-cute names. He didn't much care for the cats either as far as that went.

Olivia adored them. She was as close as she got to happy whenever one or the other won a ribbon. She fussed over them at home. She found their behavior endlessly fascinating. They chased a tied-up pair of pantyhose across the floor! They sat in a box! She had concocted intricate personalities she professed to see in them while to Nick, it appeared that they only ate, slept, batted around sparkle balls, and were almost totally indifferent to Nick's and Olivia's presence in their lives. The cats were part of the ticket price to Olivia. He'd keep buffalos, if that would make her stay. It always felt to him as though she had one foot out the door, although whenever he asked her about this, she looked completely surprised, as though the thought hadn't occurred to her.

"You just be a good boy and I'll stick around."

With their head start, they drove through the day, down from Missouri into Arkansas. Country stations spanned the dial. The car swelled up with fiddles and pedal steel. Olivia rolled the knob, trying to get some George Jones. They were huge fans, went to his concerts wearing matching cowboy shirts. Corny, but so what? They got into country through Emmylou Harris and Randy Travis, but by now they had gone way back to Buck Owens and Hank Williams, back to the Stanley Brothers and Lefty Frizzell.

A quick stop for gas and Cokes. They were careful not to disturb the cats, who were topped off with Valium, meek in their carriers on the backseat.

Through the afternoon, with her head propped against the open window, her foot with its swollen toe up on the dashboard, Olivia read a romance novel. She could get totally wrapped up in these. Which seemed so peculiar to Nick. She was the least romantic person he had ever met. He read a couple to try to understand where she plugged into them. As far as he could see, they were just pages and pages of longing and bogus historical crap leading up first to a big ravishing, then to a royal wedding.

"Good one?" he asked her now.

"Mmhmm," Olivia said, deep into the story, which, from the cover, appeared to be about a man and a woman with matching long, wind-blown hair.

It was late afternoon when they reached Eureka Springs, where the cat show was being held.

"This town is made of motels," Nick said as they wound around, profoundly lost. "And every one has a sign for a whirlpool bath. It's like they took the 'spring' concept way too seriously."

"I think we've been on this street already," Olivia said. She smoked in a dreamy way, exhaling out the open window. "We're going in circles. Maybe turn left there. That street just past the Goofy Golf."

But the left turn was yet another mistake followed by another half hour of winding around before they finally pulled into the Blue Jay Inn, where they had a reservation. By this time, the cats were coming off their tranquilizers, pacing inside their carriers, wailing.

"Stage butterflies," was Olivia's diagnosis. "They always get worked up before they have to face their public."

The room—Number 217, on the second floor, a long haul up with luggage and cats and cat-grooming equipment—had blue everything—carpet, bedspread, walls. A coin box on the bed's headboard activated the mattress with a Magic Fingers massage. Across from the bed, against the opposite wall, a full-size refrigerator took up a good part of the room. Nick wondered if this was supposed to count as a feature. The room was small but the bathroom was huge—to accommodate a large, blue, molded plastic Jacuzzi.

"Whirlpool," Nick said, poking his head in, reaching around behind himself to slide a hand between Olivia's legs. Playing around.

"Later," she said, backing away to open a carrier and pull out a cat. "We've got to clean these girls up. They lost their lunch in here. Oh, this is bad. Poor babies." She pulled on long rubber gloves and handed another pair to Nick. He could see that the cat was crusty with dried vomit.

The next half hour was a blizzard of flying suds and spray, bared claws, the high whine of the cat dryer, and finally, a soft falling mist of fur spray.

When they were done, Olivia slumped into the room's only chair. "Cats think they should be left to do their own grooming. Lick, lick, lick. They don't get the bigger picture, like that they have to be ready by tomorrow morning."

• • •

They had sex in the Jacuzzi.

"I think it's mandatory," Nick said. Olivia sat on his lap and rode him hard as he held her and bit her shoulder from behind. This was a favorite position of hers, not just an aquatic adaptation, and he hoped it wasn't because she didn't want him to see her expression while he fucked her. In his worst vision she was staring into the distance at something he couldn't see. Fundamentally, Olivia was unknowable.

Never much for lingering in the afterglow, she hopped out as soon as they finished. She dried off and jumped into her fancy sweats and set herself up by the bedside phone to set off the flurry of social life that was part of these show weekends. Nick soaked on by himself. He pressed the small of his back up against one of the jets. A decade of carpentry had left him with stretched tendons in his neck, a tricky rotator cuff. All of which he could smooth out with a few heavy-duty painkillers, but these were, of course, not allowed on his current program. It was ironic that, due to long, recreational use of these drugs, he was unfamiliar with ordinary pain, and experienced it in a fresh, crisp way—and could not defend himself against it. But, as Olivia would say: tough. This was how he saw himself: balancing on the event horizon, trying not to get sucked into the black hole, trying to hang on to the light.

As he came out of the bathroom, she said, "You might want to put your jockeys back on." She had the phone to her ear, waiting for whoever to pick up. The cats had gone feral; this always happened after they had been groomed. They bounced on and off the furniture, chasing each other in a game without a point. "You know." She covered the mouthpiece. "If you want to hang on to your nuts."

Nick didn't kid himself that what he and Olivia had was love. It was more serious than that. He could still smell the prison on her. She'd had to forge a hard interior to make it through all the days she was inside, all the small humiliations, and this had left her composition slightly metallic. There was something erotic about this. He heard from her about the truly tough women inside, and the elaborate hierarchy and the endless rituals. Goods exchanged for services, services exchanged for protection. Having to get permission to walk by certain cells. Doing laundry, cleaning toilets for women higher up in the pecking order. He knew Olivia slipped under the wing of someone powerful and cruel. "All you need to know is anything I did in there, I did to save my ass."

She kept him on a tight rein. It was the only way, he understood. Her terms for coming back were that they play by her rules. They married quietly. They didn't and wouldn't have kids. Olivia believed they had forfeited that privilege. Fine if Nick wanted to fool around with astronomy, but she wanted to see a regular paycheck, which meant steadily working construction jobs. They didn't do drugs or drink. If he fell back into that, she'd be gone. He found both comfort and fear in the knowledge that she stood between him and the past, also between him and the world beyond her, where very bad things could happen fast. He didn't really know why she was with him.

They ate at a restaurant outside town that was on the premises of an abattoir. The red neon STEAK HOUSE sign was surrounded by killing barns.

"Here we are," he said as they pulled into a parking spot, "the aorta of the American heart of darkness." They were here at the insistence of Olivia's friends, Randy and Gia—part of the cat crowd who had been here before and thought the place was loaded with local color. By the time Nick and Olivia showed up, Gia and Randy were already half in the bag—flushed and jolly, waving at them from the table. Now that he wasn't one, Nick found drunks extremely tiresome.

Randy ordered New York strips for all of them. The dinner, he said, was his treat.

"At least you know your meat here is fresh," he said.

Randy and Gia were from Port Huron, in Michigan. Gia described herself as a fitness specialist, which really meant she worked at a health club teaching classes in ab busting and cardio striptease. She wore a lot of makeup, but in a nice way. She wasn't particularly large breasted, but must have worn some kind of bra that pushed what she did have into a perky rack. Randy was an aging frat boy who sold high-end speedboats—broad shouldered, with hair plugs that were still healing. They had a teenage daughter who was off-limits as a conversational topic. She did something so terrible she could never be mentioned. This secret was by far the most interesting thing about them.

Randy talked about his job, which he loved. He said he could sell a boat to anyone, even if they'd never given a thought to boating before.

"I can get people to part with so much money, sometimes I want to cry for them, cry for this whole country full of idiots. Cry all the way to the bank." He slapped the table a little too hard and set the water glasses jingling. They were in a booth, but Randy sat next to Olivia, Nick next to Gia. This was Randy's idea, to "mix things up a little."

Randy and Gia had only one cat, the Duke of Earl, but he was a champion. So what, Nick thought. They had a good cat, but they also had that daughter. Nick thought neo-Nazi. Maybe specialty call girl.

"The Duke is on a winning streak. The Duke can do no wrong," Randy said as Nick tuned out for a while. He had heard enough cat competition talk to last nine lifetimes. When he tuned back in, he noticed that Randy's arm had wound itself around Olivia's shoulder in the middle of some hilarious cat moment Gia was describing and they were all three of them laughing in a way that made it necessary for Randy to give Olivia a little shoulder squeeze. But now they were talking about cat shampoos and the hand lingered. And just as he was noticing this, Nick felt a light pressure on the inside of his thigh, just grazing his tackle. He looked over at Gia, but she didn't look back, just kept talking shampoo, moving on to a silk conditioner she'd found that made fur positively gleam under the show lights.

"You have to get it by mail order," she said as she continued to tickle Nick's balls.

"There's something about the adrenaline before a show that really gets me going," Randy said. Nick could see his hot dog fingers cupping

Olivia's shoulder. Nick looked across at her in what he hoped was a readable code. She looked back and for a nanosecond opened her eyes wide, like a character in an old movie, tied up in a cave with a long fuse sizzling toward a powder keg.

"Have to see a man about a horse," Nick said, sliding out of the booth as though Gia's fingers were not hard at work between his legs.

"We must have synchronized bladders." Olivia gave Randy's arm the slip.

They didn't dare look at each other until they were in the long hallway to the johns, which were marked STEERS and HEIFERS. And then they laughed so hard they fell against the walls.

"What are we going to do? I don't want to insult them. They're going to be at every competition from now until the end of time. They probably try this out on everybody. Oh, I'm seeing it all in my mind. I'm screaming in ecstasy, yanking out Randy's hair sprouts."

"We could say we've been passing a nasty marital infection back and forth."

"They won't buy it," she said. "We'll say we've found Jesus. We belong to something scary now. Jehovah's Witnesses. Or we're Mormons. I can talk a pretty good game. From my time inside."

They turned out to be great, embellishing liars. They said they had some religious literature back at the motel and maybe Randy and Gia would like to come and pray with them. Nick worried they wouldn't buy this, but whether they did or not, the conversation quickly sanitized itself, and moved on to Reagan and Bush, whom Randy thought of as a baton of greatness passed. He thought America should just elect a Republican king and get rid of all the crooks in Congress. It hurt Nick's teeth to listen to Randy.

At the motel, he put a quarter into the bed to get it jiggling and they fell onto it laughing all over again. Olivia wasn't a big laugher and so he got her to go over the whole story again just so they could keep laughing and vibrating.

"I wouldn't mind getting a little fresh air," he said when things had quieted down. "You want to take a walk with me?" He knew she'd say no.

The Blue Jay was at the top of a small hill. He passed several other motels on the way down. Spring Waters. The Babbling Brook Inn. The All Inn. From the bottom of the hill, it was ten more minutes walking, past a decent restaurant, then two diners, around the corner at the 7-Eleven, and there it was—in the deserted lot of a defunct Midas Muffler shop. There were three cars waiting, parking lights on, radios laying a drift of melody on the heavy summer night air, the glow of cigarettes the only thing visible inside the cars. Nick pulled a pack of Marlboros out of his pocket and lit up in a spirit of communion. These strangers were his compadres.

Most people think drugs just waste your time and screw up your life. They don't understand the happiness. They think you're off drugs a few months, a few years, you forget about them, put them behind you and good riddance, but this is not the way it goes. Drugs have mass and density. Thick and delicious, they fill every crevice inside you. They offer absolute comfort and well-being. In reverse, their absence leaves you empty and arid.

Sober, he had to keep busy and purposeful, always moving. If he stopped, he immediately heard the sandstorm inside himself, and it terrified him.

He hadn't smoked his cigarette halfway down when the dealer rolled in, in a Trans Am, flipping his lights off, ready to do business. Nick waited until a transaction got going between the dealer and a woman in a Lexus, then turned to walk back up the hill. He himself was not buying. He just liked to know he could still find the marketplace, wherever he was. This wasn't difficult. Every place was basically the same. It was like kitchens. You could usually find the silverware drawer and the garbage pail on the first try. You just had to pay a little attention.

game show

Walter and Gracie were by now a rolling ball of dust in the vacant lot, what the old-timers in Chicago call a prairie. Gracie was twice Walter's size with a bear head and tiny ears. They were good friends, boxing enthusiasts—paws around each other's necks, grunting and growling, phony as TV wrestlers. Pinning down, sitting on, rolling over, pushing their noses into each other's privates, then finally lying on their backs exhausted, side by side, occasionally flopping their heads over to lick each other's mouths.

Gabe was their best audience. He jumped up and down in a squiggle of delight. The dogs were done; they didn't have an ounce of boxing left in them.

"I think they've had it," Carmen said to Gracie's human, a young guy named Jack who brought his dog over here for these matches. They agreed this was something dogs needed, a good rumble. Something their humans couldn't supply.

She and Gabe rushed Walter back home. They were perfecting a system for launching into their days. This involved making their lunches the night before and getting Gabe's books into his backpack and letting him sleep in his school clothes. He was fine with this. And he only looked a little rumpled, not so bad that anyone had said anything. Walking back, Carmen looked at her watch and saw that time had closed in on her. She grabbed the dog's leash and Gabe's hand, and broke into a slow run. Not just in this moment, but globally, cosmically, she had lost her advantage against daily life. Weeks, whole months passed beneath her notice, or off to the side while she was on the game show that was her life. She ran from pillar to post then on to the next pillar, ringing bells, pressing lighted buttons and buzzers, making wild stabs at answers to questions she wasn't sure she had heard correctly, walking when she should be skipping, speaking when a song was expected. The show was called Single Parenthood. Added to this was time lost to surgeries—last week was the third—to reconstruct her ear. She would never know who hurt her, or if it was deliberate or inadvertent. The cops closed off the area and did some questioning, but the pro-lifers closed ranks, and no bystander had noticed where the flare had come from. This was not so important to her. She didn't see herself so much as the victim of a single crazy person as of a whole crazy movement, and of its unfortunate collective unconscious belief that women are the property of men.

Tomorrow, she would have one pair of clean underpants left in her drawer and this was not a good pair. Once while polishing a pair of black shoes, she mistook them for a rag. She really needed all new underwear, and had made a mental note of this, but realistically couldn't see a day in the near future when she'd be able to go down to Field's. The only store nearby that sold underwear was on Broadway and it was a sex shop. The only underpants they'd have would be either leather with little zippers or a thong with a heart patch in front. She would just have to do laundry tonight, come what may.

The laundry was the least of it. Really, the whole house had gotten away from her. The crappy mini-blinds were felted with dust. The soles of any shoes crossing the kitchen floor stuck then peeled off with a ripping sound. The bathtub had a grimy ring with an embedded, historical character; moldy grout framed the tiles in a disturbingly colorful, shimmering way. The refrigerator had filled itself, not with meal-making elements, rather with a hilarious number of jars of mustard. Assorted supplements—bilberry and black cohosh and blessed thistle—that someone swore by and Carmen then bought but as yet had not actually taken, and eventually would forget what ills they were supposed to remedy. Pushed to the back of the fridge were small crushed balls of aluminum foil and a couple of Tupperware boxes long past any point at which they could have been safe to open.

In the van, Carmen took off Gabe's glasses to wipe the grease off the lenses with a corner of her shirt. She handed him a hairbrush. "See if you can do something with that rat's nest." He hated washing his hair.

"I need red and orange and yellow construction paper," he said. "There's a project for fall—" He was reading off a Xeroxed sheet he'd just pulled out of his backpack. "Colors of autumn. I'm on the project committee."

"How could you be on a committee? You're nine. And you had to have the paper by today?"

"They told us a while ago. I forgot to tell you."

"Oh. Okay. Let me think." She U-turned and headed back in the direction of the Walgreens. Because of its expansive hours, she wound up doing a lot of shopping there. In the same way, she bought a lot of groceries—spotted bananas and wildly overpriced head lettuce—at the 7-Eleven. These stores were light-up buttons on the wacky game show.

Gabe sat silent once he had the construction paper on his lap and they were on their way again. She interpreted his silence as a guilty one, but when they pulled up across from the school, he hopped out quite chipper with his backpack and his drawing folder and came around to the driver's side window. He stuck his right hand in for Carmen to shake and just as she was thinking what a little gentleman, she felt a sharp, sudden buzz run up her palm into her wrist. And Gabe was laughing so hard he dropped his stuff on the street. In moments like this, everything else, all the trouble fell away and Carmen was just the luckiest person in the world.

"Where'd you get that piece of evil?" she asked as she plucked the joy buzzer out of his hand. It looked serious, professional strength, from the high end of practical joke devices. "Do they sell this to children?"

"Alice got it for me," he told her.

"That was so nice of her," Carmen said, shaking out her zapped hand. "I'll have to thank her for that." What she was thinking was how did she deserve this wonderful child. As difficult as it was for them to manage in the day-to-day, she missed him if he was gone, even overnight. Missing him was the worst part of her recuperation last winter. He stayed a week with Alice while Carmen had more surgery on her ear.

Gabe was picking up his backpack when a car came around the corner way too fast. Carmen reflexively reached out the window and pulled him flat to the side of the car—a rush of relief at having gotten him out of harm's way, followed by a vague drift of guilt for protecting him where she had failed the girl.

The next segment of the game show—the part with tunnels and chutes—was Carmen's workday. She was now executive director at Hearth/Home. As she hurried through the activity room on her way to her office, she was flagged down by Maureen McCrachy, and spent the next fifteen minutes or so on a plaid sofa next to Maureen, who believed the mice in the shelter were not only multiplying, but growing in size. Maureen was not a lovable client. She was dismissive of the shelter, thought the food was terrible, the bingo rigged, the temperature too warm in the summer and too cold in the winter. Also, she maintained an extreme lack of hygiene. Close encounters with her were always a little swoony. An ancillary problem had developed with Maureen's mouth, which was only partially toothed, and those remaining in varying shades of black and brown. These troubles were, of course, accompanied by a breath problem to add to her body odor problem. Sometimes Carmen thought: forget food and shelter and job training and counseling, just fix everyone's teeth.

"The mouse I saw last night was big as a cat." Forming the words "mouse" and "last" caused Maureen to whistle through her dental gaps and spit a little onto Carmen's lap. "A cat," she repeated for emphasis. "And in its mouth it was dragging around a baloney sandwich."

Carmen couldn't be entirely sure this was a delusion.

"I'll check it out," she said. "We'll get rid of them. I promise."

"Otherwise," Maureen said in a mafia whisper, "I might have to move on."

The great emptying of mental institutions in the 1970s filled the streets, at least in Chicago, with some very crazy people. A good part of the clientele at the shelter were women who were not so much homeless as lacking an asylum. Part of sheltering them was finding out what meds they were supposed to be on, then making sure they took them. Not an easy business. After she got used to feeling better and more stable on a prescription, the mentally ill person often took this as a clear sign—usually from God—that she no longer needed medication. It was difficult to reason with someone in this position. And, of course, it was particularly difficult trying to talk down someone with a mouse phobia when your facility was infested with them. Almost as soon as Carmen sat down in her office, one skimmed out from under her desk and across the ancient linoleum floor, making a mad dash from one crack in the wall to another. She didn't know what to do about the mice. All the alternatives were terrible. She could poison them, or snap their heads under a sprung bar, or let them get stuck on a glue pad until they starved, or worse, gnawed off a leg to free themselves. None of these methods survived a pass through her conscience.

Still, she couldn't just let them run free. The mice seemed to spend their vast amounts of free time dining in the pantry and having sex, so where there were only a couple of mice two weeks ago, their current number seemed to be several verging on many. Until recently, she only saw them skittering around the pantry and the back of the kitchen. Now they'd migrated into her office, where there wasn't any food. Which meant they were going back and forth for meals. They were commuter mice.

"Is there something that gets rid of mice, but doesn't hurt them?" she asked Slawek, the building janitor. He looked back at her from under the heavy eyelids of a man who had lived through harsh winters in an under-heated Krakow apartment block by stuffing his clothes with newspapers. He had had several root canals without Novocain, just gripping the arms of the dentist's chair. He traveled the first leg of his escape to freedom in the trunk of a car. The suffering of mice did not enter his field of moral vision.

The silent end of their small conversation was interrupted by a layered ripple of screams and screeches from the activity room. In her mind's eye, Carmen saw ladies in sweatpants standing on chairs.

"Do whatever you have to, I guess," Carmen told him. "Just don't let me know what it is."

"Got a minute?" Ann Welch poked her head into the doorway.

Ann was Carmen's assistant. She had been working through the morning with a young woman and her little boy. A referral from the hotline. The woman—her name was Nadine Mooney—was on the run from her partner.

Days earlier, Nadine had arrived too hysterical for a conversation, Carmen gave her a Valium from an infinite-refill prescription her mother passed along to her every once in a while. She supposed this wasn't exactly kosher, but tranquilizers, she had found, were extremely helpful in getting someone bent out of shape back at least into a sort-of shape where she could begin to be helped.

Ann had found a room for Nadine and her son at a halfway house; Hearth/Home was too small and underfunded to offer overnight shelter. She had the boy enrolled in the closest grade school and a job interview lined up for Nadine at the McDonald's on Wilson at Sheridan. Nadine was nervous about this. Her only work experience had been picking—tomatoes and berries. She came up on a night bus from a place in Mississippi so rural it didn't even have a McDonald's. She said she came up to Chicago to be near her sister, but then the sister turned out not to live here. A lot of the stories women came in with had these sorts of narrative trapdoors.

"I need you to pep talk her a little. She's losing her nerve. You're so good at this stuff."

As Carmen made her way back to Ann's office, she tried to gather up an inspirational air. Women like Nadine, barely free of the clutches of the boogeyman they'd been trapped by, always thought these were the scariest days of their lives. They never saw that the truly scariest were the ones they'd just lived through, usually with husbands, but sometimes, as in this instance, with girlfriends who beat them and drank up all the money.

Nadine, Carmen saw as soon as she came into the room, had been hit so much and so often that one side of her face appeared to be not just bruised, but softened. Some of the wounds were fresh, but Carmen saw, beneath and behind the recent trauma, that this woman had been beaten for a long time.

Carmen sat with her, pulled out some toy trucks for her boy, who was both shy and surly. She talked with her about what she was going to have to do, getting things down to a task analysis—Step One followed by Step One and a Half. Step Two was way too far off. Nadine appeared so grateful Carmen couldn't look at her directly. Still, when she had gone, Carmen leaned against the doorjamb to Ann's office and told her, "She'll fold. Two days tops and she'll be on the bus back to Big Mama."

This was a discouraging part of Carmen's work. She tried to put it out of her mind, tried instead to imagine this woman six months on, working at a decent job, her face healed over, her kid not traumatized every night. Sometimes this did happen.

◆ ◆ ◆

When she got to his school, even though she was a little late, Gabe was not out in front. She tracked him down to the art room where he was lost in a painting, a detailed interior of what she assumed was his bedroom at Matt and Paula's. Back from Nigeria, they had moved into a huge, ramshackle house on Byron. They got it cheap because of its disrepair. Not broken windows or tacky paneling, nothing easily fixable like that. In this house, the floor of the upstairs bathroom was almost entirely rotted away. A nest of rats lived inside the engine of an abandoned car in the garage. The elderly man who owned the place died in an upstairs bedroom and hadn't been found for some time and the whole place reeked of both his sickness and his death. Carmen knew these details from Gabe, who was an eager gossip. The only thing the house didn't have was a corpse in the crawl space. But even if it had, Matt and Paula would have bought it, they so desperately needed the room for the orphans they'd adopted. Nigerian sisters, seven-year-olds, twins—Cheluchi and Chetanna—adorable, but with a penchant for setting small fires. Also, just a couple of months ago, they got a depressed, colicky Romanian baby who came with the name Vlad, which everyone agreed was too vampiric, and so they changed it to Mike. Gabe seemed totally good-natured about all these instant siblings.

It was so peaceful in the art room; the only noise came from a radio turned low.

"Hey." She came up behind Gabe at a table easel. He turned and smiled, twirling his hands a little, singing, "Yabba dabba dabba dabba dabba dabba dabba said the monkey to the chimp." A song she taught him when he was first starting to talk. He often surprised her with what he remembered.

"Don't blame me," his art teacher said. "I told him to go home." The teacher, Ryan Hadley, was fresh out of art school, impossibly full of energy. At the moment, he was painting a mural of the first Thanksgiving on a long piece of brown wrapping paper stretched across four tables. "Bulletin boards," he told Carmen. "The cornerstone of elementary education. I wanted to make a panorama of how we sold out the Indians, took their land, got them into alcohol and shoved them into reservations, but that didn't fly with management."

"A casino," Carmen said. "You'd want to put a casino in there somewhere."

Gabe cleaned his brushes and racked his painting. Although Ryan always had one or another reason he needed to stay late, Carmen suspected he hung out this extra hour to give Gabe a casual sort of instruction. He thought Gabe was hugely talented, had told Carmen, "I just want to be around this. To see how much can happen, even in the beginning."

In a brewing turf war, Alice was suspicious of Ryan without even having met him. She worried he was turning Gabe into a "decorative" painter. Yeah yeah yeah Carmen told her. She figured that, at nine, he was not being hopelessly corrupted by one or another artistic faction.

"Hey, can I drive?" he said, swinging his backpack as they went through the parking lot. He liked to ask. He had only seven years to go.

She had a sitter for tonight. One of the two high school Jennifers who lived on the block. Thursdays she and Alice went to a Proust class at the Newberry.

"I don't think we're supposed to park in here," Carmen said as Alice swung into the lot behind the library, clearly marked EMPLOYEES ONLY. Alice didn't hear this. She pulled into a spot designated for Mr. Fox.

"Come on," she said to Carmen. "We're late."

The class had about a dozen students and an earnest teacher, Mr. Costello, who loved Proust, and tried to spark a sophisticated literary conversation about the book and the architecture of Parisian society at the turn of the century. He swam against the hard current of the class bores—there were three—who could relate every incident in the book to something in their own lives. Proust spoke especially to them. Alice wanted to follow each of these blowhards home after class and deflate their car tires with needle-nose pliers.

"You know. Send a message."

During the break, one of the few guys in the class came up to Carmen and Alice in the hall. "M&Ms?" He offered a pack with the corner torn off.

"Who'd say no?" Carmen said and he tapped a few into her palm. Then another few into Alice's.

"Where'd you get these?" Alice asked. "Is there a machine?"

"I picked them up on the way from work."

"That just seems like incredible forethought."

Carmen was glad Alice was doing the talking. She had trouble making conversation with guys like this. "Like this" meaning anyone who might be flirting with her. Of course, he might well be, probably *was*, flirting with Alice. Carmen had noticed him in class. They all had name cards propped in front of them. His said Rob. He wore expensive sweaters, cashmere v-necks, but with nothing underneath. Also something gold on a thin chain around his neck. His hair was manicured. Every hair had its exact place. He wore some kind of manly cologne. From his remarks in class, he seemed to be clueless about what Proust was trying to get across. He thought Charles Swann should give up on Odette and get out of Paris. Get over being so French. Get his head on straight. Maybe move to New York. This bone-headedness made Carmen think he was only in the class to pick up women. And that once he saw he was barking up the wrong tree with Alice, he would turn to Carmen. She knew she signed up for the class mostly to meet someone, but that someone was not Rob. That someone was Ralph Fiennes.

The thing on the chain around his neck, she saw at closer range, was a little Egyptian ankh symbol. She could already imagine his apartment. The leather sofa, the dimmer switches. The Luther Vandross collection. Rob was art director for a chain of hair salons, whatever that meant. She was being a hideous snob, she realized, particularly for someone who got left by a guy she thought she was doing fine with, and further was now a person with only half her hearing and one ear that looked as though it had been drizzled onto the side of her head from a melting candle. This was a guy she'd probably be lucky to get, and before he had even put himself forward she was already rejecting him. The social road ahead looked like a bleak highway, post-apocalyptic, overblown with dust, gray and lifeless except for mutants popping up here and there.

portraits of girls at windows

[alice in amsterdam]

Zombies lurched and hobbled across the screen on the wall in front of her, slow and hungry. Watching them, Alice was temporarily, but enormously, happy. Watching a zombie movie in business class, eating heated nuts on a flight from Chicago to Amsterdam. Things were quite different, she was finding, when you were famous, or even just loitering at the edge of fame. You didn't hang your own paintings anymore. You didn't crate them or uncrate them. Craters and uncraters and hangers took care of all that. When you traveled for exhibitions, you didn't fly coach on Icelandair. You didn't stay on the sagging sleeper sofa of a friend of somebody you met once at a group show in Milwaukee.

Days later, in Amsterdam, she was still feeling the buzz. She was being put up at a hotel on the Herengracht, with caviar on the room service menu, linen sheets on the bed, a spa on the top floor. All expenses taken care of by the museum that was putting on a solo show of her recent work. All that was required of her was her presence and, for the moment, her absence. The time had come when the curator and her assistants needed the meddlesome, overanxious artist out of their hair. Alice took the hint and headed off to blur out a few anxious hours with tourism. First to the Van Gogh museum, then to the Anne Frank House. She knew only the outline of Anne Frank's story. The hiding. The diary. The death camp. The death. Before today, she had only considered Anne Frank as an emblem, the face put to the fate of the millions. On the Prinsengracht, she found her way to the end of the line of pilgrims that hugged the house. She shuffled forward with her silent companions up the steep back stairs hidden behind the revolving bookcase, into the small secret annex, the only sounds an ambient sanding of soles on wood, a creak of leather handbags, here and there coughs. As though they themselves were slipping into hiding.

Inside the bare rooms time stopped; they moved like sleepwalkers. Alice touched the faded ochre wallpaper, frayed at its seams and edges from the erosion of thousands of brushing fingertips, air-stirring whispers. She peered at Anne's taped-up rotogravure pictures of movie stars, celebrities whose fame had been dissolved by time, the girl who taped up their pictures, in the end, more famous than any of them.

Standing in the back, where Anne and her sister Margot slept, looking out the windows onto a chestnut tree, its branches bending to a light breeze, Alice realized this must be the same tree Anne Frank saw, the sum of the natural world available to her for those two years in hiding. Suddenly Alice was sucked pneumatically through a tunnel that brought her to thoughts of children broken by instruments of fate—both by huge, deliberate killing machines and small, foolish accidents. A child stopped dead in her tracks, held back from moving into life, everything in front of her rendered perfectly smooth, free of footprints.

She realized she had been standing too long in the same spot, the traffic of visitors forced to eddy around her. She moved along, but only to circle the room again; she wasn't ready to leave. Although she was always working on one or another painting of Casey, Alice had come to a dead end in thinking about the accident. By now the memory was filtered, reflected. In this moment Casey came to her along with Anne Frank, a quick flip of snapshots in an album—two girls, one looking out a window, the other flying into one.

And then Maude flipped into the album. Maude straightening out the broken girl on the grass just beyond the road's gravel shoulder. Alice remembered the almost painterly composition of a patient in pale madras and denim, a nurse in silk, shimmering in the drifts of moonlight that fell through the gently rustling tree branches. Finding the girl's vague pulse, trying to breathe her own life into the girl's mouth. All her memories of Maude, beginning with this one, were so vivid, their focus so sharp, that Maude's current absence was kind of irrelevant, just something trivial cloaking her continued presence.

Of course, added to this was the nuisance of Maude's presence on television, as Ginger Slade, the tough but tenderhearted cop she now played on a terrible show called *Blue Light*. Any Wednesday night, Alice could watch Ginger jumping a high fence in a chase sequence, or interrogating some poor Colombian woman being used as a drug mule. Or standing with her booted foot on a chair, a serious automatic holstered at the small of her back as she leaned in to stare down an insolent coke dealer. What Alice hated most about the show was Ginger's tough-talking love affair with a crime scene expert. It wasn't that Alice was jealous of this stupid fictional romance, but it burned her that some dumb actor with cultivated stubble got to make out with Maude now, while Alice didn't.

Worst, though—the particular torture devised for Alice—because of Gabe, Alice's and Maude's paths still occasionally crossed. In this small, maddening way Maude was still available to Alice. The chocolate left in the box, still in its crinkly wrap, beneath its tissue cover. These points of contact only added to the confusion. Gabe's tenth birthday brought her back to Chicago last year. This was after her breakup with the guy who rented out period cars for movies, before her marriage to the cameraman.

The birthday party was at a bowling alley. Gabe was currently a bowling maniac; no one knew where he came by this interest; all his friends played soccer. Maude and Alice eventually drifted away from the lanes, out to the parking lot and stood leaning against the front of Alice's van, looking down at their comically colored rented shoes until Maude turned suddenly, pressing the length of herself against Alice, kissing her then saying, "Do you think I don't still want this?" And Alice, who had never been able to ask Maude the tough follow-up questions, just stood in the middle of that moment emotionally naked. But this kiss was followed only by a little more bowling then a lot more absence and silence and, for Alice at least, more of the low, rumbling roll of finding and loss, retrieval and flight that began the night of Carmen's wedding and had not yet come to rest.

She had tried to outrun the past. She had tried to find a replacement for Maude. For a while, she was running through the muscular carpenters and electricians in a group called Tradeswomen. Most recently she had been seeing the most serious woman in the world. Ingrid. Carmen set them up. Ingrid sat on the board of Carmen's shelter. She sat on a lot of boards, gave speeches and presentations on women empowering themselves. She was a vegetarian. She wore plastic shoes. She used Z-Tar soap and always smelled a little like fresh roofing. Spiritually she defined herself as Druid. Alice found all of this dead seriousness kind of hilarious in the abstract and in the retelling, but in Ingrid's presence, it was somehow intensely erotic. Like bedding a saint—rough sheets, silent sex. Their days together were numbered. For sure Alice would slip and use the term "history." Or, in some heated moment, ask to be fucked. Soon she and Ingrid would have a small, nasty breakup that would look as if it was about something, but would really only be about Alice not having enough passion to go on. This was Maude's legacy; she had left Alice with her heart weakened, its chambers bruised. She was no longer up to the enthusiasm required by love.

• • •

She found herself sitting on a bench overlooking the Prinsengracht. When she idly checked her watch, she sprung to her feet. The light had fooled her. She was running very late.

At the hotel, she showered hot then cold, changed into skinny black pants and a silk camp shirt—a sort of uniform for opening nights. She walked over to the museum, along ochre canals, over bridges, under heavy awnings of leaves, past buildings of brick, their doors painted in high gloss colors—dark green, navy blue, vermillion. Instead of ending, the day had stretched out. Instead of being dusk, six o'clock had the look of mid-afternoon in these fabulously long days of early northern summer when it stayed light until eleven. Staying out as the day pushed toward midnight was like playing hooky from the regular rules of clocks. Café tables spilled out onto the narrow streets to accommodate swells of customers. The canals were filled with salon boats, cigarette boats, tiny fishing dinghies with outboard motors. Salvaged lifeboats were jam-packed with partiers, everyone standing, still dressed from work, holding glasses of wine, bottles of beer, ducking a little to clear the bridges, their chatter and laughter reverberating off the brick retaining walls.

The streets along the water slipstreamed with bicycle traffic. Men in suits, women in loose skirts, their purses dangling daintily from the handlebars. A musician with a cello strapped to his back. Parents with toddlers in rigged-up seats, front and rear. A woman with her dog in a box cantilevered out over the front wheel. There were no stop signs so the mix of traffic—the bikes, but also cars, motorcycles, delivery vans, pedestrian tourists five abreast—dismantled then reassembled itself at each intersection, in this or that nick of time.

She thought she might be able to be happy here in an interestingly sad way.

The curator of Alice's show, Anneke Morren, waited at the museum's entrance, smoking languidly. Anneke was thin in a way that reeked of control; you could almost smell her flint, her metal. Her favorite beverage seemed to be hot water with a slice of lemon. Alice had never seen her eat anything. She had dark eyebrows and white-blond hair, glasses with square frames. Tonight she wore a lightweight purple cape over something else, something black. In any lineup, she would be immediately recognizable as the museum curator. She exuded a heavy musk of calm. Openings were all in a day's work for Anneke, no cause for fluttering. Besides, she had people whose job was to flutter on her behalf—two young guys in black trousers and white shirts who were laughing continuously, as if they were being tickled, when they were actually only setting up a white-linen-covered table in the museum's lobby, arranging wineglasses, silver trays of canapés, and vases extravagantly crammed with extravagant flowers—purple lisianthus, golden calla lilies. This was Holland; they had flowers to burn.

"Your show, it will be a great success," Anneke predicted as she draped one of her bird-wing arms across Alice's shoulders, guiding her inside. "I always know a little ahead. It is something like a scent, it precedes the crowd. This is hard to describe. But I am always right."

They walked through the gallery, taking a last-minute look at the twelve paintings that made up the show, which the museum was calling American Vacation—a series of big canvases, 48" x 72"—that imagined a low end of tourist postcards. Narrative scenes of gas station restrooms, grim motel rooms, mangy petting zoos, third-rate roadside attractions. Alice was proud of this work; if it had been made by someone else, she would have been envious. She suspected it had found favor in Europe for being exotically American. She would have preferred it was liked merely because it was good, but she'd take approval where she could find it.

"You are pleased?" Anneke waved a swath of cape around the large gallery. A few years ago, Alice would have burst out laughing, but by now she had been subdued. Now she could keep a straight face in front of the most pretentious statements or gestures.

"Oh yes." In addition to the paintings, the room had been lightly cluttered with old hotel desks and writing tables with postcards of two of the paintings, pens and sheets of stamps set out. "But this is really your part. The terrific presentation. For me, the best part was when I was making the paintings."

She hoped this sounded like the truth, which it was, although more and more of what she said about her work sounded canned to her as it passed her lips, pre-formatted for the interview, or the short chat with the collector or gallery owner. When she had been painting in obscurity, she could just paint. Now she had to paint *and* articulate her process, her themes, her palette; be flattered by approval; try not to appear defensive in the presence of criticism. These were luxurious burdens, of course.

"You know," Alice said, trying to make it sound by the by. "I visited the Anne Frank House this afternoon." She wanted to talk about this with someone. What was it like in Amsterdam during the war? Anneke's parents would have been alive through the occupation. Immediately Alice saw that she had brought too serious a subject into this upbeat moment. The silence elongated. A pulse became visible at Anneke's jawline. Alice suspected she was hardening against having this conversation with a foreigner. But she was polite as she closed the subject. "Anne Frank," she said, "is complicated."

Maybe a hundred people came and went during the next couple of hours. The language barrier Alice had been dreading turned out to be nonexistent. Everyone spoke excellent English, as opposed to her phrase book Dutch, which consisted of being able to say *alstublieft* and *dank u wel* to shopkeepers and the hotel maid. Everyone at the opening offered kindness and praise, of course. She took the chat at openings with a grain of salt. She wasn't sure what she would hear if she had the room bugged. Once, after a group show early in her career, Alice was overflowing with self-congratulation until she got smacked with brutal reviews and a sudden chill from the gallery. Over time she learned to not take the bubbly atmosphere of these evenings too seriously. The bubbles had more to do with seeing and being seen around the art than with the art itself.

While Alice was talking with a couple who collected electronic sculpture, Anneke rushed up (which is to say her low-key, discreet version of rushing) and whispered at Alice's ear. "Kees Verwey has arrived. This is a great honor for you. He comes to few openings. At this point, he hardly ever leaves his studio in Haarlem."

Verwey, Verwey, Alice thought. Then her memory gained purchase. Kees Verwey. Still lifes. Gestural portraits. She couldn't call up any specific paintings. And wouldn't he be dead by now? Wasn't he painting in the 1930s? Then she saw him across the gallery, thickened and slightly stooped with age. Comb-over hair, bristly mustache. She only knew it was him by the way the crowd deferred and dispersed, as though street-sweeping brushes spun in front of him while he moved slowly along the perimeter of paintings.

He examined several paintings quickly, then stopped at *Wish You Were Here*. The painting's setting was the pool of a down-and-out motel, its colors a constrained palette of worn pastels. Leaves floated in the corners, a plastic water slide dangled over the lip, broken off halfway down. Its subject, faded to a ghostly presence, was a family. Alice had tried to render these figures as shadows, valiant humans trying to make a vacation in this place where any initial impulse of hope had long been abandoned. She spiraled down inside herself watching the old man stand in front of it, then move back across the gallery to look from a remove. Suddenly his opinion held weight. She anticipated his worst criticism. She shared the curse of many artists—that praise beaded up and rolled off her while criticism stuck like glue, glue embedded with ground glass.

When he finished looking at Alice's work, he was accompanied by the middle-aged man who brought him, toward the buffet table where he made himself a substantial sandwich of dark bread and smoked salmon. Alice thought, well, at least she wouldn't have to talk with him, then saw Anneke glide across the gallery, snag him, and guide him slowly over.

Alice told him she was honored he had come.

"I had an appointment here anyway. With my dentist." He tapped his cheek with a thick index finger, tipped dark green with paint. His suit had the tight, boxy cut of an earlier era, its sleeves and pockets specked and dabbed with patches of paint. He went on insulting her. "It is nothing that I came here. The painting on the notice interested me a little. Now I have seen the others. I would say to you that these are good paintings. But they are part of your apprenticeship. Something is yet held back, I think. I would like to see what you do after these. You may contact me and bring me the paintings. I will look."

Alice felt heat rushing across her face and turned away so he wouldn't see this. When she turned back, he was still looking at her, waiting. She saw, finally, that he was offering something of value.

"I don't know when that would be," she said. "I don't live here."

"No matter. I am usually at home. You can bring me work when you are ready."

Alice nodded and shook the hand he extended and started to say something, but he was done being social. He worked his hand free of hers, turned, and headed off toward the bar table.

"It's remarkable, really," Anneke said, "that he still paints."

"I think," Alice said, "he does it in that suit."

"It's true." This was someone new, who had come up to join the conversation. "He always wears a suit and tie. Like painting is a business. Or at least he puts on the suit when visitors are coming." Alice had been tracking this woman since she arrived—1940s gabardine jacket, T-shirt and long, baggy, foreign-legion shorts. Unattractive in an extremely attractive way. Like a minor figure in some artistic circle of the recent past. Those American dykes in Paris in the twenties. Someone on the fringe of the Bloomsbury group. Edith Sitwell maybe.

She was Charlotte somebody; Anneke introduced them. She was an artist herself, also the art critic for a local arts and entertainment weekly. She spoke excellent English, but with little slang and few idioms; she sounded like a friendly alien. "I have been to visit him two times. For interviews. Once he was happy to see me. The next time he pushed me back out the door. His studio was like an explosion. Now he does not often leave. He paints whatever he finds in there, also what he finds inside his head. When he is hungry he pushes aside the mess on the table and puts his meal in the space he has made. Then he paints some more."

Alice listened to the small echo created by this conversation, the space outside the words that told her she would sleep with this woman tonight. Everything between now and that eventuality was just filler.

"Do you have any of his paintings here?" Alice asked.

"Well, of course," Anneke said, sounding a little insulted. "We have a gallery given to his work. On the third floor."

"I could show her," the Charlotte person said. So helpful.

The walls of this gallery were painted a dark, dusty red. The color worked to hold the paintings in place. Alice looked first at the watercolors, which were amazing in their layering and opacity. But what knocked her out were Verwey's oils. The way they enlisted both vibrant color and near-total darkness. The paint thick as frosting, the casual brushwork nonetheless giving an architectural precision to the chaos, as though chaos were just a slightly more interesting version of order.

"This guy is great. Why hasn't he gotten more recognition?"

"Well, maybe because he is not such an easy person."

Alice made her way around the room a second time. "Man," she said, "for all the time I've been at it, people have been saying painting is dead. But here, this is why painting won't die. Because someone can make pictures like these."

A little later, Charlotte asked, "Maybe, when you're done here, you will let me take you away a little?" Alice's original plan—to head back to the hotel to beat herself up a little, to recapture the melancholy of the afternoon—no longer seemed so compelling.

Charlotte had a favorite coffee shop, which was about the size of someone's living room. They got Cokes in little bottles and shared a joint of some weed called White Widow and Alice was soon stunningly high. Their conversation slowed and expanded. They talked about art and women, the difficulties of both. Rough commonalities in their childhoods, although Charlotte's was grounded in an epic sort of poverty. Lard sandwiches, walls patched with newspaper, wearing other people's shoes. Alice lost the thread here and there. When they emerged from the coffee shop, the sun had still not set; the day was staying open late for them. Charlotte stopped Alice and kissed her against the side of a church. They walked along the cobblestone streets, kissing some more as they went, the kissing a part of the walking. Boys on a boat passing along the canal beside and beneath them shouted out.

"What are they saying?"

Charlotte burst out laughing. "They are telling us to get a room!"

A few blocks over, on a side canal, Charlotte pushed open her front door and Alice pulled herself up the spiral stairs by the railing, Charlotte behind her. At the top, she reached past Alice to unlock a door and they were inside. The walls of the small entrance hallway were tacked full of drawings—extremely articulated studies of human organs.

"Being art critic at *The Daily Planet*—the name is from *Superman* so we keep it in English—well, it is not really a paying job. This is how I make money to live. Medical drawings. For textbooks. It is not such terrible work."

"No, no," Alice said, peering at the drawings, which were quite good. "I used to do meat."

"You are saying meat?"

"Yes, for a market. I could show you how to draw an excellent lamb chop."

"That would be so useful," Charlotte said and it was as though she had made the funniest joke ever. Alice laughed so hard her knees went wobbly, and then Charlotte was also laughing. They laughed for what seemed about an hour. Everything had moved into slow motion. And then they weren't laughing, and Charlotte was running a finger, tracing Alice's ear, the line of her jaw, lavishing kisses on Alice, or more accurately, started one long kiss that went on until they'd lost all grace and technique and were only eating each other's mouths. Beyond the little foyer, the apartment was a blur of blue linoleum, walls the color of green tea ice cream, an old manual typewriter set on a wooden table, books and more books—in bookcases, but also in high stacks. Then an old iron bed they fell upon and Charlotte was undoing Alice's pants, pulling down the zipper as Alice tilted her hips slightly, to help Charlotte slip her hand inside. Alice filled with gratitude.

In the morning, which arrived a little after four-thirty according to the clock by the side of the bed, Alice woke halfway and watched a gray-and-white cat eat kibble from a small bowl. A row of high, tall windows on the other side of the room sluiced watery sunlight into the room. She looked over at Charlotte, sleeping on her stomach, the side of her neck stained with hickeys. Without knowing it, this woman had been a Good Samaritan. She had saved Alice from a gin-soaked night alone in her hotel room, self-indulgently conflating her remorse with all of Europe's.

Alice woke again. This time Charlotte was lying on her side, head propped up on her hand. She dipped to kiss Alice softly with sweet breath and slightly puffy lips. "So," she said. "It wasn't a dream. I really did spend the night with Alice Kenney in my bed."

Before Alice left, Charlotte asked if she would sign her copy of the catalog from the show. The pen leaked a little black ink into Alice's hand and Charlotte blotted it off, then kissed the palm playfully. Clearly she meant to flatter, but Alice felt snapped with a little whip. She hadn't factored in that success was going to be a little tricky. Last night, she saw, had already been framed for retelling, a small prize this woman would show off to her friends. Alice saw the standard equation of attraction had been altered for her. Not only would she not have to hang her own paintings anymore, she would no longer have to rely on her own charms. From here on, for a time anyway, her name alone would be enough to slide her into the beds of admirers. A flinch of sadness caught her.

hammam
[carmen in paris]

Carmen pretended to read *Out of Africa* (which had been gathering dust on her nightstand for the several years since she enjoyed the movie and thought she'd get right down to reading the book). As she pushed through chapter three, she was peripherally distracted by Heather in the seat next to her, felt-tipping a black spider onto the back of her hand.

Heather didn't acknowledge Carmen's interest. She was masterful at making it seem not as though she was ignoring Carmen, rather that Carmen simply wasn't in the frame. To avoid any possible engagement, she had worn her Walkman through the five-plus hours they'd been on this flight.

On the other side of Heather was Heather's father, whom Carmen had been dating since they met in the Proust class. Rob hunched over an open folder of paperwork. His calculator ran out of solar juice, and as he shifted in his seat and reached up to rejuvenate it with the light from the reading bulb, he looked over at Carmen and winked. Like they were linked in a conspiracy of fun.

program, which meant big bucks if she stuck with it, cutting hair in a first-tier salon instead of at Sharon's Curl & Color on Irving Park, the only place Olivia applied to that would accept her prison cosmetology certificate. He definitely had a big heart.

Basically, Carmen had been worn down. She felt lucky to have come up with someone even kind of possible. Rob was older, in his mid-forties. But as she cruised through her thirties Carmen noticed that friends her age were sometimes dating men twenty-five years older than they were. Which meant these were not older guys, but actual old guys—guys with ear hair and white belts and the solid paunches Alice called "front butt." Rob still had a hungry look about him, a bit of future left. He still held the possibility of a few surprises.

He wasn't perfect. She could see this. There were too many different names populating his relationship anecdotes, and once he let slip that he had been forced to change his phone number four times in the past few years, since he got out of his last (third) marriage. She knew that when somebody told you these sorts of things, they were pebbles cast into the pool and you ought to look carefully at the ripples of implication. But who ever did? To hell with implication say the weary veterans of dating.

His politics were not that great. He wasn't a Republican, nothing out-and-out repulsive, but he was shifty on certain issues—like welfare and the death penalty. He thought people ought to work harder, the way he did. He thought it was okay to fry certain criminals. He picked the least sympathetic examples. Guys who chopped up their victims and served them in stews. That sort of thing.

But the fact was, she wasn't offering perfection herself. She wasn't as open or optimistic as she once was. She was already too formed for some guys, too serious for others. A little too demanding, she supposed, although she liked to think of this as rigor. Just having Gabe would rule her out for some guys, on principle, without even getting to know him. But Rob professed to like Gabe, claimed to be unfazed by the superciliousness and the send-ups he must have known happened behind his back. (Once, she was sitting in the kitchen and looked up to see Gabe, out of Rob's view, standing in the hall with Brillo pads stuffed into the open collar of his shirt.) His willingness to keep taking it on the chin from an eleven-year-old gave him huge points, and made her feel obligated to keep trying with Heather.

Before he left, Rob asked Carmen if she would go along with Heather for the afternoon.

"Don't make it look like we've talked, and you're chaperoning. Just—if you could pretend to be interested. Whatever it is."

"Why do I have the feeling it's going to be that tour of the sewers?"

Heather longed to escape into the Paris promised by her guidebook—*The Hip Pocket Guide to Paris,* with the emphasis on "hip." She was interested in exploring the margins of the city, and this guidebook was ready to take her there. On the plane, Carmen noticed her circling an entry on anachronistic matinee dance halls, like the one in Bertolucci's *Last Tango in Paris*. Heather was into film, particularly old and/or foreign films, particularly those that offered critical reevaluations of the culture, indictments of "civilization." Civilization always wore quotation marks when Heather said it. She had the pretensions, not just of youth, but of a youth that happened twenty years ago—actually, a youth much like Carmen's own, which made it even more frustrating to Carmen that they short-circuited rather than connected. She wished Alice were here. She would immediately find a way to plug into Heather. She'd beat Heather at her own game. Take her to an absinthe bar.

"She's really a good kid," Rob said on his way out the door.

Yeah, Carmen thought. Maybe.

She arranged to meet Heather at three.

"What about if we find each other in the Luxembourg Gardens?" Carmen suggested. "By the boat pond." This purely childish place stood out in her memory from the otherwise culturally hard-driven, museum-centered vacations on which Horace took the family.

"I don't know if I'll be able to find it," Heather said.

"Oh I'm sure you will."

Carmen arrived late, but not terribly. Scanning the mid-afternoon crowd around the pond, she spotted Heather, reading her guidebook, the headphones of her Walkman buzzing as though bees were trapped inside their foam covers. She sat in a verdigrised metal park chair, one black-booted foot propped on the other. Although the day was warm, particularly here in the park in the steeply angled afternoon sun, Heather wore a black leather jacket that was scuffed to brown in places, and torn away altogether at one shoulder.

Carmen knew from Rob that Heather spent a great deal of her weekend time dressing and making up and disheveling her hair for nights spent with the black leather and silver-stud kids who milled around the parking lot of the Dunkin' Donuts at Clark and Belmont. Whenever she used to drive past this regular weekend scene, Carmen assumed they were all on their way somewhere, waiting for someone to show up or something to begin, but Rob said no, often Heather just hung out all night in the parking lot, then took a bus home.

It could be the girl was not being looked after enough. She didn't talk about friends, or a boyfriend, but then she wouldn't, of course, not to Carmen. Her mother, according to Rob, was wrestling with some tricky bipolar disorder—on, then off, then on her meds again. There had been bad incidents at both poles.

Carmen sat down on the chair next to Heather, and when the girl still didn't look up, Carmen announced her presence by tapping her rolled-up *Pariscope* against the ripped knee of Heather's jeans.

To which Heather responded by jumping with a shout of "No!" She dropped her book, ripped off her headphones and went into a martial-arts position, half crouched, her hands circling smoothly through the air in front of her. Only then did she realize—or rather only then did she pretend to realize—that it was Carmen approaching her, not a madman.

She then placed a hand over her heart, as if to subdue the wildness of its beating. She was just, Carmen now saw, going to keep making it impossible.

"Look—" she said, pushing at the air with the palms of her hands, a gesture usually reserved for talking lunatics down off ledges. "Just, let's say—don't ever touch me like that again."

Quite a few of the people around them—loungers and readers and nappers and mothers of the small children pushing toy sailboats around the pond—had stopped and were watching this showdown.

"Hey, sorry," Carmen said, trying to bring this stupid situation down from its hysterical heights, while not really giving Heather anything. As she apologized, she held her voice as far back from sincerity as possible, as close as she could get to the synthesized voice on the machine at her parking lot at work. The voice that said "Please take your parking ticket. Thank you." This was the voice she also used with obstreperous women at the shelter, to not give them the satisfaction of getting a rise out of her.

At first Carmen thought Heather's toughness was a protective exoskeleton, but on closer acquaintance she had come to think the girl might be hard clear through, harder than the young hookers who came to the shelter when they were desperate. Often they were on the street because of circumstance. Usually they were addicts, and hookers only by bad luck. Many of them slept with teddy bears. Heather—Carmen would have put money on it—did not have a teddy bear.

"Have you found us something good?" Carmen nodded at the book dangling from Heather's hand.

"Oh," Heather said. For a suspended moment Carmen thought this might be all she was going to say. But then she began again, with seemingly great effort. Like someone trying, despite the ice pick in her chest, to cough out the name of her murderer. "Yeah, well . . . there's this hammam. It's, like, a steam bath."

"Oh yeah. My sister Alice went to one once when we were teenagers. We were in Morocco with our family. This was during a period when my father was painting deserts. I didn't have the nerve myself. For the hammam. It sounded too—I don't know—too exotic."

"Right," Heather said, as though Carmen had pulled up a potbelly stove and a rocking chair and a piece of whittling, and had begun telling Heather about each of the big snows in a lifetime of winters. "So do you want to go, or what?" She followed this with an impersonation of sign language, a little roll of her hands then a pointing away, a lifting of eyebrows to indicate a question. She did this when she wanted to be particularly nasty to Carmen, brought her ear into the mix.

It only now occurred to Carmen that Rob not only asked her to look after Heather, but probably asked Heather to pay some attention to Carmen. Which would explain why everything Heather said sounded Novocained. So Carmen would understand that her attention was not voluntary.

"Sure," Carmen said to the idea of the hammam, even though it was the worst idea Heather could have picked of all the terrible ideas in her guidebook. The actual reason Carmen hadn't gone into the hammam in Morocco with Alice all those years ago was her ridiculous modesty, which she still dragged around. But maybe this hammam would be an updated, Westernized version, someplace where everyone bundled up in large, fluffy robes.

On the Métro, though, she borrowed the guide from Heather and read, with a heavy heart, that this place came highly recommended (of course it would) for its cultural authenticity. "A bit of the ancient medina in the heart of Paris with mysterious rituals of ablution," she read, translating this into "everyone will be stark naked."

The hammam turned out to be part of a larger building, white-walled as it would be in its native desert setting. Once through its portals, they were in an interior garden where many people, mainly men but some women, all in Arab dress—veils on the women and, on the men, wool robes and pointed leather shoes of a lurid yellow—sat drinking glasses of mint tea and talking in what gathered up into a mild din, a pleasant hubbub. Through another archway, in a tearoom, a sea of men huddled over cigarettes or ate from low tables a variety of vividly colored pastries, as well as some that looked to be sealed, like souvenirs, in honey.

"Here it is," Heather said.

On a large wooden door to their left a cardboard sign hung at a tilt:

AUJOURD'HUI—LES FEMMES

"What luck," Carmen said as Heather pushed against the door, held it open behind her with just the tips of her black fingernails, and they entered.

With a few stairs down then a short hallway, they went back several centuries. They stood in a room that was ancient and cavernous, detailed with Moorish arches and tiled floors, the walls narrative with worn mosaics.

To their immediate left was a high counter.

"C'est votre premiere fois?" asked the red-haired woman behind it. She towered over them, like a schoolmistress in a dark dream.

"Oh," Carmen said. *"Oui."* It was most definitely their first time. And with that, she had run out to the end of her hammam vocabulary, and put up the palms of her hands in defeat and supplication. The counter woman took pity and exchanged their shoulder bags for a single claim check and two towels.

"Là-bas," she said, pointing with a hand whose fingers bore at least twenty rings. *"Déshabillez-vous là, et ensuite entrez dans le hammam."*

Carmen nodded and stared around the room. In the center a small stone fountain was lapped by water. Brushes, like shoeshine brushes but bigger, lined the base of the low surrounding wall, also sandals, all of a uniform wooden type. Around the sides of the room were raised platforms covered with padded gym mats, on which women were sitting or lying in various states of dress, more accurately in various states of undress, as hardly anyone wore much more than underwear. Most were naked. They ranged in age from young teenage girls with their mothers to extremely aged women. Most appeared to be Arab—Algerian, maybe Moroccan. The rest were French, Carmen guessed, although two had such an assertively blond look she figured them for Scandinavian tourists. They also came in an amazing variety of sizes, from cigarette-thin women to women larger than any Carmen had ever seen. Women who, naked, looked like giant soft-serve sculptures, their bodies great, graduated, overlapping fountains of flesh.

Some of these women were sleeping, curled up and lovely in their being both unclothed and at the same time not vulnerable, there being nothing in the situation to be vulnerable to. Most, though, were awake and socializing in an unfocused way that Carmen—her own friendships maintained through agenda-heavy meetings or the camaraderie at political actions—had never encountered other than with her sister. She could definitely imagine being here with Alice—well, if everyone wore a little more clothing.

Along with the socializing there was a lot of languorous grooming, the way cats lick each other, the way monkeys pick through each other's fur for nits. In this assuaging fashion, the women here rubbed each other's limbs with oils, or combed each other's hair or applied henna. Many of them, Carmen now noticed, had hair of the same muddy red color. So much here was strange to Carmen, that for the first few moments she was taken out of herself, her fears left far behind. They came back in a rush only when she realized this wasn't a TV travelogue, but rather a ritual in which she was immediately going to be expected to participate.

"We don't have to do this," Heather said in a low voice next to her, the first words of kindness she had ever spoken to Carmen.

"No. Let's go on." Carmen nodded toward the open archway at the far end of the room, from which steam rolled out like a low-lying fog.

"Like the entrance to hell," Heather said. "You know. In cartoons."

• • •

As they stood there, leaning in slightly toward each other, an attendant—a wiry woman who had just scurried in from the bar area with a tray full of jiggling, clinking glasses of mint tea—came up to them and motioned with a cock of her head for them to take two adjacent mats. After she had set down the tray, she cleared the towels of the previous occupants, then pointed at the pegs lining the wall.

"I think we hang our stuff there," Carmen said.

Heather hopped up onto the raised platform. Carmen followed, stepping onto the squishy mats next to an ancient woman who had also just arrived. She was wearing a chador, her face covered by the traditional veil, but she also had with her an Adidas gym bag.

None of Carmen's old locker-room routines of disrobing would work here. There was no dark corner, no locker door to slip behind. Worse, they were on a platform that created the effect of a stage. She felt bereft of her clothing as she stepped out of her skirt, unbuttoned her blouse, unhooked her bra, transferring all this protective coloration onto a couple of the wall pegs. She was profoundly chilled, even though, only moments earlier, the room seemed too warm, too close with the sighing breath of all these women. Who—Carmen suddenly realized—had now become quiet, as if holding their breath collectively. She found herself awake in the middle of her worst nightmare. They were turned, looking her way. She instinctively crossed her arms in front of her breasts, and felt a flush spreading through her.

Only when she was able to look up again did she see it was not her they were fascinated by, but rather Heather, who had emerged from her leather and denim and gender-generic underwear looking like the poster girl for famine relief. The head of an adolescent on the body of a child. Her ribs bowed out below her tiny flattened breasts, her arms looked snappable as dry twigs, her collarbones jutted like stones at the base of her neck. The flesh stretched over this frame was the watery blue-white of nonfat milk.

Heather, snapping her underpants off a toe, looked up and caught the stares of the assembled. She didn't seem offended, or put off.

Carmen saw she might find their interest flattering. She had, after all, gone to a great deal of trouble to come to this, and might well want to show off her accomplishment.

Suddenly Heather wasn't just a jerk or a spoiled little rich girl. In a rush of pure impulse, Carmen wanted to fold her up in her arms, stand Heather's toes on her own and dance her around this ancient room like she used to do with Gabe when he was little and having a bad day. But, of course, she couldn't.

Carmen feared for girls. After Casey Redman, they all seemed fragile, vulnerable, miraculous in making it through girlhood. And Heather, Carmen now understood, might well not.

"Ready?" she said now, challenging Carmen with her nakedness, daring her to show pity or revulsion or fear.

Carmen looked away, at nothing. "Okay." She saw that some women were emerging from the steam bath in their underpants, and so she left hers on. She kept her arms crossed over her breasts and followed her Virgil, into the depths.

Which began with a bank of showers surrounding two tables with padded, cloth-covered tops, on which lay women undergoing what must certainly be the

NETTOYAGE DE PEAU-55 FR

advertised on a paper sign taped to the wall.

"What does it say?" Heather asked.

"It's some kind of skin cleansing," Carmen said, and they stood for a moment watching the women on the tables being ministered to by huge, hulking masseuses with massive arms and red hands, who looked to be sanding down their victims with rough, wet cloths. Carmen couldn't tell whether this process would feel heavenly, or torturous.

Beyond this they found another large cavern with raised, tiled cubicles lining the walls. Within these, women in pairs and threes were taking amateur turns at rubbing each other down, and pouring water over each other from the sawed-off plastic liter soda bottles that littered the floors. There was water everywhere, from the fountains and the hoses snaking around on the tiles, also standing water in all the many depressions worn through the ages both in the floor and in the sitting platforms.

With Heather leading the way, Carmen followed so closely that, to counter a slippery step, she put up a hand and touched the sharp blade of Heather's shoulder. She seemed so insubstantial and vaporous, and with the steam rolling up and around her, it almost seemed an outstretched hand would pass through her.

They moved slowly over the slick floors, through a third chamber and into a fourth, the heat growing progressively more oppressive, the steam clouding ever thicker until finally Carmen could barely see anyone else, and only a misty specter of Heather. Which relaxed her a bit in her modesty, and made it easier to look straight at Heather without flinching.

"Want me to dye your hair?" Heather asked over her shoulder, the first joke she had ever made with Carmen.

"How could anyone stay in here long enough to do anything?"

"Challenging, though, in a weird way," Heather said, holding onto Carmen's arm briefly, for support.

They tottered over and sat down in a shallow lake on the edge of an empty, tiled alcove. "Let's see how long we can stand it," Heather suggested, and disappeared behind the drape of vapor that closed around her as she reclined.

Carmen moved to the back of the niche and collected water from the small fountain carved into the wall, pressing her face into it, then spilling the water down the front of her body, over one then another shoulder. For the next small stretch of time, she lost Heather's terrible troubles along with her own small ones. For a few moments in the depths of this place, so far inside it was almost impossible to think of an outside; she became someone she felt only vaguely acquainted with.

◆ ◆ ◆

When she tried, she had great difficulty standing up. She waited an extra beat for some confidence of balance to return, then reached through the mist to find Heather, and finally made contact with a hip that was an immodesty of bone, thinly veiled with flesh.

"You okay?" she asked.

"It *is* kind of intense," Heather admitted.

"Let's go back," Carmen said, taking Heather's hand, the two of them moving forward with the smallest, most tentative of steps. Carmen was still a little woozy when she entered the previous room, but at least she was freed from the weighted air of the deepest chambers. They progressed—or rather regressed—slowly, until they reentered the first, mildest steam cavern, where they stopped and sat for a while and watched two women large as sumo wrestlers, in black thong underwear, one scrubbing the other in a slow, trancey way, cooling the cloth under a running tap, wringing it out, then scrubbing some more.

"This place is a trip," Heather said, and Carmen could see she was trying to cut the experience down to size, trim it into a tidy story to tell some night, to someone else in black, in the Dunkin' Donuts lot.

"Let's cool off," Carmen suggested and they stood again, much steadier now, and retreated into the showers, which only ran cold, and were stunning.

"Ahhhh," Carmen said.

Heather moved in next to her, under the same flow of what felt like brilliant liquid ice. Carmen sensed her presence through the water and opened her eyes to meet Heather's vacant, wash-blue stare. She saw that Heather was putting herself through a decompression process, pulling herself out of this unalterably shared experience into the pale Paris afternoon they were about to reenter, once again separate. But she wouldn't be able to get there. They could no longer retreat into their previous positions exactly because they had been here together. Carmen saw that everything up until this afternoon had been prelude between them, overture, that now was the exact starting point, the place where she and Heather might begin.

• • •

At the hotel, she called Matt and Paula's number and mercifully Gabe picked up.

"How's it going?" she said.

"Big doings here." He was talking not in a whisper exactly, more like a TV golf announcer during an important putt. "The twins started a fire in a new house going up on the next block over. Then they stuck around to watch their handiwork. The cops picked them out of the crowd right away. The toes of their sneakers were melted and charred. Dad's furious. And freaked. Those girls are so sweet looking, but they are total criminals." He stopped and for just a beat, they were both listening to the same soft ocean of fiber optics. Then he said, "Hey, how are you? Heather try to push you off the Eiffel Tower?" And Carmen unfolded with gratitude for him. In contrast, she envisioned the road ahead of Heather, the next few years. The creepy boyfriends. The unsavory interests, the phases and episodes and therapy and medications. All requiring enormous amounts of parental attention and intervention. Getting Heather through to adulthood looked like a staggering proposition.

The three of them went for dinner to a restaurant Rob knew, in the Marais. Filled with diners at the far end of their youth, riding a surf of conviviality, ordering cigarettes, which were then brought to the table on silver trays, the pack opened, the matchbook folded back, everything in a state of readiness, as if smoking were an urgently necessary element, an integral part of the hilarity, along with the many bottles of champagne brought up the circular steps from the basement, their popping corks punctuating the laughter and conversations—French in the upper registers, underlaid with a few more pedestrian languages.

Rob ordered them a Bordeaux, something excellent he knew about, something he'd written in a thin leather notebook he kept in an inside breast pocket. Rob hadn't gone to college. He'd attended a cosmetology academy and in the years since had risen to a social level he'd had to cram for.

For dinner, he ordered the steak frites. Heather, who, like Gabe, was vegetarian, ordered a spinach terrine and the vichyssoise. Carmen—an ocean away from Gabe's censorious gaze—ordered quail. She had never eaten them, but here they were in the capital of haute cuisine, so why not be adventurous? She imagined small, delicate chicken-like pieces in some complex sauce. What arrived were two very dead birds with their heads bowed.

"Oh gross, how could you possibly?" Heather said, throwing the back of her hand across her eyes, an actress in a silent movie. "Really," she said, "I'm going to be sick if I have to watch her—" here she stopped and turned away from her father, toward Carmen, granting her the concession of direct address—"watch you eat them."

"Maybe we should send them back," Rob said, grazing Heather's cheek with his knuckles. He asked her, "Would that be better?" He was careful with his daughter. The same way he approached Carmen, to whom he said, "Would that be okay? We could get you something else, something less tragic?"

He acted as if the problem at the table was a small one, merely another matter to be smoothed out. He persisted in relentless cheer until the shoals of the evening had been cleared, and the rest of the meal took on a light, peppy rhythm. Carmen sent back the quail and ordered the sole. Rob, in a gesture just shy of a toast, lifted his glass and rolled the red wine so it coated the inside, leaving a film of itself behind as it washed up the other side.

"I know I should feel exhausted by now, but I don't. I feel hyper-alive. It's Paris. That's what this town does to you."

Carmen and Heather sat by, not looking at each other, but strongly in each other's presence, and pretended to listen while Rob overpainted their frictions with a fantasy in which they were three sophisticated people enjoying one another's splendid company in the City of Light, in a Brassaï photograph.

Carmen's sole arrived and Heather only then began to address her terrine, taking a few bites, then just picking at it, pushing broken-off pieces under a shell of radicchio. As soon as the waiter had cleared their plates away, and was setting out small cups for espresso, she excused herself from the table to find the toilette.

"Let's be corny tonight," Rob said to Carmen as Heather passed behind him, occupying a sliver of space. "Let's go up to Montmartre and have our portraits done by terrible artists. Go to a cancan show." He took Carmen's hand. He was still enjoying the beginning of their romance while Carmen had moved much farther down the road of their cluttered, now intersected lives. Or rather she saw that the road was rushing crazily toward all of them, the way it did in Pole Position, an old video arcade game that used to make Gabe scream in fake terror as he steered out of the way of falling boulders and sudden oil slicks.

This was not what Carmen had in mind. She'd been looking for something fun and manageable and sexy, but now it was clear that a lot about this, if it went on, would be large and messy. She imagined merging herself and Gabe into Rob and Heather, making one of those awkward, reconstructed families that create a new geometry out of everyone's already existent problems. She didn't know if she loved Rob, or even liked him enough to shoulder into the yoke next to him so they could share their burdens. Until now she hadn't had to ask herself these questions.

black earth

Nick was taking I-90 north through Illinois. The traffic, for no apparent reason, was crazy. He had to swerve twice to avoid spaced-out lane drifters.

He hadn't mentioned this pilgrimage to Olivia. He just told her he was meeting Bernie Cato up at the observatory. She was easy to lie to these days, distracted by her new job. Carmen's boyfriend, Rob, had brought her into his company. MarcAntony. A new Roman empire. They had a huge salon just off Michigan Avenue. Olivia was now on the receiving end of the sort of tips wealthy women considered appropriate. She had quite a bit of extra income. She'd bought another cat.

He was fairly certain she would eventually leave him. She wouldn't be enough to protect him from himself. Himself was such a formidable enemy. And if he started using again, she'd be out. Those were her terms and she was a hard-ass woman. If she disappeared he wouldn't be able to manage on his own, and his sisters wouldn't be able to save him. They couldn't see how puny they were in the face of his need to be high. They were ants saying, "Hey can we help you hold up this huge building that's toppling onto you?"

He was trying out good behavior, shifting his focus from what he needed to what he might provide for someone else. He got the idea for driving up here from Alice. According to her—and she got it from Jean—Tom Ferris was hoping to revive his career with a song about the accident. And Nick thought, just in general, but particularly in this instance: What would be the exact opposite of what Tom Ferris was doing? What he came up with was this private pilgrimage. He imagined the girl's family had been hollowed out by their loss. He would offer himself up to them in whatever way they might need. Someone to talk to, grieve with.

Out of Illinois he headed up through southern Wisconsin, past the cheese curd shops, then, at Madison, caught Route 14 west toward Black Earth, which he had not visited since Carmen's wedding. He remembered, with a surprising Technicolor vividness, driving out that day with Olivia, Willie Nelson on the tape deck as they passed through the already-fading green of high summer, looking out at the heat shimmering over the crop rows. As he took this road again through a different weather system, in a better car and a more serious frame of mind, he remembered something he had totally forgotten about the accident—that it had started out as a wonderful day.

Not too long after he passed Cross Plains, farm fields gave way to woods as he reached the spot. Surprisingly he didn't need any markers. Some primitive part of his memory, some pigeon-like homing device knew how to find this exact place even though he had been totally stoned that night, even though that night was now a dozen years back. He pulled over to the side of the road, got out of the car, and walked toward the old oak—big that night, bigger now—that Olivia swerved into as she tried, too late, to get out of the girl's way. There was no longer any sign of that maneuver, no scar remaining on the tree's trunk. In nature, what happened here had healed over, filled in.

He stood absolutely still. Branches above him flickered with new leaves. He squatted as close as he could remember to where the girl lay twisted on the ground. He remembered Maude working so hard, giving the girl mouth-to-mouth, then CPR, then listening for breath or heartbeat. While he and Olivia sat there as useless as Raggedy Ann and Andy.

He scooped up a handful of the soil, which was the same deep carbon black of the fields he'd been passing. When he stood up, he had no idea how long he'd been there.

Back in the car, he took a run out past the town to what used to be the co-op—long since taken back by the ordinary. The house still stood on its majestic rise, but was now painted an undistinguished, drab white. The multicolored barn where Alice had her studio was now back to red, and from what he could see, had been reclaimed for storage and livestock. From the road, he couldn't see if the flower garden remained behind the house. He sat parked on the side of the road for too long. A state trooper drove past him, then stopped, but didn't back up, just waited. Nick turned the key in the ignition, made a U-turn and headed into town. He stopped at a no-name bar, a cement-block shack with a neon OLD MILWAUKEE sign hanging in the small front window. A bar-fight bar. He had been in enough of these that he could smell blood without even opening the door. Inside, he asked around in a low-key way for Terry Redman, made up some bullshit about repairing his septic system, which got him directions to the house, on a dirt road not far from here, very close to where they hit the girl.

Then he found the house he was looking for, sided in a weary tan with bent, paint-flaked gutters—where the girl was most likely headed that night. There was a scrappy front lawn being idly dug up at the moment by a sluggish basset hound. Nothing here signaled pride of ownership; this was not a place that would prompt a glance backward when leaving it behind. A carport sheltered a small Toyota pickup, and four very old cars parked one behind the other on a semicircular dirt driveway. An ancient Falcon, a Pontiac Bonneville, a boxy convertible Packard, an early Mustang. As though a ghost party were going on inside.

The front door was open, so he knocked on the storm door glass.

No one inside heard him; the TV blasted out an old episode of *Roseanne*. He could hear Roseanne tell one of the kids, "Go ask your father . . . your real father."

He pulled the door open slightly, the basset nudged by him into the living room. Nick poked his head inside.

"Hey in there," he said, then listened. Creak of Naugahyde, heavy shuffle of feet, then the TV clicked off.

"What do you want?" An adolescent voice, followed up by a fat boy in T-shirt and sweatpants coming to the door. Security guard material. The girl's brother. The kid who lived.

"Your folks home?"

"He's around back." The kid had mastered an absence of interest that was almost a vacuum. He pulled the door shut and disappeared back into the house. A click and the TV blasted back on.

Behind the house, Terry Redman rode a tractor hitched to a wide-blade mower, circling to cut down a meadow. Eventually he saw Nick and pulled up in front of him, but didn't shut down the engine.

"Hey!" Nick shouted, then signaled "TALK?" Made a yakking sign with one hand. This got Redman to cut the ignition, leaving Nick awash in a thick, oily current of gasoline fumes. The guy was still the scrapper Nick remembered from the police station that night, now with the addition of a small paunch.

"You don't remember me," Nick said. He no longer had his ponytail, now wore glasses for driving.

"No, I remember you, all right," Terry Redman said. "I never forget a guy in a dress." His face was composed of jutting jaw and brow, a knifelike nose, teeth that were stained in various shades of brown. A face forged in the fire of too much bad experience. Fights, lost jobs, accidents with machinery, domestic disputes.

"I don't want to waste your time," Nick said.

"You know, I'm not really interested in anything you've got to say, and Shanna—she's not here."

"I could wait."

"That would be a problem. Right now, she lives a couple of states away." He dismounted from the tractor and came to stand in front of Nick, a little too close. A well-like sourness seeped from his mouth, a plug of chewing tobacco made a slight bulge on his cheek.

"I'm just here to try and make amends is all," Nick said. "I want you to know I haven't put this behind me. That night sits inside me as if it were yesterday. Time passing doesn't touch it."

"Why would I care about that? What do you want from me? I hope you haven't come around for some kind of bullshit forgiveness."

"No, just that . . . I just want you to know that someone shares your sorrow. I think everyone needs to think there was something they could have done to make it different. Otherwise it's all just chaos and flying crap hitting a flying fan. And I'm thinking maybe you've taken some of the blame on yourself, and I wanted to—"

"What the fuck are you talking about?" Redman stepped forward as he said this and started flicking a really dirty fingernail sharply at the collar of Nick's shirt.

"Just that, well, your daughter being out alone in the middle—"

"Look. I don't know who you are now. Looks like you've cleaned yourself up a little. But back then you were a freak like your friends. We live a different kind of life out here. At three a.m., we don't expect cars out on the road. Or if there is somebody, it's somebody we know. Somebody who knows there are kids here, and kids can be up to anything, even in the middle of the night."

Nick had more to say, but saw he wasn't going to have a chance to say it. Terry Redman shot a fast brown glob out the side of his mouth; it splattered about an inch from the toes sticking out of Nick's thick sandal. Spit hitting dirt was the last thing Nick heard before the snap of something coming loose in his head, and then there was only the fierce and sudden seizure of pain, the blistering red, then black.

* * *

When he came to, he was lying where he'd fallen; the left side of his face felt as though it had gotten in the way of something industrial. He saw a small puddle of vomit and a bloody tooth on the ground in front of him. It took him a moment of poking around with his tongue to understand this tooth had recently been secured in his mouth. He put it in his pocket. He touched his nose to see if he was going to once again need a new one, but this time it was still intact. Slowly, with several pauses for regrouping, he stood then walked around to the front of the house. It was quiet inside now, the pickup truck gone. All that was left were the ghost cars.

He stood in a whippy wind, watching a darkening sky, a spring storm fast approaching. He understood that by taking this, his second punch from Terry Redman, another extremely small adjustment, a minute recalibration had occurred in an as-yet-unsolved equation. This must have been what he came for.

in the corner, in the spotlight

"I hate her." This was a new Gabe, one Carmen hadn't seen before. Part of the new Gabe was about the old Gabe turning twelve. Another part was that first Rob, and now Heather, were living with them.

"I know she can be difficult." Carmen was having a small talk with him. Yesterday he and Heather got into a bad fight. She teased him about something neither of them cared to disclose. In response, he slapped her hard enough to leave a bruise on one side of her face. This was unacceptable, of course, but also not a parenting issue she'd ever contemplated.

"I just hate her. I think her anorexia is boring. Her stupid punk style—also boring. She's on the phone all night with her stupid friends. They talk about nothing. There are all sorts of weird little dishes of food pieces under everything, or between the sofa pillows, like there's a squirrel in here storing up for the winter. This used to be our house. Now it's just like Dad's—crowded with other people all the time."

When Carmen and Rob got married, Heather was living with her mother. Then, when she got down to ninety pounds Heather went into a residential program where they got her to examine her relationship to food, or whatever, and eventually she beefed up to 102, and she was ready, according to the doctors and psychologists, to rejoin the regular world. But Rob didn't want her going back to living with her crazy mother.

Carmen always took the supposed craziness of Rob's ex, Louise, with a large grain of salt, given what people (herself included) will say about whoever they used to be married to. But then, at one of the family support meetings at ReNew, she finally met Louise (and the two not-quite-housebroken dogs she insisted on bringing with her), and it was case closed. No one, let alone a seventeen-year-old girl, should live in the same small apartment with her. Not to mention that Louise herself weighed maybe 103; funny Rob never mentioned that.

Clearly the better situation for Heather would be to live with her father and Carmen and Gabe. Theirs was the most stable situation available to her. When Carmen and Rob were looking for a new place, instead of moving, they painted Carmen's rooms with more contemporary colors and bought some new furniture and established their own occupation of the house on Ravenswood. The neighborhood used to be a hodgepodge of dilapidated frame houses and low brick factories with vague industrial activities, and was farther west than anyone lived, anyone she knew. In the past few years, though, it had become fashionable. Architects had revamped the industrial buildings into studios, yuppies had bought the houses and renovated them with narrow-board siding and Victorian gingerbread trim. All she had to do to become hip was stay put and get the right siding. Sort of how staying in exactly the same position politically had moved her from liberal to radical. She had left the moving to others.

But the house was small and they had to move Heather into the room Gabe had been using as his art studio, so of course he hated her from the start.

"I know, I know, it's not the best situation for you. Just maybe look at it this way, that we are helping her stay alive. Alive and out of the asylum."

He didn't answer, just looked at the ground and made the little buzzing sound he made when Heather wasn't around. This was about the bee she had tattooed above her eyebrow, which had tiny motion marks on either side of it.

Carmen believed they were doing the right thing taking Heather in. But she also saw how Gabe legitimately felt displaced, and she didn't like putting anyone's well-being over his.

She talked to Rob. His idea of how to fix the problem was completely crackpot. The four of them were going on a trip to Alaska as soon as the kids were out of school for the summer.

"Trust me on this," he said, standing in his underwear, looking critically at his profile in the mirror on the closet door. He patted his flat stomach. "The baptism-by-fire method. We all go together to someplace wild and unknown to any of us. Someplace where we can heave and ho together, fall on each other, form a bond. It's a management trick. A variant of the corporate retreat."

Both kids rejected the idea out of hand, then were told the trip wasn't optional. A lot of complaining (Gabe) and silence (Heather) followed, but one day at the end of June they took Walter over to Gracie's house (a mutual dog-sitting arrangement), then headed for O'Hare.

"Man, this is an amazingly long trip," Carmen said as they ran through the Minneapolis airport to make their connecting flight.

"You were looking at that map and forgetting Alaska's drawn in there as an inset," Gabe explained. "It's actually way over by Russia."

When they got off the plane in Fairbanks, it was bright and sunny and nine p.m. They picked up a rental car and drove to a hotel they picked out of a travel guide, an old lodge for mining executives.

"That would have been quite a while ago," Carmen said as they pulled up in front of a scattering of maybe historic, but definitely collapsing, cabins. A pair of teenagers checked them in, a boy and a girl. They were sharing a fork and a Tupperware container of macaroni salad. The next morning, when Rob checked them out, the same couple figured up their bill.

"I think they killed the real owners," Gabe said.

Heather smiled very slightly. She was in the backseat with Carmen, eating miniscule pieces she broke off an energy bar. Part of her recovery was eating frequently. This had turned out to be eating energy bars in this labor-intensive way.

They drove south through the morning to a huge national park where they waited for a school bus that would take them six hours into the park to a nature lodge. None of them had much interest in nature. They were urban creatures. Out the windows of the bus they saw elk and rabbits. In the distance a bear prowled in a circle. He had killed a cub—one of his own—to eat, and was guarding his food. This was upsetting to the guide driving the bus. It was deviant behavior among bears, killing their own young.

"Well, but, it's an idea to consider," Rob said, one of his lame jokes; he was a master of the form.

That night they had dinner at the lodge. Heather ordered a Caesar salad with the dressing on the side.

The waiter said, "Would you like that with or without halibut?"

They went to an orientation lecture in the sod gathering house. They were told that if they encountered a bear while out walking they were supposed to cluster around each other and begin singing, so the bear would think they were bigger than he was, also merry, not threatening.

"Right," Heather said. "You'll see me clustering and singing."

The next morning they took a guided nature walk, the easiest of three offered. They picked wild blueberries. They stepped lightly, as cautioned, on permafrost.

"It's like the scrubber side of a dish sponge," Gabe said.

On their third day, they were flown in a tiny prop plane up to the face of Mount McKinley. The plane was made of metal the thickness of a license plate. The sound inside was deafening. All of them wore headphones and microphones to talk with one another. The mountain was coming at them. They were about to crash into it.

"You could turn anytime," Carmen told the pilot. She was in the copilot seat, in charge of the fire extinguisher.

"We're still a ways from the mountain," the pilot said. "Distances can be deceiving up here."

No one else said anything. They just stared at the mountain. Finally Rob took charge.

"I think we've all seen as much of the mountain as we can stand," he said, and the pilot turned and for an instant they were all happy—happy together.

And in the end, Rob was proven right. The trip, once it was over, was a shared experience. A stamp in the beginning of a collection book. The frost between the kids seemed to thaw. Carmen found them in the kitchen together in the late summer mornings, Gabe eating a mixing bowl of Cheerios and a quart of milk; Heather having a piece of dry toast and tea with lemon, or saltines and a Diet Coke. The two of them talked in an encoded adolescent way, employing the nasal inflections all their friends used. They themselves were becoming something like friends! Carmen and Rob congratulated each other with little high-fives. Then in early August Carmen tagged along with Rob to the annual MarcAntony style show in Atlanta. Four days later they came back to things having shifted yet again. Gabe and Heather were back to avoiding each other, but in a different way.

The two of them hung out around the house a lot, not so much interacting as hovering, circling. Carmen kept her suspicions to herself and watched for clues. Eventually she resorted to room inspections and a little journal reading. What she came up with were some entries in Heather's diary about "G's" crush on her, and how she was "pimping it." Then Carmen came home from work a little early one afternoon and found them together on a blanket, tanning.

Carmen brought the matter out of the realm of the unspoken, shutting the bedroom door one night, putting her forearms on Rob's shoulders, butting her forehead lightly against his. "Houston, I think we have a problem."

"No, he's way too young for her." As though this was the relevant factor, the thing that made it impossible. "And I'm not sure about this, but I think she's still a virgin."

"She is not a virgin," Carmen said. "She has been in three eating disorder places and one drug rehab. Somewhere in the middle of some unsupervised night, I can assure you she slept with someone. And at the moment she is taking advantage of Gabe's innocence." She told him about the journal entries.

Rob listened in a serious way, so she thought he was getting it, but then what he said was, "So nothing has actually happened?"

"Yet."

"At the salons, we usually leave the stylists to sort out these sorts of issues on their own. Crushes as well as fights."

"What are you even saying?! We aren't talking about comb poaching, or adults dating. These are our children. This is our family. Gabe is twelve years old!"

From there the argument careened around in bumper cars. Rob thought it was a phase and they should just wait it out, until it passed. Carmen thought Heather needed a talking-to.

"That'll only turn it into something she can rebel against," Rob said.

Up to now, Carmen had always thought of Rob as a smooth operator, managing temperamental stylists and bitchy clients. Now she saw that his indirect approach to problems was not a superficial mode, but rather, at bottom, deep passivity. She realized she had never seen him discipline Heather. Also, until this, the two of them had never had a fight. He was totally non-confrontational. Non-confrontational but intransigent. An unbeatable combination.

"We can't let this go on," she said. "It's too backwoods. If you won't help me, I can't negotiate with them alone. I'll have to send Gabe to live with his father."

This was a false threat and they both knew it. Sending Gabe to live with Matt and Paula would mean letting them know what had been going on, and Carmen wouldn't be able to bring herself to that. So instead she stewed awhile. She gave Rob the silent treatment while she tried to figure out what to do.

On the third day of being not spoken to, Rob gave in, sort of.

"I still think this will pass on its own, but I can't take any more of this silence. I'll stand behind you. But you'll have to do the talking."

This was not what she'd been hoping for. She'd been hoping for a meeting of the minds and this was only a weak concession. But she said okay even though it felt like giving in.

The talk with Heather went very badly. She was indignant that her privacy had been violated.

"Look," Carmen said. "The problem is your having done this, not our confronting you about it." She paused, waiting in vain for Rob to chime in while he sat off to the side, like an unwired stereo speaker.

Heather sighed in a stagey way and stormed out. Storming was one of her main modes of transportation.

"I think that went pretty well," Rob said later, when he and Carmen were alone.

She realized that in the long run this would just be a speed bump. She had driven a wedge between the kids; knowing their parents were watching would put a damper on things. Gabe would get past his crush on Heather. Heather would go off to college to get into some more major-league trouble. And Rob would continue to massage away every problem. And Carmen would stay with him and accept this. But inside, she had begun the process of losing her religion, the certainty of her own assessments. Also, from here on she would always consider the marriage a small mistake.

She got up and opened the kitchen door for Walter, who had been patiently waiting for her to reshuffle her worldview so he could go out and pee.

emma goldman's grave

Walter was sacked out at the foot of the bed, on his back, four paws splayed up in the air, snoring in a small, wheezy way. Although he was edging past middle age, sometimes—when he was sleeping, or playing, pretending that a rawhide chip was a mouse, backing up as though he was scared of it, then pouncing—he could still look like a puppy. Mornings after showing off, though, boxing with Gracie, he would look like a guy with a hangover. His muzzle had gone white, a big tooth was missing on one side of his mouth. Carmen could see this when he was upside down as he was now, the leathery edge of his mouth flopping onto the quilt.

She rolled over and got stared down by Emma Goldman, from the cover of the invitation propped on the nightstand. Today was her birthday. Every year on June 27th, a small contingent of anarchists in Chicago held a memorial at her grave. Jean and Tom would be there singing union songs. Carmen had persuaded Alice to come along. Rob was at work; Saturday was the biggest day of the week in the hair business. Carmen vaguely remembered hearing him leave earlier. Today he was grading stylists on their way up the ladder, making surprise visits to three local salons, which were inspections really, but he tried not to give off an inspection vibe. Stylists could be prickly.

Since the episode with Gabe and Heather (off at college, but who knew how long she would stick with it) last year, she had scaled back her expectations of him. She had accepted that their marriage was not a merger of beliefs. They were not de Beauvoir and Sartre. Lillian Hellman and Dashiell Hammett. Frida Kahlo and Diego Rivera. What she had with Rob was nothing like that. Seeing the marriage as a mistake took the pressure off it and freed her up to see what he did offer her. An enormous amount of kindness for one thing. And she was able to be physically intimate with him in a way she hadn't with anyone else. He also provided something less definable; his presence was something like a weighted vest, holding her more firmly to the ground. When she came home, she was always happy when he'd gotten there before her. She saw that all this added up to something.

"Hey." Carmen stretched to shake one of Walter's limp paws. "Let's see what's cooking." Still half asleep, he hopped off the bed and groggily followed her downstairs. They both got a happy surprise. While they were asleep, Gabe had slipped back into the house from his overnight at his father's. He had taken over the kitchen table, simultaneously eating a plate of toast slices with peanut butter and working on a paint-by-number landscape. He had been doing a lot of these lately. He picked them up at junk shops then followed the pattern, but transposing the colors, not in any obvious scheme like red skies and blue lawn—rather an alternate order, but an extremely subtle one. A code.

Alice said he was creating an ironic parallel geography. Carmen was not so sure about the irony. His own paintings, which he worked on in his room here, also over at Alice's studio, were almost comically dark. An alley with a Dumpster, eyes peering out from its slightly opened lid. A midnight junkyard, its gate swung open, someone inside waiting. She decided not to bother worrying about this, that it would pass and something else would turn up to worry about.

"How come you're not still over there?" she asked him, opening the door to the backyard for Walter. She ran a hand through Gabe's hair. It was filthy. She let this go. She didn't want to start his day with nagging. She counted herself blessed. At thirteen, he was still an extremely decent person. A little lazy, a little dreamy, a little self-absorbed, but hey, he was a teenager. Sometimes Carmen luxuriated in thinking of all the ways he could be terrible, but wasn't. Silent. Sarcastic. Arrogant. None of these worries had materialized. Not yet anyway. She had found a magnet school specializing in visual arts, where he was just ordinarily talented, and would have trouble getting an inflated notion of himself.

"I kind of slipped out early." He looked up at her, his eyes enlarged by the lenses of his glasses. "You know. Before the pinball machine really got rolling." By arrangement, Gabe spent Saturday nights with Matt and Paula. The twins were big on setting booby traps for him, also big on food fights. Plus he got conscripted a lot to try to find what might interest his sorrowful Romanian stepbrother, who was indifferent to play of any sort.

Of course Carmen was delighted any time Gabe opted to bail out of there, even if his preference for here was based on a search for dullness, sameness. Also, Sundays here did not entail a long morning spent in church. It was pathetic, she knew, that she still counted moments like this—when he came back early—as winning. Doubly pathetic because while she was still pissed off at Matt for leaving, he was so far along another path that when circumstances forced them into each other's company, he seemed kind of fuzzy on the fact that they were ever married. He had a superficially chummy manner toward her, as though they used to work in the same office.

Matt and Paula were no longer, if they ever were, a scandalous May–December match. With all her responsibilities, Paula was acquiring an ageless worn-out look. Now the two of them just looked like every other couple with young kids. And then they were further worn out by their good deeds. The adoptions were just the start of it. They also tithed their modest income. Every year they played one of the three kings (Matt) and Mary (Paula) in a giant outdoor Christmas pageant put on by their parish. Before they got the kids, they stuck out their year in the fly-covered mission in Nigeria, proselytizing natives and putting in a water filtration plant for the village. This was good for the villagers, not so good for Gabe, who was without a father for that time.

In the fridge she found a can of food for Walter, a bagel for herself.

"Hey," she said to Gabe, "maybe you want to come with me today to the Emma Goldman thing?" Although she tried not to show this, it mattered that Gabe came along. She wanted him to move into adulthood, not just along some artistic path or into some happy marriage, but also instilled with the history of the American left, and with a sense of his part in it.

"Bo-ring," he said.

"No, not boring. Inspirational. Alice is going to take us. We're making a little outing of it. We need to get her outside today. Lately she looks like she lives in a crypt."

"Crypt dweller," he said in a horror movie voice, still painting.

Alice was in the crypt because she had mono (the kissing disease, she liked reminding everyone), and on doctor's orders had put her life on hold for a couple of weeks while she laid on her sofa. Gabe adored Alice and so Carmen knew he'd say okay.

"Okay," he said.

Upstairs, Carmen took a long shower next to a window propped open with a paint stirrer. A hawthorn tree just outside was in its white blossom phase, which lasted only a couple of weeks. Although the morning sun was benevolent, the breeze that sifted through the branches and then through the window screen was still a little sharp and sour, sighing out the last of a wintery spring. She shivered and turned up the hot water.

She made her bed, first scooping up her glasses and the paper she'd been reading last night. A long report by Human Rights Watch on the aftereffects of rape and sexual mutilation on the women of Rwanda. Two years after the genocide, Rwanda still weighed Carmen down.

Two years ago, she spent every Saturday through the spring, in front of one or another Jewel or Dominick's, gathering signatures on a petition urging U.S. intervention. Accomplishing absolutely nothing. Clinton, Madeleine Albright—dithering, worthless. The U.N. mission hobbled. Humanitarian workers fleeing for their own lives. Eventually she was sunk by the futility of standing in front of a supermarket in Chicago, trying to get shoppers with long grocery lists and little time to care about tribal people in a small country in Africa whacking their neighbors to death with machetes.

She tried to explain to whoever would listen what was happening, how the Hutus were obedient, docile killers egged on by propaganda coming off the radio. How they learned to kill efficiently, practiced on those left for dead, then graduated to the fully alive. Some they killed by cutting off their hands and feet, leaving them to writhe to death. Tutsi victims willing to pay could ask for a bullet, the quickest way out. Babies, for the sake of ammunition economy, were just thrown against the wall. Carmen had photos, blown up and laminated. She taped these to the front of her card table. No one looked at them. No one wanted to see piles of hacked-up body parts, human junkyards.

She couldn't talk with Rob about this, of course. Before she corrected him, he thought there were seven Supreme Court justices. He'd never heard of Mao's Cultural Revolution or Rosa Parks. He was an extremely decent person within his limits, but these did not include Rwanda, which he had called—only a couple of times, but still—Rhonda.

And now the killing had ended, but there was all this aftermath—women degraded, ashamed of having been raped, now raising the children of their rapists. Carmen worried this period was only a lull. How would the Tutsis forgive neighbors who murdered their whole families? She used to think in terms of discrete issues, but now saw the worst problems as long narratives. She studied the mechanics of genocide, to try to understand. She lectured occasionally on the subject. Everyone, she thought, must keep a sharp eye out for another mass killing, to get in its way before it began. Her belief was waning, though, in the sort of enlightenment that would save history from repeating itself. When she read lately that Mother Teresa had said she was unable any longer to hear or see God, Carmen thought: well, yes.

They brought Walter along. Carmen and Gabe had just read a book by some monks who raised German shepherds and the book said bring your dog along, wherever. It also said to sing him a song with his name in it. They were pulling together a tortured lyric that rhymed Walter with "never falter" and "not a hair would we alter."

When they pulled up to Alice's building, the converted laundry, she was waiting outside for them. Carmen had always loved her sister, but since the moment Alice rushed her out of the crowd at the abortion clinic, one hand on Carmen's shoulder, the other holding her detached ear, Carmen had come to be—in a grave and profound way—in love with Alice.

"Let's take the ragtop," she said.

"Are you sure you're up to driving?"

"I can drive. I just can't kiss."

Even sick she looked great. Wearing jeans and a worn green T-shirt, she was sitting on the hood of her new car, which was someone else's old Mercedes convertible. The top was down; the car was ready for adventure. Alice looked, Carmen thought, like an ad for something, but not the car. A jazzy cologne, maybe. Some kind of tampon for women too active and important to be bothered with bleeding. A big part of Alice's appeal was that she traveled with the slightly sheepish air of someone much plainer. Everything about the picture—the old car, the fragile early summer day, the industrial decay of the neighborhood—set off a light envy in Carmen. Recently she figured out that she herself had put on about a pound for every year since she left grad school. These sneaky pounds had not made her fat so much as sturdy, also in possession of a butt to reckon with, to obscure with long jackets and pleated trousers. Alice hadn't put on an ounce, not even when she finally quit smoking. She could still, in the middle of her thirties, sit on a car hood in a thrift shop T-shirt and jeans and look only a slightly different kind of great than she did in her early twenties. Carmen considered re-approaching the stationary bike in the basement, which she had been using for some time as a rack to dry sweaters.

This was a good time for Alice. She won a Guggenheim last year, now had a Near North gallery representing her work. She had begun to make real money from her painting, something she said she never anticipated, and this left her in a slightly uncomfortable position, richer and more famous than her friends. She tried to obscure her success by staying on in the old loft, although with some new furniture, a real bathroom and kitchen, a thick mattress on her bed—something she special-ordered from Sweden. And her Mercedes was a very old one, well over the line into ironic. In the same way, she had an assistant she never mentioned, who spent a day a week replenishing Alice's paints, stretching her canvases, cleaning her brushes. The way Carmen saw it, Alice was tiptoeing softly into her new life.

On the way over to the cemetery, Walter put his nose to the wind and Gabe leaned in from the backseat to tell Alice about the American Revolution, which they'd been studying at school. He had taken it upon himself to spruce up Alice's education, which he thought was tragic. Carmen and Nick had gone to the Latin School where the basics were well covered. Alice, on account of her artistic promise, went to a free school in Old Town, one of those staples of the late seventies where the teachers went by their first names and field trips were to violent or naked performance-art presentations, and reading was not really stressed. The curriculum encouraged Alice's painting, but left her with certain gaps, like most of history except for how it framed artistic periods.

"Okay, so while Washington was fighting the British," Gabe told Alice, "Benjamin Franklin was over in France forming an alliance with them."

"You mean we didn't even have a country and we were already being diplomatic? Wasn't that, I don't know, kind of nervy?"

"The whole thing was nervy. Totally nervy," he said.

"What about Thanksgiving?"

He looked at her for so long that she turned her head quickly to see the stare accompanying his silence.

"That was earlier, right?" she said, eyes back on the road.

"Uh, yeah."

"I knew that," she said. "Way earlier."

"You did not. You thought Ben Franklin was having turkey with the Indians. And after dinner they all went out to fly the kite. I'm going to make up weekly pop quizzes for you. What if you're around other adults and you make one of these horrible errors? I have to keep an eye on you. You and the twins. They're even worse than you. Dad bought them a globe. And then it kind of came out that they thought we live on the inside of the ball."

At the cemetery, he gave Alice a little rundown on the Haymarket riots, the information that several of the rioters were buried in this cemetery. From there, he moved on to the labor movement around the turn of the century, the fight for the eight-hour workday, the Wobblies, the bomb tossed into the crowd, the dead a mix of workers and policemen. Alice played dumb to humor him. Her academic gaps notwithstanding, she was, thanks to Carmen, well versed in the history of America's progressive movement. Gabe was good on the facts, a boy thing. Carmen's concern was that he also got the bigger picture. She had tried to show him that there's always the history and the secret history. That there were always beneficiaries. To understand how things work, you had to follow the circuit all the way back—to who was getting something out of it. Follow the power or the money, or both.

With friends, more and more, Carmen found injustice talked about in some new abstract vocabulary of large and amorphous concepts, rather than in the old fired-up rhetoric of specific actions against the powers that be. Now the problems had become huge, systemic wrongs not approachable by the remedies of individuals. She hated this. And she didn't want Gabe to grow up in this new, morally lazy climate. So she brought him along to events like today's, to see the left as a path.

She was surprised at the good turnout for the memorial. Maybe a hundred people had gathered. Carmen allowed herself the vanity of pulling her hair behind her ear, to show it off. The ear had made her a local hero.

Tom Ferris and Jean were already there, on guitars, banging out rousing union anthems, old songs like "The Springhill Mine Disaster," and a few new ones they'd written together, like "Barred Doors and Blazes," about the Triangle Shirtwaist Factory fire.

Gabe and Walter loped off to play with a puppy they'd spotted. Carmen waved at Jean and Tom.

"He looks different," Carmen said.

"He lost the sideburns," Alice said. "He's exposed some face no one has seen for years. He's rejuvenated his career with 'Black Earth Blues.' Fuck him."

Carmen said, "I know. I've heard it a couple of times on XRT."

"Jean said it might be big. Moving up the charts or whatever."

"I don't know how he can do this. It's invading the girl's privacy, like claiming an intimate relationship with her."

"Yeah. But really, how much closer to someone can you be than having killed them?"

"Alice."

"Here's what I hate. I hate that it doesn't matter if we see each other. There's still this connection, between me and him because we were both in the car. Like in arithmetic. Because of the accident, we're not just separate numbers. When you add us up, you always have to carry the one."

Carmen looked around to find Gabe and saw Walter peeing on a grave. She hoped it was not some historical figure's plot. The music stopped, and an old Wobbly, glasses taped together, jacket lumpy with a sweater underneath in spite of the day being so mild, stood in front of Emma Goldman's grave and started to read an earnest speech. Barely a paragraph or two in, the anarchists showed up. They sprung onto the scene like jack-in-the-boxes.

Carmen flinched in the way she did now at sudden, peripheral movement, a change in the tone of a situation. Then saw this was just the usual harmless theater and unclenched her jaw. The anarchists hopped all over the grave; they sat on the headstone playing kazoos and tambourines and heckling the earnest speaker.

"This is so cool," Gabe said.

"Well, when you're an anarchist," Carmen said as they watched the Wobbly shrug and finally give up on his speech, "I think you have to expect a little dancing on your grave."

Gabe went over to join the fun.

A refreshment table. Lunchmeat roll-ups, carrot sticks, onion dip. Terrible punch the color of melted cotton candy. Alice drank three cups straight down. Part of her mono was a constant sore throat.

Carmen wanted to say something to Tom about his song, about using tragedy for personal gain. But she didn't want to make Jean uncomfortable. Jean, who for some inscrutable reason, was still with him. Now the two of them were heading Carmen's and Alice's way.

"Jean still thinks he's something," Alice said before they came into earshot. "She's stuck on his fifteen minutes of fame." Then she put on what she hoped was an extremely insincere smile and greeted Tom. "Looks like you've found a way to take those old lemons of ours and make lemonade."

Tom didn't flinch. Years onstage had thickened his persona. "I'm just singing out of my own experience, Alice. It's all we really have in the end to make art with. Like Clapton—" He looked over toward where Jean had been standing, but she had walked off a ways, into the crowd, probably smelling an attack coming. This freed Carmen up.

"Interesting comparison," Carmen said. "Only Clapton was on the other side of the equation. It was his kid who died because of someone else's carelessness. I don't think we can bend logic to the point where the accident was our tragedy."

Alice added, "Like the Menendez brothers crying because they were orphans."

"Oh boy. The Kenney sisters are out in force today. Moral Mighty Mouses. But hey, sorry, I'm just here to play some songs." He flipped his guitar over his shoulder, and walked away.

Carmen said, "What kind of humans are we if we forgive ourselves? That's what he's done, just forgiven himself."

Back in front of Alice's loft, she asked them up.

"You're too tired," Carmen said.

"I'll lie down. You can take care of me a little."

They all got into the enormous, groaning freight elevator. Walter stood stock-still. Elevators bewildered him. He didn't seem to get why they had to go into the box, then out of the box. In the studio, Carmen set out a bowl of water for him, and Gabe propped up a painting he had been working on. The subject was a set of steps leading down to a darkened basement. He loved painting at Alice's, in a serious studio. They watched him set up in his fussy way. Everything needed to be exactly here, or right there.

"Sometimes I worry he's too easy," Alice said once he was out of earshot. "I mean, what did we do to deserve him?"

"But you know he's going to have to hate us for a while, probably soon. He almost hated me over the Heather thing. He's going to get to that place a few more times."

"I know. So he won't be living with you when he's thirty-five," Alice said. "Like in some Tennessee Williams play."

"Right," Carmen said. "So he's not hanging around doing my hair."

"Washing out your dress shields," Alice said. "By hand." She was clearly happy to be home, perched on her sofa—the old ruby red velvet monster she'd hung on to, from the co-op. In her new prosperity she had had it recovered and refinished back to the lurid glory of its youth. It was more than a sofa; it had the authority of a davenport. Perching turned out to be too strenuous and Alice let herself fall back on the bed pillows propped against one arm. They gossiped a little. Carmen told Alice that Jean had inadvertently got knocked up. That Tom had behaved badly. Now Jean said she was doing some serious thinking.

"Is she going to keep the baby?"

"I don't think that is the direction of the serious thinking."

Alice said, "I have to tell you something about Horace and Loretta. They asked me to dinner last week. They had some good news and, blahblahblah, could I meet them at Geja's?"

Carmen nods. "They love Geja's." To show solidarity with Nick, Carmen had seen very little of their parents since the birthday party debacle. Which was a little ironic since Nick himself still saw them. (At least it was the last of those hideous birthday parties; at least it killed that tradition.) Alice saw Horace as the ticket price to Loretta, whom she still—for reasons Carmen couldn't fathom—cared about.

"I know. Give them their long forks and their bubbling cheese and they're happy. Anyway, when I got there, I told them I wasn't hungry. On account of the mono. The mono is great that way. I can get away with anything I don't want to do. And I really can't eat fondue with them. There's just something, don't you think, queasy-making about plunging bread into the same cheese bucket as your parents?

"They're already having wine when I get there—drinking it out of glasses; mercifully, Horace didn't bring that goatskin thing with him. Anyway Mom says he's been offered a show at the Walker in Minneapolis. And I say something like 'Hey, that's great!' I mean it's years since he's been taken seriously. And then she says it's a very special show and I start smelling a rat. A big rat."

"I'm smelling it a little, too," Carmen said.

"I could see Loretta was the designated hitter. She told me they want it to be a father-daughter extravaganza. 'Kenney: Two Generations.' Horace told me that was a title they're bouncing around. I, of course, haven't been included in the bouncing."

"They didn't approach Dad at all, did they?" Carmen said.

"Of course not. It might have been his gallery that called them, but it was probably just Horace on his own hook driving up there one day. He's still totally capable of that sort of ballsy behavior."

"What'd you say to Mom?"

"Well, what could I say without looking like Camus's stranger? I told her it sounded great. Gabriella is going to be totally pissed off. They're so serious over there. The Walker might be sentimental, but my gallery won't be."

Carmen noticed the pillows on the sofa were pretty bedraggled. "Let me put fresh cases on these," she said. When she came back, Alice was making a wimpy attempt to straighten up her sick bay.

"I'm reading all these cheesy dyke novels from the forties and fifties." She gestured to small, soft, teetering piles around the couch. Carmen bent to scoop up a handful. The covers had a sinister tone, usually represented by a woman in a black or red slip. "They're all great," she told Carmen. "They're like Greek tragedies. Everyone gets horribly punished in the end. Or they hang themselves with a belt over the steam pipe."

"But weren't these somebody's real, tortured life once?" Carmen said.

"Well, sure, but now they're more like folktales. Hardships of our ancestors. Like Lincoln walking ten miles to school every day through the snow. That sort of thing, only in bars."

"So sad for them," Carmen said.

"Yes, of course," Alice said. "But don't you think the sex was probably great?"

"Just lie down now and rest," she ordered Alice, gave her a little push for good measure. "Do you have any of that soup left?"

"In the fridge."

"I'll heat it up." Carmen got this stuff for Alice from a Tibetan place on Sheridan. It was a remedy soup, hard to tell what was in it. It was extremely herbal and aromatic, the flavor was something like mushroom/VapoRub. But it really seemed to help with the sore throat.

When she came back with a bowl, she sat on the floor in front of the couch while Alice ate.

"What do you think?" Gabe came out of the studio holding up his painting, bracing the sides of the canvas with the palms of his hands. His method was using the smallest brushes he could find, starting in one corner, without gridding the rest, and just painting his way out of the corner by assembling a huge number of tiny details. He now had his staircase completely done. He had put in the first cobwebs.

"Cool," Alice said, leaning forward over her soup to see the painting's detail. "Very cool. You sure you want to be painting in that shirt, though?" It was a lurid Hawaiian shirt, luscious with flowers. "Where'd you get that anyway?"

"It's a surfer shirt. Maude brought it for me from California. Last week at Grandma's birthday party."

The conversation clenched. This would be Gabe's other grandma, Matt's mother, Marie. Maude was crazy about Gabe and took the opportunity to spoil him a little whenever she was in town. Carmen didn't mention these visits to Alice as they invariably induced the same look she was getting now. Grim, crazed bravery. The French Lieutenant's Woman on hearing that the lieutenant had just been seen riding through the village. Carmen hated this look, hated that Maude was still able to elicit this much pain from Alice just by her existence somewhere in the world, out of Alice's reach.

Part of Carmen's opinion of Maude came from her being Matt's sister, guilt by association. But really, she was annoying enough all on her own. She came back once, after her divorce, for about ten minutes, the length of time she could apparently bear to be queer. Then she rushed back to being a straight person, or to some more complex idea of who she was that wasn't defined by Alice. Somewhere during these ten minutes, Alice, after putting up a pathetic impersonation of indifference, let her defenses completely crumple and threw herself at Maude. She sold the farm. Carmen told her not to sell the farm, but Alice sold it—a quick and complete liquidation of agricultural assets. Followed by Maude leaving yet again.

It was usually not, Carmen had told Alice, a good situation when the same person provided both the pain and the analgesic. Also, Carmen didn't understand Alice's ability to maintain such a renewable present. For Carmen, the present had become so heavy with past. She could be going up a flight of stairs in an old apartment building and suddenly she was moving through something invisible but dense, something a decade thick. Some particular combination of landings littered with sneakers and earth shoes and moon boots and bicycles. Groaning floorboards and worn carpet and varnish and incense and cat litter and curry would drag her back through compressed time like an undertow, up a hundred staircases—to birthday parties, babysitters, the sofa of her Jungian analyst, the tables of massage therapists, the hearty dinners of chicken baked with rice and mushroom soup, rent and fire parties thrown for friends in crises, political strategy meetings. By now the present had become a very crowded place for her. If only she could impress this idea—factoring the past into the present—on Alice. But she didn't have the heart to hammer on her now, sick as she was. And in any event, Alice had moved from disturbance and sorrow to having fallen asleep.

"No offense intended," she said, waking a little, groggy, and reached down to touch Carmen's mangled ear. "It's the mono."

"None taken," Carmen said, then just sat on the floor, her back against the sofa, her head by Alice's, Alice's breath passing over the hair at her temple. She pitied everyone who didn't have a sister.

pad sieu

If Nick weren't Alice's brother, if he were just a friend, she supposed they would have drifted apart long ago. But they were not friends. They were here to keep each other from spinning off alone into the dark matter of the universe. They never said this aloud. Instead they held small rituals, concocted ordinary traditions; they tried to seem like everyone else, like two people in a snapshot. For instance, the two of them had November birthdays a week and three years apart; every year they found a midpoint and treated each other to dinner. This year Alice was turning thirty-five, Nick thirty-two. She suggested they meet at a Thai restaurant up on Broadway; they'd been there before.

When Alice arrived, Nick was sitting alone by the door on one of two chairs provided for take-out customers. Although the windows were steamed over and it was about ninety degrees in the restaurant, he seemed quite comfortable in a heavy flannel shirt with a red quilted vest over it. Both looked as if they were from L. L. Bean. He enjoyed ordering from catalogs. He looked like he had just arrived from a logging camp.

At the moment, he was fascinated by a little electric fountain near the entrance that ladled water out of, then back into, a synthetically steaming, miniature wishing well. This piece of Asian bric-a-brac had been ladling and steaming through the two or three previous dinners they'd had here. So it fell into the category of peculiar, but no longer remarkable. Alice took Nick's fascination as a bad sign.

He was holding a thick, plastic-sleeved menu—the cover a collage of lurid color photos, which at first glance appeared to be underwater shots of amorphous sea creatures, but when you looked closer were snapshots of various curries and noodle dishes.

"These pictures are just so fucking colorful. I'd really like to Xerox this for this woman who just moved into my building. She's a photographer. Tina. No. Nina."

From this neighborly impulse, Alice understood that Nina was a woman with large breasts. Nick went on.

"Do you think they have a copier in the back there?"

"Sure. Probably a color copier," Alice said. "And a postal substation. Like most storefront restaurants."

He twisted in his seat to peer back toward the kitchen. "Do you think it would be okay to ask them to make a copy?"

Alice said, "I think we ought to just get a table and use the menu to order the meal we're going to eat here. You know—now."

More bad signs cropped up when they were seated across from each other at a glass-topped table giving off a blue astringent smell. Alice noticed that Nick's eyes, usually a clear green, were currently crusty pinholes. His face had too much definition, the skin was stretched a little too tight over the bone and muscle beneath. She was reminded of faces in Lucian Freud's paintings.

He seemed to be in a hurry, although when she asked if he had to be anywhere, he said no. As soon as they ordered, he popped off to the bathroom.

Alice looked around. The restaurant appeared to be an extension of the life of the family that owned it. An old woman in a back booth worked on an adding machine amid piles of paperwork and long loops of register tape. Two small kids sat doing homework at a bamboo bar against the far wall. Above the bar, a Thai video ran on a TV hanging from the ceiling. In the movie, two Asian women—one in a sarong, the other in a jogging suit—were having a heart-to-heart. Then one of them turned to hide her tears and the music swelled and the scene changed to a jail cell.

Nick came back. He wrestled himself out of the vest and the flannel shirt until he was down to his T-shirt. His left forearm was mostly taken up with an aging tattooed portrait of Olivia. He didn't talk about Olivia. She was a non-subject. A couple of years ago, she found a pill in the cuff of his khakis. That was all. One Vicodin. She left on the spot—left their apartment, her job at MarcAntony, apparently left Chicago—and he hadn't heard from her since. He didn't say a thing about her, ever.

He picked up his menu and scrutinized it for a long time. Whatever he'd loaded up on in the john was kicking in; he had pumped up from cold to hot, dropped from agitated to dreamy. He sat awhile without speaking. When he finally said something, what he said was "coconut." Like this counted as conversation, or he had just taken conversation to some higher plane where everything was encrypted and compressed. While Alice was still working the old-fashioned way, with sentences.

When the food arrived, he did not remember having ordered it, and seemed to not be particularly hungry. He only poked at the curry and *pad sieu* with his chopsticks, which he was holding by the thin—wrong—ends. After taking a sip of the iced coffee, he tried to set the glass back down on the table. They both sat silent for the maybe minute-long stretch during which he brought the glass in for a difficult landing. Something heavy and slippery fell inside Alice watching this.

He said, "I'm okay. Talk to me." He pulled a pill bottle out of a pocket in his vest. "Actually, why not join me?" He put a long white tablet on the table.

"Thanks anyway," Alice said. "I might find out I like it. That would be a bad piece of information. But listen, before you fade out, can you talk to me? It's about the girl."

"About the paintings?"

"Sort of. They keep coming to me. It's like I'm her portraitist, and she won't fire me. And the paintings she has me make are always better than any I make on my own. Whoever is painting her is a better painter than I am. It creeps me out."

"Plus it's depressing."

"Thanks for mentioning that," Alice said. "So much time has gone by. I feel like everyone else has put the whole thing behind them, except me."

"I haven't put the whole thing behind me. I still drive down to Missouri to see Shanna."

"The mother? I thought you only did that once."

"No. I try to get down there every year around the time—you know. I don't know about Tom Ferris. I guess his way of keeping her alive was making a bunch of money off a song about her. He's just a jerk, but I don't think anybody else has put this behind them. It's like—" He drifted out for a moment. Then back in. "I think we altered what was supposed to happen. And we can't go back and make it happen right. So we're stuck in some kind of endless loop, trying to improve the past. Which, as you might notice, is resistant to revision." He furrowed his brow and nodded, as though giving consideration to what he'd just said. But then he kept nodding, like a bobblehead doll in a rear car window.

"Come on. Please," Alice said. "Don't fucking go away."

"This is the best I can do right now. I do my best for you." For several minutes they were silent. Alice ate a little, Nick kept a close watch on his plate. "I do appreciate that you're not trying to save me. Like Carmen. I feel like she's wearing vestments when she approaches. Like she's just putting up her hand to bless me. Like she's riding by in the Popemobile. Fuck that."

"That's just her. She's trying to save all of us. I'd miss it if she weren't trying to save me. You would, too. What's this?"

She tapped her finger on a manila envelope, the interoffice kind with a grid of senders and recipients listed and crossed out.

"Oh yeah," he said, then with some difficulty, unfastened the string clasp, and pulled out a photo. "I brought this for you. A really excellent nebula."

Orange sparks and a kind of roiling aqua steam burst off a deep, inky background. Like a storm made of vapor.

It was amazing to Alice that Nick still occupied a place in the world of astronomy. He had become a weirdo hotshot. His expertise got him off a lot of the usual hooks. He didn't have to show up for classes or department meetings. He took on individual advisees and made and broke a lot of appointments with them. The students were apparently willing to put up with this for the opportunity of studying with him. He wasn't pressured for regular performance of any kind. What got him all this latitude was a talent for ferreting out black holes. Envelopes arrived by overnight mail, as though understanding celestial activity that was thousands, millions, sometimes billions of years old was suddenly urgent. He also got flown to various radio scopes—Kitt Peak in Arizona, the Parkes in Australia—to observe and interpret what he saw. Incidents had occurred. He still had his little trouble with flying and airports, their temptations. But these missteps had, so far, been swept under various carpets. He had made a small success of himself in spite of his limitations. Everyone was surprised, Horace not so pleasantly. He'd been counting on Nick continuing to fail. He was totally unprepared for Nick succeeding. Now all he could do was feign overwhelming happiness for his son, so overwhelming that everyone would understand the sentiments were a parody.

"This is very, very cool," Alice said, then looked up and saw he had already drifted off. She reached over and pulled some hairs on his forearm.

"Hey," he said. "You think because I'm high that doesn't hurt?" He then paused so long she thought he had finished speaking, but then he started up again, this time as though he was being forced to tutor a dullard. "It's really just mapmaking. Eventually we'll chart it all. It's just a big project. Do you know how many stars there are? Just in our galaxy, the Milky Way?"

"Thousands," Alice said. She knew she was going to be wrong no matter what she said.

"Billions. And billions of galaxies beyond ours."

"I hate when you tell me this stuff. It doesn't make me feel the majesty of the cosmos or anything like that. It makes me feel like a speck."

"You *are* a speck. This whole life that seems so huge to us?" He gestured widely with his arm, nearly taking down a tiny waitress passing with a tray full of cocktails in ceramic pineapples. "All of human enterprise even? Fuck us. We are so tiny." As he said "so tiny," he bent over until his forehead was nearly touching the tabletop, as if he was homing in on the speck that was them.

"I can't stand to think we only add up to a blip. I need to think we're more than that."

"Deal with it." He looked around, as though someone had called his name.

He counted a lot on people being too polite to confront him about being high. Alice was not too polite; she just didn't want their whole conversation to revolve around this. Easier, really, to ignore the problem and just let him take the time he needed to set down his glass of iced coffee. Or listen to him speak in small, deliberate word packets. Or watch him gaze for way too long around this restaurant. What did she know? Maybe he could live a sort of okay life even though he was on drugs most of the time. And anyway, her nagging wouldn't make any difference. She left the reforming to Carmen. Carmen could keep pressing books and articles on Nick, dragging him to meetings, trying to keep him on track. By now Alice questioned even the notion of a track.

• • •

"I know I don't have much credibility at the moment," he said. "That you'll just think this is all about the drugs, but I swear it's not."

"What are we talking about?"

"Something new. Keep an open mind. Please. The thing is, if I wait in just the right way, I can tell when it happens. It's very easy to miss. The first time I noticed was a couple of months ago when I was making a pot of coffee, but I was out of creamer. On my way out I glanced at the clock on the stove—3:17. Okay?"

"Okay."

"I drove to the White Hen but things were peculiar, don't ask me how."

"I won't."

"I mean I was clearly in my car, headed the right way, and the weather was exactly what I'd noticed out the window—a cool, brilliantly sunny day. And the Indian guy at the counter was the same one who's always there. Everything about the errand was routine, except it wasn't. Something was off. The colors were too high contrast, as though some dials had been turned up, others down. The breeze was a little too warm, or with little bits of warmth inside the colder air. The Indian guy, who is usually very laid-back, was slightly impatient, as if he was nervous to be doing something else with this moment other than taking my money and asking if I wanted a bag for the Coffee-mate and Marlboros.

"Okay, so when I came back and was pouring the coffee I'd made, I looked at the clock on the stove, and it said 3:17."

"And the clock wasn't just stopped," Alice said.

"Please."

"Sorry."

"Now I can tell when it's happening. I don't need the clock. I just exit regular forward momentum, then I come back in at exactly the place where I left."

"Have you told anyone about this stuff?"

"What would be the point?"

• • •

Over dessert, which was beige and sweet and quivering in little dishes, they exchanged birthday presents. Alice had found Nick a boxed set of his namesake opera, Verdi's *Nabucco*. He had two gifts for her. The first was a Chicago Bears keychain. (Alice didn't follow football.) The other was a turtleneck sweater she had seen him wear a few times. He smiled graciously as she pulled it out of the grocery bag he brought it in. Like it was a real gift. Like he had handed her a check for a million dollars, the keys to a yacht, like he was waiting to see how thrilled she was going to be. Tonight was beginning to depress her. She tried to keep in mind that it was only through some stroke of good fortune that she herself was not a junkie or an alcoholic. That she was not the one at this table thinking an old sweater of hers with a food stain on the front was a pretty good gift.

A lull entered the conversation, out of which Nick emerged trying to be social, to appear to have social skills. "You seeing anyone?" He always asked this, but Alice had become leery of exposing her love life to his inspection. It only fed his interest in girl-on-girl action. Plus he found it hilarious that Alice was still looking for love; he found that quaint. "You still getting lucky at those women's issues groups?"

"This woman is too good-looking," she said. "It's not going anywhere. I'm trying to steer clear of gorgeous women. They've dragged me under too much barbed wire. Over too many deserts. Deserts made of shattered glass. Plus this one has a kid and a husband. She's still coming out. Everything has to be very quiet."

"Sounds kind of interesting."

"Interesting at first, but gets old fast. Like waterskiing."

"Like drag shows," he offered, then asked, "What's her name?"

"What does it matter?"

"I'm putting a picture together in my mind."

"Nora."

He grew quiet, savoring this little nugget of information, a hard candy. He looked down at his plate.

"I've got someone new, too." This turned out to be his new masseuse.

"I thought you went to that guy, Earl. The one who put your rotator cuff back in business."

"This is different," he said. "Her name's Celeste. She does an herbal oil, hot stone thing. You have to go to her apartment. There's this kind of Malibu atmosphere."

"Right. That would go with the herbal oil thing."

"And, well, it's a nude thing, too," he said.

"Well, of course. I mean I just don't get people who keep their underwear on. I always just take it all off. Let them really dig into those glutes."

"No," he said. "I mean her. *She's* nude while she does the massage."

"Oh man," Alice said, caught by surprise. "Boocs, I've got to tell you if I were on the table and popped open an eyelid and saw Eleanor—you know? my massage therapist—saw her prancing around in the altogether, I'd be flipped."

"This is kind of a different thing. Celeste is a different kind of person."

"Different like a hooker?"

"It isn't just that. We take her dog for a walk afterward."

"Oh, well then, sure. Sounds meaningful."

Although he had spent much of his adulthood avoiding real life, what small contact he'd had seemed to leave him embittered and edgy. Although he still sought out women, he appeared not to like them very much. He didn't have real dates anymore; it was all hookers now. When he was flush with funds from Loretta and research grants, these were call girls. When the money ran out, the hookers he could afford were junkies he picked up on North Avenue. "You have to buy them dope and wait until they shoot up," he told her once. "Then wait some more until they stop shaking enough to fuck them."

In order to keep liking Nick (as opposed to loving him, which was non-negotiable), Alice sometimes had to look at him obliquely, or with her eyes half closed, or through a pinhole in a piece of cardboard. Straight on would burn her retinas.

After dinner, they hugged on the corner and Nick insisted on taking a cab home. Alice drove around for a long time. She was thinking about the married woman. Nora. The husband, Alice knew, was out of town. Tonight started coming together as an opportunity.

The lights were off except in the basement where she could hear the TV going. That would be the daughter. Alice used the secret key the family kept in a fake rock by the front steps, slipped up the stairs into Nora's bedroom, shut the door behind her, all without a sound, Alice thought, but still, something caused Nora to wake.

"Hmm?"

"It's me," Alice said as she shrugged her jacket and jeans and underwear into a fireman's pile at her feet. Nora lifted the covers, still half asleep. She was wearing only a black T-shirt, and soon not even that.

the limited palette

Alice awakened into the first morning of the new year—the last of the current century—a little groggy. For a moment, she wasn't sure whose bed she was in. Then life rolled back in like a tide. Last night she and Charlotte went to a party thrown by a collector friend, an apartment with a roof deck overlooking the Amstel. By eleven-thirty the sky was on fire with luminous anarchy. Afterward, they walked up through the city zigzagging along the ring canals among maybe a million other celebrants, ducking and weaving around all the amateur pyrotechnicians—many of them, of course, drunk—setting off crackers and cherry bombs inside trash cans, near the exhaust pipes of parked cars. They traveled through a fog of gunpowder so thick they could barely see across the Herengracht. If war were a happy thing, it would look like this. Even as they were going to sleep, late crackers were still popping sporadically, the last kernels in the bag of microwave popcorn.

Now, although technically morning, it was actually still night outside. The seasons this far north pushed the light around in dramatic ways. In mid-winter, the sun didn't arrive until after eight, then slipped out of the sky before five. Alice checked the bedside clock—twenty past seven. The flat, narrow radiator was gently clanking and hissing. Then a distant, machine gun–like burst, then another, enlivened the air. The racket awakened Charlotte.

"These are crazy people!" she said, burying her head under her pillow. Her cat Melke—who was only middle-aged when Alice first slept over here the night of that long-ago museum show—was now skinny and stiff with arthritis as she walked along the wide windowsill of the bedroom. Quietly, Alice climbed out of bed; the lifted comforter released a small gust of sex.

They did this sometimes, Alice and Charlotte—slept together. It didn't jostle their friendship. Neither of them was spoken for, neither precisely free. Charlotte had an on-again/off-again girlfriend who was a film critic in London. Alice wasn't in the market for a girlfriend in any country. She was resting up.

She and Charlotte went to movies together and of course, to galleries. If they spent a Saturday night together, they lingered through Sunday morning reading the papers. But if they didn't see each other for a week or two, it wasn't a big deal. Whatever element causes romance to flare was simply not present in the air between them. This was a huge relief to Alice. Romance no longer looked like so much fun, more like a repetitive stress injury—beginning with Maude, but by now also including all the failed and pathetic attempts to replicate that constellation of emotion with someone else. She could measure this past effort in all the underwear she had left behind in apartments, all the bottles of pricey wine she had brought to dinner, all the recitations of bad childhoods and adult disappointments she had earnestly listened to. Sometimes she made lists in her head, little catalogs of experience. The first list was, of course, all the women she had by now slept with. Taken individually, they seemed, at their various times, to hold the possibility of lasting love. As opposed to now, so far down the line, when they could only be looked at in accumulation, as one then another fool's errand. An offshoot list to this was the figure for how far she had gone for sex. (Thirteen hours on a flight from Chicago to

Tokyo then back to Chicago the next day has held the top spot for quite a while; she might never better this.) Books she had read to get into somebody or other's bed. (*The Four-Gated City. The Fountainhead. Linda Goodman's Sun Signs. Women Who Run With the Wolves.*) Terrible music she had listened to because it was someone's idea of a mood enhancer. (Hall & Oates. Holly Near. George Winston. The Carpenters. Celine Dion.) Topics in which she had feigned an interest during the short term (Juice fasts. Rugby. Celtic dancing. Bikram yoga.). The longest list was of the kinds of tea she had drunk in moments structured around the pretense that tea drinking was the reason for being in this or that café (Pergolesi. Kopi. Café Boost.) or kitchen, or side by side on this or that futon sofa or daybed, sipping. (Earl Grey. Lapsang Souchong. Gunpowder. Rooibos. Sleepytime. Morning Thunder. Seren-i-tea. Every possible peppermint and berry. Plain Lipton.) There was a stretch of time when tea became fetishized for her for being so linked with sex and romance, so reliable a harbinger of one or the other.

She could scare herself with the renewable ingenuousness implied by this catalog. Still, the alternative—the development of an acidic cynicism—seemed worse. She tried to steer clear of that. Instead, she made a quiet life out of a limited palette—grays and the paler hues of blue and green. And it was easier to do this half a continent and an entire ocean away from Maude. As a mechanism, this at first seemed a little ludicrous, like the heiress in a novel of manners being sent to Italy to cure a broken heart. But the move had turned out to be successful in a small way. Back home, her initial injury was repeatedly supplemented by insult. After Maude's move to L.A., it was absurd for Alice to care where she was if she never saw her anyway; nevertheless she did. Then there was her coming back that one weird time, then fleeing. And then there were the Gabe-related events where Alice had to good-naturedly go along with the two of them being mutually doting aunties. At one of these birthday parties, she met Maude's husband and immediately threw up in the restaurant bathroom. Ridiculously, each of these encounters was ferociously difficult, each a new configuration of Maude's absence.

Over here it was better. She had managed to shrug off a significant amount of her obsession. She could now go about living a life with only a shadow of Maude lying softly across some edge of her. Nothing so terrible, really. Maybe distance and quiet were all she needed.

She stood at the window looking down at the dawn-lit cobblestone streets. At first glance it seemed as though a belated autumn had blown through; the pavement was covered in what appeared to be pink leaves. These, she then saw, were the remains of spent firecrackers. This was her third winter in Amsterdam. She had been right in her initial assessment; the city's mild melancholy matched her own. Something about the mist and damp, the dark water of the canals. And in these months with so little light, there was the pleasure of walking along the water at night, watching the life of the city through the uncurtained windows of its canal houses.

"Will you come to the party Friday for Jan Doorn?" Charlotte asked, still half-asleep. Doorn was a photographer from The Hague. His work was impressive.

"I'll think about it." Alice came back to the bed in her coat and knit cap, to say goodbye.

"Which means no," Charlotte said.

"But I will see you soon, yes?" Alice said. She avoided the art scene. Arriving with possibly too much fanfare, her last sequence of paintings—portraits of hookers she had connected with through Nick—was savaged by the critics. She was badly stung. She had grown so accustomed to success that she forgot to keep a guard up against failure. Maybe the paintings were simply not very good. Maybe there was no way to paint prostitutes that wasn't sentimental, like sad-eyed clowns. Whatever, she couldn't sort anything out back there, couldn't hear herself. In this foreign city she could hide in a corner and lick her wounds and think about painting in a solitary way without background noise and, she hoped, make new, better paintings.

Elements of her muted, smallish existence were purchased—the streamlined, lubricated daily life of someone modestly wealthy. She had a woman who came twice a week to shop and clean and do laundry. She had an assistant in the studio. This help allowed her to spend much of her day working. Nights she read, or entertained friends. She took Dutch lessons Tuesdays and Fridays. Two mornings a week she taught at an immigration center—kids mostly, but sometimes also their mothers. They painted the stories that had brought them here, and Alice tried to help.

She biked the few streets over from Charlotte's, then three bridges up, to her own apartment, the top two floors of an eighteenth-century row house on the Singel, overlooking the bridge at Tornsteeg. This morning, halfway there, she was forced to stop and button her jacket. The cold in Amsterdam was nothing so fierce as the winters in Chicago, but it was impressive in its own way—a damp that settled in the bones, to be drawn out with a steaming tub at the end of the day.

Sunlight drifted down through the high windows. She was an orderly studio keeper. She had a drawered cabinet for paints. On top were two coffee cans stuffed with brushes, a row of bottles—medium, linseed oil, stand oil, assorted glazes, Turpenoid for cleaning brushes. In front of this paraphernalia, she taped down the thick pane of window glass that was her palette. She mixed her colors. Then pulled a high stool about ten feet back from the canvas, sat, and plotted her course.

Hours had passed by the time she came up for air. She was hungry and had to pee. Painting was a world without clocks. Once she was out of the bathroom, and had made herself a cheese sandwich, she checked her message machine. Nick, asking for money. For something very important, an investment opportunity, top secret at the moment.

"So I'm going to need you to wire twenty-seven hundred thirty-two dollars and seventeen cents—"

Alone in her kitchen four thousand miles away, Alice burst out laughing at this absurdly exact amount he had concocted. She replayed the message. She missed him. He would like it here so much, although not in a savory way. Missing Carmen was more complicated. When her sister had come up from Rome in the summer, off-shooting from a business trip with Rob, Alice cried herself bleary after putting her on the train at Centraal Station. Still, she was happy to have a time-out of no one bullying her to get her teeth cleaned, or work for this or that progressive candidate, or read some actual literature instead of true-crime stories.

It wasn't quite homesickness that afflicted Alice, more a nettling sensation that life back home wasn't on PAUSE while she was over here. Nick was going down the tubes again and it was unfair to dump him on Carmen. Also, Horace had the beginnings of Alzheimer's and Loretta was overwhelmed creating a comprehensible environment for him. Drawers with signs so he could find SPOON or TOWEL. Clothes set out for him in a particular order. Long walks in the early evening, when his agitation peaked.

Alice knew she probably shouldn't linger in this idyll much longer.

She heard the door to the street open downstairs, then a good deal of bang and clatter up the staircase.

"I got everything on the list yesterday, except they were out of Naples Yellow." This was Pim, her assistant. He dragged a little whip of wind in with him on the fabric of his jacket. He had ferried across town on his bike several tubes of paint, along with stretchers and a roll of canvas. He was incredibly agile, born on a bicycle like most Amsterdamers. Unlike Alice, who, when she first arrived, pretty much fell her way across the city, frightening pedestrians, bringing out Good Samaritans to pick her up and help her collect herself. She went around with chronically bandaged knees and elbows, an ankle that stayed deep purple for weeks. She was better now, hadn't fallen in some time. Still, she left the tricky or cumbersome supply runs to Pim.

"It's okay," she told him, about the Naples Yellow. "I can mix some myself. I'm just being a lazy butt. I feel guilty about you even coming by today, on a holiday."

He wasn't really listening to any of this. He wanted to see what she had done this afternoon.

"This part is great," he said, crouching to see details of the final Casey Redman painting. These canvases had been a large part of her work through the time she had lived here.

In one, a gallon of milk rests on the hood of a pickup in the parking lot of a convenience mart; next to it Casey in her twenties leans back against a fender as she looks at the night sky. In another, Casey is lying in a field with somebody not her husband. Even though a husband isn't present on the canvas, Alice somehow understood that he exists. In all the paintings, the girl is wearing the denim cutoffs and madras plaid shirt from the night she died. This last of the series had been the hardest painting to get right. Its setting is indeterminately tropical. Casey is sitting on wide, mossed-over stone steps. Behind her is a large wood door. Although it is inset with glass, what is inside is not visible, only the reflection of her back, the pale greens and pinks of her shirt darkened in the glass to crimson and viridian. It is night. Loose greenery and languid flowers play in the wind. Alice had to paint an exact tempo into them to make the painting accurate. The other element Alice had to imply with subtleties of gesture and expression was that Casey is waiting for someone. She is also holding something small and obscured at her ear, a small dark seashell maybe. Alice wasn't sure. She was only taking dictation.

Pim was so tall and thin that when he crouched or sat, he collapsed in on himself, like an ironing board.

"I was just fooling around here," she tried to show him. "I was trying to ruffle these ferns off to the side. I'm not sure I quite have it yet, though, the motion I'm looking for."

"No, this is good painting here, I think."

"I'm nearly finished. Verwey will see me next week. It's time." Alice was making a small pilgrimage to Haarlem, to see Kees Verwey, taking him up on his offer, now years back. But he was still alive and still painting and, remarkably, when she returned to Amsterdam, he remembered her. She had visited him a few times, to look at the work he had in progress. He reluctantly mentored her by showing her how he creates an effect (the eyes in his portraits, for instance, which are small starburst miracles), how he pulls back from representation into gesture. He talked to her about ways of folding dark into light.

This would be the first time she had brought her work to him. Fourteen canvases, each of them 36" x 36" square to approximate the boxiness of snapshots. These were all the Casey Redman paintings. She understood this was all there would be.

She had to bring the paintings to him. He was very old now, and did not leave his home much anymore. Although he knew she was coming, he could very well not receive her once she arrived. He was still very temperamental.

Tuesday, when she and Pim arrived at the door of his house on the Spaarne, they rang the bell. Nothing happened. She didn't want to ring again so they continued waiting, shuffling from foot to foot in the damp cold. After maybe ten minutes, the door opened and it was Verwey, in his suit of course, looking a little disoriented, and not entirely happy to see them.

"Go away," he said, waving his hands as though he was trying to shoo out a bird that had come down the chimney. "I am disturbed by this ringing and ringing."

"I only rang once," Alice said. "I would never ring twice."

"Yes yes, well come in then if you must," he said, as though they'd been dragging their feet.

After they'd brought the canvases in, and Pim had gone back out to the rental van to listen to a tape of what he said was "very new music, almost not music," Alice set out the paintings. At her own studio, she liked to show work, even just for herself, to its best advantage. She had a long wall she had painted a perfect green—the color of green tea ice cream. This was her curing wall, for nearly finished work, to see what else it might need. Verwey's studio was of an altogether other sort, a squalor of props that had itself been the subject of many of his paintings. He didn't really need to go outside these walls. The inside of his head, she figured, must be filled with explosions of light and color. Like Nick's nebulae.

She made room for her work amid this light chaos, tilting her paintings against chairs, amid unfinished lunches, vases of dead flowers, aged newspapers, rolled-up rugs. She could sense him growing impatient behind her.

"Don't bother with this, I will do it."

She tried to tell him it was still tacky but he waved her away, taking the last canvas from her hand. It took him maybe an hour, standing in front of each in turn, his hands clasped behind his back. When he was done, he settled slowly into an armchair across from her.

"The girl, she is not alive."

"Right. I never knew her alive. There was an accident. It was night. The car hit her with almost no sound. The first I saw her, she was—I think—already dead. When I see her now, she's suspended in one or another piece of time we stole from her. I can't paint her to life. I tried a couple of times early on, but it read false."

At first she worried he was about to say something very bad, and was working up to this. Then she thought he might be slipping into a nap. Finally he said, turning away from her, as though speaking to someone across the room, "These are very good paintings. They are, perhaps, something new."

"Thank you. But what do I do with them? She'd be twenty-five now. What I think is she doesn't need me painting her anymore."

"But you should show them, of course. They would almost certainly bring your reputation back."

Alice flushed with humiliation. He was clearly aware of the critical beating she took on her last show.

"I think they might be private paintings," she said.

"What, you think maybe these were a conversation you were having with the girl? You were what—you were looking for her *vergiffenis?*"

Forgiveness. Alice pauses to think. "Maybe. Something."

"But you are honoring her with these, giving her a kind of life. What if these are the best paintings you will ever make?"

"Then maybe not showing them is the terms of my atonement."

Verwey looked at her with an expression that seemed to signal impatience. Of course, it could just be indigestion. He was a difficult person to read.

"I think you brought these to me to tell yourself what you need to do with them." He put his feet on the floor so forcefully it was nearly stamping. He stood in creaking stages, then began making little sweeping gestures. "Now go away, please. I am tired of thinking about this work of yours and these old troubles of your life."

One of the great things about him was that he never let Alice swoon into hero worship.

"So?" Pim asked her when she got back into the van.

"Just help me rack them back in here," Alice said. "I'll drop you at your place on my way home. I can take care of unloading them. I'll take the van back in the morning."

She waited until early evening and headed out. It took her a little while, but she eventually found a secluded spot in a picnic area along the A6 heading northwest out of the city, toward Lelystad. With twigs and fallen branches doused with Turpenoid, she made a good fire in a trash barrel. She pulled each of the canvases out of the van, leaning them against the bench of the picnic table, then hiked herself up onto the tabletop and watched the flames snap and surge against the night sky. She waited for the courage of destruction, but it never came. She would never show these paintings, especially now that she was fairly certain they would buy back her reputation. But neither had she the heart to burn them. Alice knew the girl had been telling her something with the paintings, but she still didn't know what. All she knew was the paintings were something very good she had made, and destroying them pulled against everything she believed about the intrinsic value of art no matter what its subject. She would store the canvases, over here where no one would find them. This was the best she could do.

Which left her in the position of the timid high diver who, unable to make a dramatic surrender, now had to creep backward down the rungs of the ladder. A flutter of sorrow and shame rushed through her. Along with a crazy sort of love for someone she never met. She searched for the girl amid the blue slips of flame but couldn't find her, waited for something last-minute in the nature of guidance but there was nothing. Finally the blaze shrunk down inside the metal container, everything settled back to the ordinary, and it was just a cold night on a northern highway.

social life

It was bitter outside. The glass doors to his balcony were frosted halfway up. Nonetheless Nick had nothing covering him. He lay naked on a damp mattress which, he had to admit, didn't smell all that great. It was very dark except for a path of light running across the carpet from the TV in the living room. It could be just past nightfall, or almost dawn. He had no idea what day it was. Forget days, even months. It was winter, though. He was sure of that. He didn't know if he was lost because he had stepped outside time again, or just because he had been high. Whatever, this had been a wonderful set of days. Driving around, then here at home, it had all been very busy. Watching movies from his video collection. *Thelma and Louise. The Double Life of Veronique.* He had a girl over, one of the new hookers. Fleur. They had fun, he remembered, without being able to recall many particulars. They took a lot of Polaroids.

When he came into the living room, a commercial for a complicated exercise machine was on the television. He tried to focus. It was for abs. You looked great when you used it. It folded up and out of the way when you were done. The commercial provided no help in getting his bearings. The world of the ab machine was as sealed off from regular human life as he was. Good concept, though. Excellent abs could be part of the personal revision he was planning. New, improved packaging could definitely be a part of the whole thing. From there he drifted into a long, pleasant sequence of memories about some girls he met in Lincoln Park one night. In the chess pavilion. This was in high school.

He got up and roamed around and rummaged through the bottles lying everywhere on the carpet. All empties. Dry as bones. He sat down on the sofa, then lay back to map out a strategy.

✦
✦
✦
✦

Still dark, or maybe dark again. He went into the kitchen, like a detective, following a trail of blood and broken glass. The apartment must have been broken into. The kitchen floor was sticky with spilled beer and in peeling one foot off it, he lost his balance a little. Looking down, he could see that something was wrong. His big toe. It wasn't really secured to his foot, not the way it should be. It kind of flapped and wiggled with each step. It was crusted over, but blood seeped out anyway. He was going to have to do something about this. This definitely had to be put on the agenda.

Inside the fridge. A jar of tartar sauce and a Styrofoam clamshell. DO NOT OPEN said the clamshell.

No beer. No bottles on the counter either. On a cabinet shelf, he found a creased piece of paper dusted with a cocoa-colored powder. He ran the paper under a nostril, but there was not enough left to get a mouse high.

He would have to get supplies in soon. He was getting the cranky feeling, and bad thoughts were muscling in. Time to find the sofa and lie down for a minute.

✦
✦
✦
✦

He called Martin, the dealer, but only got his machine. He left a message and smoked a couple of cigarettes. He tried to be patient, but patience was hard when you were coming down, when you had sandpaper routing out your veins.

Finding Martin was the best option because for a little extra, he would drop off the dope. All Nick had to do was pull some cash across the street at the ATM, and then come back here and wait. There was plenty of money in the ATM. Until he fell off the wagon this time, he'd been working construction with a lot of overtime. He was going to have to see about getting back to work. Not just yet, though.

When Martin didn't call back, Nick prepared to go out. There would be no dope tonight. He would have to default to booze and none of the nearby stores would deliver to him anymore. Going out presented challenges. Getting dressed, for one. So many tricky steps. Finding clothes. Finding clean clothes. Clean enough. Getting into them. Shoes were always a problem. His feet had swollen after so much time in bed. And now there was the added factor of the toe, which had a bad color and an impressive largeness. Impossible to get it into any shoe.

He pulled stuff down from the high closet shelf. He got hit on the head with an old wood tennis racket in its press. He knew by how much this hurt that he was getting too close to sober.

"Yes!" He found his old slippers—a present from Carmen during one of his stints in rehab. They were plush-lined and didn't have soles and had Donald Duck on their fronts, but he decided they were fine, really.

He fell going down the stairs, but when he checked himself out at the bottom, he was okay. His car was parked at a jaunty angle across its space and the space next to it, and before he got there he knew Carmen had already come over and put a club on the steering wheel so he wouldn't be able to drive. She was not speaking to him these days. She had gone to meetings where they told her this was the best thing, setting boundaries, letting him hit bottom. Carmen was always doing the right thing. Fuck her.

He hailed a cab on Ashland. It pulled over and let out four, maybe five people—girls in cocktail dresses, two guys in dinner jackets. "Party on," Nick said, giving them his blessing as he folded himself into the backseat.

The cab driver was a black man in a crocheted cap. He was so small he could barely see over the steering wheel. When Nick climbed into the car, he turned around and said, "I am sorry. I cannot take you."

"You're a cab, aren't you?"

"I do not want any trouble."

"There's not going to be any trouble. I just need you to take me down to Belmont."

"I cannot do that. I must have you out of the taxi. I am off duty."

"But you picked me up."

"No. I was leaving off the party people. And now I am off duty."

Nick argued with him a little longer, but the little guy was not going to budge. Nick wasn't sure what his problem was.

It took forever to find another cab—it was weird how many people were out tonight, and how many of them were drunk—but finally he did, and this one took him down to Belmont with no trouble. The driver, who must have weighed well over three hundred pounds, gave Nick his restaurant recommendations. He loved Old Country Buffet. He was a buffet man. Nick was all edges by now, coming down fast. He sat very quietly in the back, making his presence as small as possible. When they pulled up in front of the store, he tried to get the cabbie to wait.

"Pay up first."

Nick gave him what he thought was a twenty, but might have been a fifty. "But you'll wait?"

"I'll be right here," he said. As soon as Nick got out, the cab zoomed off.

The store on Belmont wasn't a place anyone would go for regular liquor shopping. It didn't stock fine cognacs or have sales help to suggest wine pairings for your menu. It sold beer and liquor, crappy sweet wine, cigarettes, jerky, that was about it. The clerk behind the counter had no interest in chitchat. He had an air of end-stage weariness. He'd seen and heard everything already. Don't even bother, his face said. The good thing about the store—the feature for which it had gained its reputation—was that it would sell to anybody, in any shape.

Behind the clerk, on a small TV with fuzzy reception, he saw a show of people dancing in gowns and tuxes. There was a big band in the background.

"What's this? Lawrence Welk?"

"Get a grip," the clerk said. "It's New Year's Eve. It's the new millennium. They're in L.A. It's been on all day. Started on some tiny island in the Pacific. Where you been, buddy?"

"They're partying like it's 1999, because it *is* 1999." This from a kid behind him, a young guy wearing a quilted jacket liner and cloth work gloves. He looked Nick over, pointed at his slippers.

"Nice shoes," he said. He was a fashion critic.

Beer presented a transportation problem he wasn't up to dealing with tonight. (Beer was an ironic beverage of choice for a heavy-ish drinker like himself, he realized this.) He decided on two handles of Jack Daniels as a more prudent, more portable purchase. He added a couple of Hershey bars to the tab, stuffing them in his pockets.

He pissed in the alley behind the store, then had a few belts from one of the bottles. To do this, he had to hoist the jug as if he were a prospector in the Old West. To complete the gesture, he wiped his mouth with the back of his hand and said "ptwawww."

He was smiling at his own joke as he stepped out of the way for a beater truck coming slowly down the alley. Mexican junk men trawling through the night for scrap metal. No holiday for them. They stared out their window at him, as though he was a roadside attraction, but not a particularly interesting one.

He saw that the young guy had come back here, too. He had put a twelve-pack on top of a Dumpster and was popping cans and drinking them down, getting there as fast as he could. A fellow traveler.

"I didn't realize it was New Year's Eve," Nick said. "I'm glad I didn't miss the whole celebration. He tapped his bottle against the kid's beer can. He leaned against the Dumpster, looking up at the sky, picking out the few stars bright enough to make it through the ambient urban glow. Capella in Auriga. The Big Dipper. Pollux to the south. He stood like this as he waited for the whiskey to burn through his system. This was the payoff moment, when everything hungry got fed.

The young guy offered no response except to pop open another can. They were both, in their own ways, busy. Hard at the work of getting high. When they could finally stop, nicely buzzed, they sat on someone's back steps, companions. It was cold in the alley, but friendly. When they were drunk enough, they chatted a little. The kid's name was Arliss. He had dropped out of Northwestern, or was thrown out, he wasn't clear on that. He started out at a party much earlier. At that time he had a lot of company and a jacket with a lining. Nick told him a funny story about the nice hooker. Fleur. It was good to have a little social life like this, someone on the same wavelength.

"The thing is," he told the kid, "even though it's sometimes a lot of trouble, I really love getting drunk."

They were in agreement on this. Nick saw a link between the two of them, a possibility that here was someone who would understand.

"I know things. Things no one else knows yet."

"Like predicting the future?" Arliss said. He was lighting up a small, sweet cigar.

"No, no. Like understanding the universe. Sometimes I snort. You know, heroin."

Arliss didn't have a response to this. That was okay with Nick.

"Sometimes when I'm really high it's like I walk into a room and it's filled with levers and switches and I am given total understanding of how everything works. Macro to micro. I know the names of some planets far far out in the universe and understand the behavior of subatomic particles. I know how general relativity hooks onto quantum mechanics. How gravity weighs in. I understand the Theory of Everything, which doesn't even exist yet. Then I sober up and lose it all."

"Bummer," Arliss said, then after what seemed to Nick like a very long pause, but might only have been a minute, "You wouldn't have an extra hat, would you?"

prize

Alice burned her fingertips where they overlapped the pot holder. Her beer-batter crispy shrimp had been about to burn and she was careless in her hurry to rescue them. Too late she saw it wasn't really a pot holder she grabbed out of one of Carmen's kitchen cabinets, but an old Bears knit cap made of something synthetic that sizzled away between her hand and the cookie sheet she just pulled from the oven. A dozen shrimp scattered across the countertop. Carmen, taking charge of the situation, opened the freezer and stuck Alice's hand into the ice cube bin.

Ahhh.

"A secret sister bonding ritual! The Icing of the Hand," Rob said, coming in through the kitchen door. He was a compact guy, a couple of inches shorter than Carmen. Alice thought this was part of what made them adorable together. Today he wore cutoffs and a muscle T-shirt, but most conspicuously he wore an Einstein wig. He loved costuming for occasions.

"Kitchen casualty," Carmen told him.

"I'm a klutz is all," Alice said.

"Let's take a look. I'm pretty good at burns. Beauty salons are hazardous territory." He took hold of her wrist and turned her hand so he could inspect the fingertips. "Nothing to worry about. Cold was the right direction. You have a capable nurse here." He grazed Carmen's cheek with a kiss. "Put some cubes in a towel and keep icing it."

"Okay," Carmen said, then bossed Alice toward the door. "Let's go outside now. The shrimp will have to wait. We need to make a toast to Nick. Before he flees."

As Rob pulled a bottle out of the refrigerator, he said, "And remember: E equals something squared."

After initially recoiling from Rob—early on he came to a show of hers, pointed his forefinger like a gun at this, then that painting, saying "Like it"—Alice had come around to being crazy about him. Whenever Carmen complained about his passivity, or his cultural ignorance, Alice said "yeah yeah, shut up. You got yourself a good one." Alice liked how he treated Carmen, put her on a float in the parade.

Carmen was happy to throw this little party—happy that Nick, out of the blue and against all odds—had given them all an occasion for celebration. And the weather had gone along with the social plan, so perfect outside, so overwhelmingly June, everything bleeding out color—lawn, trees, the embankment of the railroad tracks scattered with wildflowers from a spring community project. Her yard, with the years and perennials and Rob helping, was now a respectable garden. Rob stood in the middle of it and popped the cork, massaging it out of the bottle, into a bunched-up bar towel that muffled the carbonated thwap to a sputter. It wasn't real champagne, only sparkling apple juice. Everyone got rid of any alcohol—threw it out or locked it up—whenever Nick was around. A lesson they'd all learned one or another hard way with overlooked aftershave, vanilla extract, and, one time, canned heat for a chafing dish.

"To a maverick explorer, a Shackleton of space!" was what Carmen came up with when everyone's glass was filled. She was quoting the introduction given Nick as he stepped onstage earlier this afternoon to accept a small, bronze trophy artistically shaped like a melted radio telescope, which was to say shaped like a hand-thrown cereal bowl. She was astounded that this turned out to be a major prize. There must have been 300 people in the auditorium down at school. Even with his personal valleys having become so deep, Nick clearly still had the ability to scale peaks in astronomy. Which made Carmen wonder what he might have accomplished if he hadn't had to drop out so often, drop out then recover, using up so much of his allotment of self on falling and righting.

He still held on to his trophy; he was clearly nervous. He had sweated through, in dark quarter moons, the underarms of his sport jacket. His T-shirt was white, his jeans black. His skin had a freshly scrubbed look, his teeth gleamed. He had dealt with his receding hairline by shaving his head. Carmen knew through Alice that he had been on an improvement program. Micro-dermabrasion. Teeth whitening. Whatever—he embodied the notion of springing back.

She feared this tiny scaffold of glory would have a trap door, but what the hell, today she figured she might as well just be happy for him.

Nick watched Rob work the cork free of the bottle. Even though he knew it was only fizzy juice, he still got a little rush—desire spun with urgency. A frothy little mix in his head. The smallest events—

a billboard featuring black people involved in situations of sex and cognac
a bottle of pills in a friend's medicine cabinet (he couldn't ever not check)
a pair of women getting physical with each other, even just hugging hello in a shampoo commercial

—any of these would trigger a glimmery surge inside him.

"Hey," he said in response to the toast, but from there couldn't find any more words. The others waited patiently until they understood he wouldn't be coming up with a speech, and then they just began to sip their fizzy juice and talk among themselves. That was okay. No speech was really required; he had already amazed them.

"Are those orthopedic?" Loretta gestured toward Alice's sport sandals. She was here by herself. Horace was not welcome at social gatherings, but for new reasons. Instead of insulting everyone, he now forgot who they were, and how they connected to him. His bewilderment was too tragic to make him and everyone else go through an afternoon of it.

Alice didn't bother answering; she understood her mother wasn't asking a real question. Loretta, even though she had retired into a life without any situations for which she needed to look businesslike, wore red pumps with three-inch heels. She subscribed to the belief that heels make a woman's calves look more shapely. Carmen says if Loretta had lived in China, she'd have had bound feet. At the moment she had a glow to her. Alice liked her mother least when she glowed like this. It wasn't a glow of true happiness, more a phony patina of nervous excitement, as though she were back in real estate, showing a dazzling house she knew held ferocious mold in the basement.

Loretta had already moved past her little swipe at Alice, and was now glowing toward Nick. "I'm just so proud of you, honey." She reached up, maybe to scruff some hair he once had, as if he were still a boy with a crewcut, then, seeing that her hand was currently headed for an expanse of sweaty shaved scalp, she pulled back awkwardly, then bent her gesture into a little hand flourish, like a circus performer beckoning applause for her trained poodles. "Proud of all my children!" she finished.

Alice looked over at Carmen, who crossed her eyes. The two of them disagreed on the subject of their mother. Alice thought she was just a little mean-spirited, a little hunched from a lifetime under their father's oppression. Carmen thought that, had Horace requested it, Loretta would have locked her kids in a bamboo cage half underwater, like in *The Deer Hunter,* and conscripted them as players in games of Russian roulette. When they saw that movie together, Carmen thought it was the perfect metaphor for their childhood.

Nick noticed his mother go into the kitchen. He followed and, seeing they were alone, waited until she finished getting herself some ice and water from the refrigerator door.

"I was wondering," he said, "if you could help me out a little." For once he wasn't hitting her up for drug money. Cleaning up his act, along with his apartment, his wardrobe, and getting the dents in his car bumped out, had put him a little behind the eight ball.

Loretta pursed her lips in a schoolmarmish way, a little kiss of disapproval before she pulled an embossed leather checkbook out of her purse. She still wrote checks for everything. She would be the last person in human history holding up a grocery-store line to write a check for two Lean Cuisines. Nick loved the checkbook, also his check, the amount written against a background of pastel cats playing with soft balls of yarn.

Heather came into the yard and got tripped up by Tater—Rob and Carmen's new dog. (*Not* a replacement for Walter. No dog could ever take his place, Carmen would say, but it did seem she was taking to this little guy.) An inglorious entrance. Carmen went over.

"It's great you could make it." Heather was in town just for the weekend. Her mother's birthday was yesterday. Heather visited her at an ashram in northern Indiana, where she had lived for several years now, practicing a life of keeping still.

"Crispy shrimp?" Alice passed by, holding a trayful in her good hand. She loved playing waitress at parties.

Heather had mellowed. After the business with her and Gabe—which left him hurt but determined not to show it—she began college then started dropping weight again. For a while she was mostly in and out of clinics, scaring the hell out of them. And then, suddenly, she just got normal. She turned nineteen and took about a pound of metal jewelry out of her ears and nose and privates, let Rob cut her hair. She still had the buzzing bee by her eye, but that was no longer a deterrent to progress in the straight world. She never went back to school. She currently lived in Manhattan and worked for a high-end realtor. The service Heather performed was staging—buffing up apartments for sale to show them to their best advantage. She ordered sets of pale, high-thread-count bed linens, filled large ceramic vases with sprays of exotic flowers, put Pillsbury rolls into the oven set to warm, lined the rim of the bathtub with white votive candles. She brought with her an array of fragrance sprays (summer cotton, sea breeze), and a batch of mood-setting CDs. Heather also replaced the worst of what the client had hung on the walls with what she called "neutral art." She took flak from both Alice and Gabe about even the concept of art that was neutral. Give me a break, she would say.

For these services, Heather made a percentage of the agent's percentage. With Manhattan real estate prices, this added up to quite a bit of money, which she socked away in mutual funds. Her troubles, which seemed to run so deep, turned out to be fleeting, adherent to adolescence, a kind of emotional asthma. And Carmen knew she should be happy that Heather started eating like a regular human and dropped the black eyeliner and got a job. And she was, happy. But she also feared for someone—so very like herself at that age—who had all her ducks in order. As if there was any reliable way of ordering ducks.

A chainsaw rip and a rubber whine preceded a motorcycle coming up the driveway out of a turn made so sharply the rider's shoulder nearly grazed the ground. Gabe had arrived.

Alice turned to watch him dismount in a choreographed sequence of movements. He was extremely aware of how he presented himself to the world. All through high school he had run, worked out with weights, kept an eye on his body mass index. He got this from his father; he and Matt worked out together at one of those new gyms that had a prison flavor. The desk up in his bedroom was piled with giant plastic containers of supplements he bought there. Protein powder, something called Steel. Whey in a plastic jug big as a tuffet.

He was about to graduate and head off to art school. He had a terrible girlfriend. Donna. They all hated her in a lazy way, the assumption being that she was temporary. For the summer, he was working part time for a sign-painting company, making art in his off-hours. He had pretty much abandoned his own painting, and now performed spontaneous pieces in public areas. Alice assured Carmen he would get past this, that he was not going to be forty and still eating tapioca in a clear plastic box on Michigan Avenue in his underpants. But neither was he the person Alice so hoped he'd become. She'd been expecting someone sweetly shy, but instead he'd turned out to be a little brash. He still wore glasses, but now with frames that called attention to themselves. He had a little of his father's puffy self-importance. Also a little of Carmen's challenging manner, and it was usually Carmen he was challenging. Striking distance was about as close as he got to his mother these days. Carmen, so tough in every other way, dissolved beneath his acidic gaze. Today, though, he came out of his helmet grinning at his mother, even gave Heather a quick, cautious hug, then headed straight toward the guest of honor.

"You the man." Gabe high-fived his uncle, who responded off the beat and they wound up whacking into each other's forearms. A white-guy high five.

"Cool bowl," he said, nodding, clueless, toward Nick's trophy.

He had brought Nick a present, which he pulled out of his messenger bag. A small, sentimental landscape, a meadow backgrounded by an unlikely volcano. He had painted Nick into the meadow, peering through binoculars at a part of the sky Gabe had painted black then salted with stars. This was pretty much the only sort of artistic painting Gabe did these days, the ironic insertion of friends into cheesy paintings he found in junk shops.

"This is so excellent," Nick said.

Gabe idolized his uncle. He saw Nick's addictions enhanced by rock star lighting. Nick was his private Kurt Cobain.

* * *

A few stragglers trickled in. Nick's mentor, Bernie Cato, proud as a parent. Jean brought a guitar and sang "Fly Me to the Moon," to Nick, who seemed not at all embarrassed. She also brought Vincent, a wiry guy wearing a T-shirt that said COLLEGE. Carmen knew nothing about this person. Jean had not mentioned him, but from the way he sat next to her and watched in a focused way as she played and sang, Carmen assumed he was a boyfriend. A boyfriend who was not Tom Ferris. A fairly stunning development.

They had chicken kabobs, grilled tofu for the vegetarians, and Greek salad. Someone hauled out the croquet set and there was a while of wooden balls thudding off the ankles of people in lawn chairs. A little after five, a consensus gathered up about leaving. Carmen looked around and thought, with Horace absent and Alice not manifestly lovesick and Nick sober and Loretta subdued and Gabe not witheringly dismissive, these people could actually add up to a happy family.

"Hey," Alice said to Jean when she found her alone getting a couple of Cokes out of the cooler. "I think I saw Tom driving by the house just now. I was getting something out of my car. He went past twice."

Jean didn't seem surprised. "He's being stupidly tragic. He has no right to tragedy. His marriage broke up. His son turned out to be queer. That bothers him. Really. His cholesterol is too high. Who cares? Do you care?"

"Sean? He's queer?"

"Tom heard him talking with a bunch of his friends at a party. He was saying 'Whatever happened to the *fourth* Pointer Sister?' And Tom couldn't come up with an example of any straight guy saying that." Jean popped open one of the Cokes, took a drink, then said, "So let him drive his go-cart round and round the track."

"This thing is new then?" Alice tilted her head in Vincent's direction, pushing in a thin end of the wedge to open the conversation.

"Kind of new. Kind of nice. We go places together. He's not married. He can stay over as many nights as I want. Imagine that."

Nick needed a lift home. His car was in the body shop. Alice's burnt fingertips still hurt; she had to hold the wheel gingerly.

"Mmmm." Nick ran his hands along the center armrest. "Fine Corinthian leather," he said in a Ricardo Montalban accent. He never missed a chance these days to jerk her chain about having bought a Mercedes, and not a reverse-chic beater like her old one. This one was brand new.

"Looks to me like your butt is enjoying that leather quite a bit. Your butt isn't embarrassed. Your butt isn't longing for a hard plastic bus seat. But I'll keep the critique in mind. Next time, I'll get something with vinyl upholstery. A Yugo. A used Yugo."

"I don't think there are any of those still on the road. I think you'd have to get a Pacer. I saw one of those still puttering around the other day."

"You doing okay?" she asked.

"I am. And I'm serious about it this time; I scared the hell out of myself with that last bender. But still, it's not easy. There are so many minutes in a day. You know. To get through unassisted. Plus the past. Now I have to carry that around all the time. No erasing it with a pill. I want to tell you something, something I want you to know. Just you. That night. I saw her. I saw her coming out of the woods, when she was still a ways up the road. All it would have taken was reaching out and jerking the steering wheel away from Olivia, taking the car off the road, into the ditch. We would have been a little banged up maybe. But the girl would be alive. But I was just so, so stoned. I thought she was so interesting to watch. I wanted to see what would happen to her. Like she was a character in some poignant movie."

"Jesus," Alice said.

◆ ◆ ◆

Carmen was in bed. Rob stretched on the floor, holding above himself a sheet of diagrams given to him by his physical therapist. He had a terrible back. He was probably going to get spinal fusion surgery. He was holding out, hoping technology would outpace the degeneration of his discs and they'd be able to fix them with a laser, or something laparoscopic, replacements made of some unrejectable polymer or something. Carmen tuned in and out on the details.

She was reading the latest issue of *The Nation*. Bush was claiming he was going to be the education president. He was going to leave no child behind. Right. What he appeared to be so far, in these early months of his presidency, was lazy. He liked to spend time at his ranch, whacking brush. Carmen wasn't sure what about the brush needed whacking. Although she had been clenched since the election, she was starting to think maybe he would just be passive and nondescript. A nothing administration she hoped would be whisked out in four years.

"Hey." Rob was up and sitting on the edge of the mattress, holding a piece of her hair between thumb and second finger, a professional assessment. "Let me give you a conditioning treatment. It'll only take ten minutes. Your ends are pretty dry."

"Okay," Carmen said. Rob did not follow politics. He voted the way Carmen told him to. She couldn't talk with him about her latent fears about who was actually running the show while the president whacked brush. She wouldn't be able to get him revved up about the bad résumés of the new cabinet. The best Rob could bring to the table tonight was a conditioning treatment, and she supposed this was something. She still thought marrying him was a small mistake, but also that someone as fiendish on perfection as she was might need to make a few mistakes. She would say he was a mistake that had turned out surprisingly well.

"We don't deserve the luxury of our lives," she told him.

"I know. I know," he said, sitting her up, wrapping a towel around her shoulders, ripping open a foil packet. The room filled with coconut.

delivery

Alice was in gear, making coffee, mixing paint. Sitting on her high stool, mapping out the day's work while she had her usual energy breakfast, an Almond Joy. The morning outside was dazzling, pouring in through the windows and skylights.

The phone rang. It was Carmen.

"Are you watching TV?"

"Well . . . No?"

"You might."

"What's up?"

"A plane just flew into the World Trade Center."

"Accident?"

"Don't think so. Gotta go. I'm trying to get Gabe to answer his cell. I know Providence is miles from Manhattan, but I want to—you know—hear his voice."

After another plane blasted into another tower, Alice decided she needed some company. Nick had the biggest TV of anyone she knew, maybe of anybody in the world, so she headed over. People were out on the streets, and for a while it still looked like an ordinary Tuesday.

But then at Belmont, a small crowd was coming off the El and down the steps, as though it were six p.m. instead of ten in the morning. A reverse rush hour. No one wanted to be in the Loop just now. Alice didn't feel frightened for her safety. If these planes were seeking out skyscrapers, the next one probably wasn't headed for La Vida Taco or the dollhouse shop just up from where Alice turned left onto Clark. The sensation was more an eerie one, the vibration of huge events. Events of unknown origin with unforeseeable consequences.

She pressed Nick's buzzer a few times, then gave up and used her key. He was stretched out on the sofa in camouflage-print jockey shorts, not truly present to the morning. Clearly he was using again. The living room smelled of something bad masked with bayberry; melted candle stubs sat in saucers all around. She put on Channel 7 and found out that while she'd been biking over, one of the towers had crumpled to the ground. They were replaying it on all the news stations. She sat down in the guest chair Nick never used, the cleanest piece of furniture in the room.

She flipped up and down through the channels. "Oh my God, two people just jumped. Together."

"What movie is this?" he said, establishing conversational traction.

"Get a grip."

In between the news networks, stations with taped programming gave the appearance of being clueless, or insensitive. On the Food Network, a celebrity Alice didn't recognize was cooking something Cajun. On another channel contestants were jumping up and down and squealing and trying to win a low-end convertible.

"Man," Nick, now focused, said when the second tower deflated in a thick cloud of ash. "Somebody's really pissed off at us. We just took delivery on a big message."

"We're so used to special effects. I have to keep checking myself, resetting my mind to this is real. There were people in there. How many?

Who could survive that? No one will survive, will they? Not the people in the planes either. Not the rescue workers."

"Olivia might have been inside. She was in New York."

"That was a few years back. We don't know where she is anymore."

"She could have been in there."

"She could have been flying the plane," Alice said. "She is not a knowable part of this story, or any story."

"Right," Nick said, and nodded as if Alice had said something immensely wise.

Carmen came by a while later, having closed the shelter early. "My ladies—not unreasonably, I guess—have decided they'd rather be outside today than in a building. Gabe was in his studio when I got him; he's okay. Rob's in Venice, so he's probably better than okay. He's okay and eating really good spaghetti. Nobody's mad at Italy." She took off her jacket, got a Coke from the refrigerator and squeezed into the big armchair with Alice. Neither wanted to try the sofa. The sofa was a hazmat area. "I'm glad you guys are here. I don't want to be alone just now."

"Mom called," Alice told her. "She heard they've cleared the airspace above the whole country. They pulled down every last plane. Have they ever done that before?"

"What's up with the one that crashed in the field?"

"Peter Jennings said it might be an unrelated crash," Alice said.

Carmen stared at her. "Right. And why are we having to rely on the bad guesses of news anchors? Where's our government? Where's our, like, president?"

"They had a scratchy little clip of him earlier. He was flying around for a while; now he's in an undisclosed location. Because he's so valuable. Because when he comes out, he's going to know just what to do."

"He'll be wearing a little president jacket. The guy loves those jackets," Nick said.

"They don't think this is a Timothy McVeigh thing, home-grown?" Carmen said.

"No. They think it's the same people who bombed the Trade Center before. The guys who put explosives in the parking garage. They think today they were finishing the job. Terrorists with a strong work ethic."

Carmen thought awhile. "This administration, their response will be military. These are old hawks in charge. They're not going to be interested in low-profile police work, in ferreting out who's responsible, going cell by cell. They'll want to find a country to bomb."

Nick stretched to pick up the phone receiver on his coffee table. "Would you guys mind if I asked Andalusia over to watch with us?"

"Don't even touch that," Alice said. "We are not keeping vigil through our country's darkest hour with a ridiculously pseudonymed hooker."

Jean called, then came by. She'd been at her studio, trying to call Sylvie Artaud, her Parisian chanteuse, who was in New York playing a small supper club. "You can't even get through. I think the lines are jammed with everyone calling their friends in Manhattan to make sure they're all right."

"I wonder what Tom's going to do with this?" Carmen said. "What song he's going to write. Maybe about the towers falling? How it was so galling?"

"Now America's bawling?" Alice contributed. Jean was done with Tom. It was now safe to say stuff like this.

"Actually," Jean said, "he did call. Anything big, he still feels he needs to tell me. The weird thing is, I don't think he's terribly interested in a tragedy so big everyone else is in on it. He's a tragedy snob. He doesn't want to stand next to some NASCAR guy, both of them waving little flags. That's what he said."

"Wow," Alice said. "Well there you go."

They numbed themselves with replay, the loop of horror: the Twin Towers, the plane that hit the Pentagon, also the one that went down in the field in Pennsylvania. They heard about the cell phone calls from people on the planes, how the terrorists slit the flight attendant's throat.

"That would definitely get your attention. You couldn't have many illusions after that," Nick said.

"Plus the people on the later planes were hearing on the cell phones from their wives and husbands about what had happened with the first ones. How chilling must that have been?" Alice thought about this for a minute. "Today is kind of off-the-meter from anything we've had to consider before today."

On the screen, Peter Jennings asked a reporter where the president was. "He has disappeared down the rabbit hole, Peter."

"They're saying churches all over the country are filling up. People are just wandering in." Jean was relaying this to Alice, who'd been out getting sandwiches.

"Well, that's what this is with us, isn't it?" Alice said, opening the sandwich papers to see what was whose. "Today, in here? Our church? Our small religion?"

By mid-afternoon, Carmen was sifting the text for the subtext. "We're through the information-gathering part. The information is now in. Now they're shaping this for our consumption, imposing a story line. The brave passengers taking the last plane down in the field. The firemen rushing in heedlessly, answering their call to duty. And pretty soon, they'll get the president ready for his close-up to congratulate us for being Americans. This huge unprecedented, unmanageable mess, all the complexity behind it—they're already starting to manage it. They're making a theater piece out of pure horror so we can watch the unwatchable then get back to the mall."

enough monkeys

Funny thing. Just when she was truly over Maude, when she even seemed to have gotten past the need to cook up exhausting Maude-like obsessions for new women, Alice ran into her during intermission at Steppenwolf.

Alice was here with her mother, who wanted to see this play. All her friends loved it. Everyone present was happy to be pampered by the lavish air conditioning of the theater. The temperature outside had been stuck in the nineties for the past few days. Loretta, at the moment, waited in a long line of women snaking into the ladies room. Meanwhile Alice was eating the world's most expensive Snickers, drifting on a wave of peanut and the human tide of intermission, people-watching in a basically uninterested way, and then a woman with her back to Alice, turned around and was, rather stunningly, Maude.

Alice had known she was back living in Chicago. Through Gabe she always knew at least Maude's longitude and latitude. And lately she had felt the slight thickening of the atmosphere that came with Maude-proximity. She was nonetheless sandbagged in this particular moment, and had to apply herself to seeming regular. She improvised a little narration: "Some years later, they run into each other at the theater."

"Had to happen." Maude smiled, as though she had had weeks to prepare.

Suddenly the air went wavy with possibility. Alice thought she might throw up. She clung to the conversational line. "Exactly. Of the billions of times we weren't in the same place at the same time, there almost had to be one time. One time when we are."

"Put enough monkeys on typewriters and you'll get the Bible. Or I suppose in your case it would be give enough monkeys paintbrushes and you'll eventually come up with the *Mona Lisa*." Maude said all this smoothly, like this was an ordinary little chat, like Alice was the third ex-lover she had run into on her way to the concession counter.

"I'm too nerved up to go on here," Alice confessed.

"Let's talk about the play."

Alice thought. "Okay. Didn't you know when you sat down that nothing good could possibly happen on that set?"

"Totally. The farmhouse with the rocking chairs on the porch. The hitching post."

"The pump," Alice said.

"And as if there really was a second story behind the fake front. A real room with a lamp in the window."

And here they were, slipping into the sort of effortlessly syncopated conversation about nothing that they always used to have. Alice crumpled a little as she thought of all she had missed, the uncountable moments that could have been just like this, but never happened. While she was sinking, Maude turned toward someone in the distance. Alice couldn't see who it was.

"Got to go," she said, pressing a fingertip hard on the exact center of Alice's breastbone.

As she watched Maude get folded into the crowd, Alice felt an implosion in her chest. This pain then gave way to a ludicrous joy at still being able to feel this much about anything. She thought all that was behind her. She also thought this was a good thing.

• • •

She was surprisingly wounded again later that night when Maude called, wanted to come over, as if all they'd been waiting for was a chance meeting.

Still, Alice said "Okay." Then, "I've moved."

"I know," Maude said, and of course this was thrilling.

When she got back from Amsterdam, Alice bought a vast loft, the entire top floor of a renovated warehouse west on Randolph, a stretch that was now fashionable. After a couple of years of not being able to paint anything she was happy with, Alice was now finishing a series of portraits of notorious serial killers as boys. She was trying to ready the last of these for a solo show at Handel, an important gallery on Ontario. This was only a few weeks off. The show was important to her, and there were a million details around making it happen. It was not a particularly good time for her to be distracted.

While she waited, she thought about the perils of reunion. Tonight could be a small, grim disaster.

It wasn't, though. When Maude came out of the freight elevator into Alice's loft, everything turned delicious.

"Still mighty hot out there." She wheeled her bike out of the elevator, propping it against a wall. "It's okay while you're going, but once you stop, you realize you're pouring sweat." She had changed into a tank top and loose linen shorts. The top was sweated through in patches. Her hair, in response to the humidity, was huge and wild. Like she just came, not out of an elevator, but out of Hawaii.

"Do you want some iced tea? I just made some."

"Not really," Maude said. "Let's talk. But just a little."

"You first," Alice said.

"Okay. But how do I compress all this time? How do I pick the most important thing to say? I guess if I could only say one thing, it would be that it doesn't go so well for me without you. So well as it does *with* you."

"That sounds like a statement written by your lawyer."

"I'm testing the waters."

"The problem for me," Alice said, "is that you scare me."

Maude and Alice waited together for the conversation to continue. They were facing each other. Instead of saying anything more, though, Maude roughly pressed Alice against the wall.

"Hey," Alice said. "I pulled my rotator cuff at the gym. I'm still—"

"Shut up," Maude whispered.

"Just. Please. Don't fuck with me this time," Alice said.

"Shh." Maude pulled Alice's T-shirt up over her head and off.

They spent quite some time at the wall, also the wall adjacent to it, banging each other around, shucking each other's clothes off, sweat washing down them in this airless corner of the loft, making them slippery as they moved against each other. In this way, they tried to reconnect with their mutual past, obliterating the sizeable chunk of their adulthoods that had happened since, in each other's absence. It was a claim-staking enterprise, seeing if they still owned some substantial piece of each other. This was about much more than old times, or flexing muscle memory, or call and response.

Of course, they weren't quite the same people they were when they left off. Older, of course, but also both had been touched by mild versions of celebrity and the attendant burn of exposure. They were more protected, more private. After early years waiting by their phones, they now had unlisted numbers, both business and personal cells, caller ID. They never picked up. They had made themselves less knowable.

"I have an idea," Alice said when they were wobbling a little. "It's a little conventional, but well, I'm thinking, why don't we get in bed?"

When they lay down, Maude formed herself around Alice from behind. "Tell me what you really want."

And when Alice rolled over and pressed her mouth to Maude's ear and confessed, Maude said, "Oh. Well, you'd have to ask for that. Nicely. You'd have to say please."

It was really too hot for arduous connection. Alice's AC was broken and her ceiling fans were not up to the sluggish heat lingering from the day. She and Maude stuck to each other and drenched the mattress with sweat. They drank all the Cokes plus the jug of iced tea Alice had in the refrigerator, then just started filling glasses of water from the tap. The icemaker couldn't keep up with them. Maude went out to the White Hen and brought back two bags, put one in the freezer, dumped the other into the bathtub while it was filling, and they cooled down by stretching out side by side in the icy water, like patients in an old asylum.

"Hey," Maude said, "You don't smoke anymore."

"It's been years. Hypnotism and the patch. I still have moments when I consider it, but then I know I couldn't stand to go through the quitting again."

They got hungry and headed to the kitchen—suddenly modest—pulling on the old T-shirts and Gap boxers that were Alice's pajamas. They made big sandwiches and ate them standing at the kitchen counter, then headed back to bed and slept for a long time, almost around the clock. Alice woke and watched Maude sleep on without her, face down. She went weak with relief, her knees buckling even though she was lying down. She had gotten exactly what she had not allowed herself to want for so long. She needed to make very sure she wasn't misunderstanding what was on offer, so, a little later, when they were in the shower, she asked, "What are we doing?"

"Keep your eyes shut," Maude said. She was pushing lather around on Alice's head. "We're fucking our way back to each other. We're trying to reach in and grab the live cable. It's going to take some more fucking to get to it, though."

The old Maude was back, casting everything between them in huge, reverberating terms, like the construction of Stonehenge, the vanishing of Shangri-la. This must be what Alice wanted; she had waited for it so long.

Over the next day and night, Alice listened and inferred and put together a rough sketch of this new, revised version of Maude. She had been back in Chicago for a couple of months. Her acting career had washed out, the modeling gigs had thinned. Now she'd hit forty and gone back to nursing. She was in neonatal care.

"The patients are little," she told Alice. "It's easy to make their beds."

Something was slightly off. Maude didn't look quite like she did before, but it took a while before Alice saw that not all the change was about aging. The overall effect was of someone still youngish, but in a slightly suspended way. Also a little beat-up around the mouth. Alice suspected Maude had had work done, a lift, a little tucking around the eyes, lip injections. Maude was upfront about this when Alice finally asked.

"The price of staying in a vanity business too long." She patted her cheeks, as though they were merchandise.

Alice said something along the lines of sure, so what? and hoped it didn't show, her queasiness around this casual surgical revision. She herself had become more and more who she had always been, the ink darker, the etching deeper with each passing year. It was disconcerting to think that, in the meantime, Maude had been editing as she went along and might by now be in some ways less Maude than when Alice first knew her.

They took a break. When Maude left to straighten out the patch of her life she had missed these days in bed, Alice did the last bits of tinkering on the final paintings she had promised for the show. She was hopelessly behind.

She answered the million messages that had piled up on her machine. About a quarter million were from Helen Roth at the gallery. Another half million were from Carmen. Alice called her cell, then listened through a small catalog of Carmen's suffering on Alice's behalf.

"First I thought maybe you were away. I can't always keep track of your schedule. Then yesterday I started to worry. I thought bludgeoning. Maybe garroting. I was about to come over and look for a corpse. Find your keys and—"

Alice cut her off. "Listen. Something's happened. Something good. Well, you might not see it as good, but—"

"Oh no—"

"I think you're going to be impressed at how much more serious she is now," Alice said, but when Carmen asked "Serious how?" Alice couldn't really articulate it.

"Oh honey," Carmen said before she hung up.

By the time Maude came back a few nights later, the heat had broken; the weather had gone back to regular summer.

"Let's go for a swim," she said. It was one in the morning.

They biked over to the lake together, peeled down to their swimsuits and jumped off the retaining wall south of Fullerton. The water—surprisingly after all the recent heat—was a heart-stopping cold. They grabbed onto each other, went under again, and kissed as they exhaled great washes of bubbles. Maude flipped Alice onto her back and pulled her lazily along in a lifeguard's cross-chest carry. They ignored a patrol car that was trolling for party animals and night swimmers. They let the searchlight brush over them, laughed when the cop started shouting through a bullhorn. They just swam on.

"Like they're going to get those fat butts out of their cruiser and jump in after us," Maude said. And she was right. The cops got a real call or just lost interest, and took off.

Alice treaded the black night water and lined up her next questions. "What about your mother? How are you going to stand up and defy her, and stay standing?"

"I'll take care of that. That's my problem and I'll deal with it. I promise I will. I'm ready to do this."

Alice tried to think if she herself was. This slight hesitation took her completely by surprise.

Eventually they emerged from the love shack, dressed up, and took themselves out to run the gauntlet of appraisal that awaited them. Carmen—leery, but as always trying to be there for Alice—had them to dinner. Rob was out of town, but Gabe was home from Providence for the summer. In the fall he would go to London for a semester to study portraiture. This seemed peculiar. Although he had returned from performance back to painting, he worked primarily with a glue gun, objects found in parking lots, and razor stubble—his own and that of his friends.

He said he wanted to submerge himself in classical styles for a while. "Then I can dismantle the whole pathetic, two-dimensional notion of painting. Implode it. No offense, Alice." He talked like this a lot lately. He used terms like "iterations" and "appropriation" in describing his work. Because Alice was famous; also, she hoped, because he loved her, he didn't patronize her. Instead he talked to her as though she was Yoda, the Old One. Like she had secrets from a time when brushes were fashioned out of thistles, colors mixed from animal blood and plant roots. Alice cut him yards of slack. He was eighteen, smack in the middle of his jackass years. She'd been there herself once. Alice had been around for his growing up, witnessed his many transitions. Still, some moments she was purely astonished that this hulking baritone, this pretentious jerk used to be the baby Carmen put on top of the clothes dryer to get him to sleep, the skinny kid who spent about five years in a magician's cape.

He was happy that his two aunts were back together, and had made for them one of his tampered landscapes. He had painted Maude and Alice into a bucolic scene featuring a thatched cottage. He said the paintings were ironic, but also not ironic. He tried to make his subjects look their best—shaved off excess pounds, filled in thinning hair, lifted a jowl when necessary. In front of the cottage, which is on a hill overlooking a dale, Alice and Maude sit in bikinis on webbed chaises. Maude holds a semicircular reflector under her chin. In front of them, next to a grazing sheep, rests a boom box.

"This is so great," Alice said, but even as she was saying this, she was getting nervous. A terrible image had floated up in her mind. She could see the painting abandoned at the back of a shadowy closet, propped against a defunct, beige computer monitor or an LP turntable, a discard at some point in the long future where it would no longer be humorous to anyone, or a reminder of anything.

• • •

Alice and Maude made their re-entrance into society at a show Jean was putting on at the Green Mill. Sylvie Artaud's farewell performance—her seventh or tenth, she'd been retiring for decades. She looked to be about one hundred by now. She sang with a wobbly grip on the hand mic, a handkerchief at the ready to blot tears shed at the sorrows detailed in the songs she sang. "At Least When I Die, I'll Forget You." "You Passed Me on the Street Today (And Didn't Know Me)."

It was a bubbly night. Jean was on a high with so many people packing the bar, itself a landmark in the history of jazz and cabaret. Carmen and Rob came with some friends of his Alice didn't know. Also Nick. He was still on the straight and narrow. It was easy to look only at the downfalls, at the weakness they implied. Sometimes she forgot how much it took for him to pull himself back up out of a well that just got deeper, and how terrifying it must be for him looking back in, over the edge. And then even though she loved her brother hugely, she thought, fuck him, he saw the girl coming onto the road.

Tom Ferris was a surprising part of the mix, a party crasher. He had thickened over the years. He often wore a hat, even indoors. He was wearing one tonight, a little Rat Pack fedora. Apparently he was still—not so often as before, but often enough to be extremely annoying—sitting in his car outside Jean's since she hooked up with Vincent.

Alice wasn't crazy about Vincent, but then she had only met him a couple of times. He was ironic. He wore his hair short and gelled up like someone in his twenties. Had a cat named Fido. His sense of humor was a little snarky. He was a vet tech, which didn't seem far enough along any career path for a guy in his forties. It sounded like the second career of a surgeon who'd lost his license for sawing off the wrong leg. But hey, he was single, and he seemed totally crazy about Jean.

Jean didn't seem particularly ruffled by Tom's appearance tonight. "He's trying to intimidate Vincent. Vincent thinks Tom's hilarious, like a corny old joke. He's a little lost is all," she said to Alice. "Ever since his marriage fell apart. Apparently our affair was an essential component to the marriage working. Like a tree spike off to the side, feeding the tree. He actually told me that. That was the analogy he used." She turned toward the stage where Sylvie was kicking her cane under the piano and pulling on long white gloves. "Hey, I've got to go introduce the old gal."

When Sylvie had finished singing her set plus three encores, she repaired to a stool at the end of the bar, was served a martini nearly as big as her head, and greeted fans while Jean sold copies of her new CD—*Tristesse et Lillet.*

Maude was also called on to autograph a few cocktail napkins. She was still recognized quite often as Ginger Slade. Guys would come up to her and Alice wherever—the grocery store, on the street—and whip around in a 360 as they pulled an invisible gun from the small of their back, Ginger's signature move, the one she did in the intro, backed up by the show's theme song.

She was extremely good-natured about this being what she was most recognized for.

"It's not like I ever did Antigone or Mamet. I was lucky to get that part. Ginger's funding my retirement."

She and Alice grabbed a booth, then Nick found them and slid in. And then Tom was there, insinuating himself. "All right if I join you?"

Whenever Alice saw Tom now, she also saw him as he was that night—his aw-shucks smile as he stood there in the gray moonlight, his guitar slung over his shoulder, suggesting that he just take off. As if he was lighter than what had happened, and could just evaporate into the void. She looked around the table and saw each of them as they looked that night, at Carmen's wedding—Tom lean and badboy, Nick with his mane of hair and his bridal gown, Maude naked. All of them in their last hours of making mistakes with small prices.

Tom said, "Well, to paraphrase Groucho Marx, here's a club I don't really want to join, but unfortunately I am already a member."

"I think we could all say the same," Alice said. "Nobody wants to be in this particular clubhouse." Silence settled on them like a pall. Inside the din of the bar, the silence at the table entered the realm of negative sound.

Maude finally said, "Are we waiting for something? Some redemptive moment? Some *closure*? Like we beat our breasts together and we're all forgiven?"

Nick, staring at Tom's glass of whatever on the rocks, said, "Bits of our energy fused together that night. Soldered filaments on the cosmic web."

"I hate when you talk voodoo science crap," Maude said.

"I'm sorry you feel that way." This was a phrase Nick had picked up from the million rehab meetings he'd sat through.

Alice said, "I do think there's a connection between us all. There's never a day she's not with us. We keep carrying her forward, and it takes all of us to do that."

Tom said, "Of course what we have here is only the Passenger Club. Those of us whose worst crime was simply being along for an extremely unfortunate ride. Where is the driver now? Does she have any regrets about the burden she put on us with her recklessness?"

At this, Nick stood up, and before leaving, picked Tom's hat off his head, dropped it on the floor, and stepped on it. "Interesting spin on the matter, my friend. Now I'm going to leave before you try to get us pissed off at the girl for ruining our lives by dying in front of our car."

"Tom is such a lovely human," Alice said when she and Maude were in the car, on their way home. "I didn't understand until tonight that the accident was actually about him."

"But great that he's forgiven himself," Maude said. "Must be nice. Why can't I do that?"

"Hey. You did the best you could that night."

"Not really. Everyone was counting on me. I was supposed to be the medical expert. But I'd barely started nursing school. Of course I should have known how to do CPR, but I was hazy on it. I was modeling for Field's then. You remember. I had to miss classes for photo shoots. So that night I was punting. Honestly, I think I was working off a poster I saw once on a lifeguard chair."

"She was still alive when we got to her. I remember you felt a pulse."

"But so feathery. I probably couldn't have saved her even if I'd known what I was doing—she was pretty busted up—but of course I'll never know. I will never fucking know."

Maude was straightforward this time around. She had come back to Alice to make a partnership. She was less dramatic about everything. She liked being a nurse again. Every week, she worked two twelve-hour shifts at the hospital. Extra money came in from a new job for a high-end catalog with a Western theme. Her slightly weathered looks, her thick, tangled hair now streaked with silver, gave her the air of a woman accustomed to hard chores, someone who smelled a little of horse stalls. A fantasy the company thought would prompt city-bound women to buy overpriced stonewashed denim and chunky turquoise-and-silver jewelry. And there was something subtly hot about the mix of younger face, older hair.

In spite of time and change, there was still some of the old Maude left. She was still a teenage guy in bed. Still a big reader, a big talker. A huge supporter of Alice's career. (At the opening of the show at Handel, Maude had been so enthusiastic Alice worried people would think she was a shill.) She was still totally invasive. She went through Alice's mail, her drawers, the paintings in her racks. She picked bits of nut from between Alice's teeth, Q-tipped wax from her ears. Alice had mixed sentiments about this, the sentiments being (a) thrilled, and (b) wanting to run from the room screaming. But for the most part, she was the Maude whom Alice would have said she wanted all along. But instead of seeming more reasonable, practical, or grown-up, this perfected version of Maude seemed smaller, diminished by her easy acceptance of reduced circumstances. A great part of her old charm, it would seem, was her arrogance and the way she held herself just beyond Alice's reach. Without it, she was less likely to flee, but definitely more ordinary.

Because of her hospital schedule, she was either not around at all, or sleeping, or around a lot. On her days off, she lay stretched out on the sofa reading Victorian novels.

"Do you want to go out for lunch?" she asked. "To the diner?"

"I need to finish this section so I can leave it to dry." Maude had no idea how much Alice worked, how many days slipped into nights in the studio. How many weekdays flowed into work weekends. How much of Alice's time was now taken up, not just with painting, but with the business of being a painter—openings and interviews, lectures and mentoring. While Maude was away, Alice's life had gotten a whole lot bigger. "Maybe you should go without me."

"No, that's okay," Maude said. She didn't start buffing her nails or noisily ruffling a magazine, but an aura of restlessness definitely gathered up around her.

This time around Alice could see Maude three-dimensionally, as opposed to just looking at the side that faced her. She saw that Maude was a good daughter to a difficult mother. Marie was still massively controlling, but now with arthritis and deteriorating eyesight. Many doctor visits were involved. Maude took her to these and they indulged themselves in family gossip and the *People* magazines in waiting rooms, and Maude came home with a temporarily smaller and more judgmental worldview. At first Alice could tease her about this, but after a while Maude became a little defensive. She loved her mama.

When they decided it was time for Maude to move in with Alice, they were up against the cat issue. Maude had one—Archie. Alice was allergic. She thought this was going to be a big deal and was prepared to take antihistamines, whatever was necessary, but then suddenly the cat was out of the picture.

"Where's Archie?"

"Oh. I took him to Anti-Cruelty. You couldn't live with all that fur around you."

In the face of this generous gesture, Alice couldn't really say "you dumped your cat?! Just like that!"

The cat was a problem. The cat was gone. A lot of how Maude worked in the world was like this. Frighteningly expeditious.

The catalog gig got bigger. Maude went into high gear. Personal trainer, four-times-a-week yoga classes. She got expensive haircuts; Alice saw the credit-card slip from one and decided it was a subject they should never talk about. Sometimes Alice would come into the bedroom to find Maude standing on her head in front of *Who Wants to be a Millionaire* (which seemed not truly in the spirit of yoga). She had biweekly facials, monthly peels. She tanned in a measured way in the basement of her health club. Alice's bathroom filled with eyecups, ankle weights, exfoliants for different body parts. There was nothing to be inferred from any of this. It was all simply part of Maude's job.

Maude was not interested in opening up her years in L.A. for Alice's inspection. When Alice asked, Maude answered, but edited. The guy she lived with who rented out period cars to the studios was "kind of a refuge," but from what she didn't say. The cameraman husband was "mostly just a beard. You can't know how creepy those paparazzi maniacs are. They have these huge lenses and wait until you bring out the garbage or something. So you never bring out the garbage, and if you want to get them off your back about who you're dating, you get married to someone." She didn't go into the actual dating that had to be covered up. That was an edit.

Alice tried to hang on to her role as the supplicant, shouldering the burden of keeping Maude interested. She couldn't admit, until the fourth or fifth occurrence, that she was experiencing short, slick patches when her interest slid off Maude. And after that came a long-ish while during which Alice thought, well a little boredom, sure, wasn't that a part of being in something long term? Wasn't it healthy even? And in their case, an overdue bit of balancing?

They took French-cooking lessons together. They doted on Gabe, loved being aunties together. In the spring, they took a vacation to England, to see him and to take a bus tour of castles and gardens that turned out to be twenty-seven retirees and the two of them. They really tried to talk about issues as they came up, not to let them fester. By rough addition, this should have been enough to count as building a new history. But it wasn't. It felt to Alice more like they were playing house, with small props—a cappuccino maker, matching rings. Marking off time together with small celebrations. The architecture wasn't, in the end, weight-bearing; the walls were bending inward. Maybe, Alice worried, she had been rendered incapable of love, maybe these past years had only made her extremely deft at longing.

Nothing dramatic occurred. No one threw crockery. There weren't really any arguments. No one had an affair. No distraction came into the picture.

She asked Jean, "Am I crazy? Or maybe I'm a terrible person."

"Maybe you're just not in love with her anymore. In spite of putting us all through holy hell over her."

"But how could that be possible?"

"Never discount the power of time," Jean said. "Time is always a player."

They didn't break up, really. It was much more stretched out and fatiguing and sadder. Maude signed an extended contract with the catalog—Lone Pine Ranch. They posed her sitting with a breakfast tray crafted of gnarled twigs, emoting comfort on a sofa draped with handmade serapes, walls hung with lithographs of pueblos. She projected casual domesticity in a breakfast scene with her happy photo family and a few authentic-looking ranch hands. She pushed playfully against a middle-aged husband (hunky and bare-chested in jeans) in front of a charming, old-fashioned medicine cabinet. That sort of thing. The company was headquartered in Tucson, and Maude needed to be there for catalog shoots. Her contract was only for a year, so the plan was that she would bounce between here and there for a while, then come back to Chicago.

Nothing is ever completely tidy. The particular slick they hit was a long, terrible afternoon with a lot of crying and very little sense making. Bogus resolutions got made about a future together. Some desperate sex cropped up. Nothing changed.

From there, little knots began to turn up in the conversational tapestry. Maude had a dishwasher installed in her apartment down there. She took a two-year membership at a gym in spite of having only the one-year contract for the job. When Alice visited her for a long weekend, she saw a book on Maude's coffee table. A photo essay of Vietnam. Because Maude had never expressed the slightest interest in Vietnam, Alice understood it was brought over and left behind by someone who hadn't been mentioned.

Then Alice accepted an artist-in-residence position at Pratt for the coming semester.

"It's as easy to commute between New York and Tucson as Chicago and Tucson," she told Maude. They talked like this now—gorgeous, decorated lies spilling from their mouths as they waved at each other from farther and farther off.

From here Alice fell into the darkest place, bottomless; there was no end to this freefall. The loss was one she couldn't have predicted. She had been left without the specter of Maude, the shimmer at the horizon that had always been her. Now that Alice was no longer waiting for Maude, she was no longer waiting for anything.

triage

The afternoon sky was opaque, horizonless, the olive green of an army blanket, sloughing off a heavy fog. Snow was headed in. They pulled up in front of Nick's latest apartment, a bleak, tan brick courtyard building just off Ridge. A wicked wind buffeted the car, inside they had the heater on high. Carmen jingled a set of keys to his apartment while Alice, in the driver's seat, her hands still on the steering wheel, started singing along with "Silver Springs," which was playing on the oldies station.

"*Was I just a fool?*" she sang, backing up Stevie Nicks.

They were building up enough momentum to get out of the car.

There was a time when Nick's chaos and freefall seemed darkly glamorous to Alice. All those shady messages on his phone machine. His allusions to sordid evenings in the company of strangers. There was a time when she would have liked to see what one of those nights looked like. Now though, he no longer had a presence in the larger abyss. These days, most of his binges played out in his apartment.

Alice lifted her forehead off the steering wheel. "Now when I try to imagine a life for him, I can only see something very small. He shouldn't really have a car. It's only a matter of time before he runs into an abutment."

"Or a busload of singing schoolchildren," Carmen said. "He's very crafty about getting the club off. So that's not going to work anymore."

"Mom could rent him an apartment near stores, farther down on Clark or Broadway so he could manage his business on foot. He wouldn't have to work. He'd have no money for drugs, but he could drink beer in that way, you know, keep a little buzz going all day. He could be a neighborhood drunk. Do they still have those?"

Coming here was hard, but it was at least possible if she and Carmen did it together, spreading the horror around a little. But Carmen said she was done; this was her last mission.

"Cleaning up his mess just allows him to keep doing this. Plus I can't find anyone in there worth saving. Basically, he's gone. All that's left is a drug-eating, liquor-drinking machine. There are people out there who really want help in changing. I'd rather be doing some actual good for somebody."

"He saw the girl," Alice told Carmen now. "He saw her in time to steer the car out of her way. But he thought she was a magical apparition or something. He didn't want to change the channel. He just watched."

Carmen didn't say anything for a long time, then "You know I'm already done with him. This is for you. So let's go."

Alice hated the blast of ice she felt coming off Carmen. Like the Good Humor guy opening that little door in the side of his truck.

"Have you seen our brother?" Alice asked the old woman—Mrs. Nolan—who lived on the top floor, just above Nick. She was just coming out the front door. Alice tried to sound casual, by the by. This was made difficult by having to shout over the wind wailing its way around the courtyard.

"He fell. Out in front here the other day," Mrs. Nolan said. "He was trying to bring in some bottles. My son was over and he helped your brother up the stairs. That was Tuesday, maybe Monday. The walk was icy was the problem, I think."

* * *

Nick's staircase was depressing even before they got to what was sure to be his stupendously depressing apartment. The carpeting on the stairs was frayed to strings along the sides. The hallway was painted a landlord odd-lot color, a syrupy blue-green Alice called Ukrainian Maternity Hospital, 1952.

"Do you notice," she said to Carmen when they were on the first-floor landing, stomping the snow off their boots, "how polite people are, how much effort they put into explaining his behavior. Like: he fell. Or: he had the flu. Someone had to help him up. His hat blew off in the wind. It's like, remember those nice neighbors of Jeffrey Dahmer? How they offered him box fans to help him get rid of the bad smell—"

"It's going to be very bad up there today," Carmen said, peering up the staircase. She handed Alice a pair of latex gloves.

A familiar detritus of trouble started to present itself as soon as they got to the second floor. A scattering of beer bottles covered a thick stack of *Tribunes* piled tidily in front of Nick's door by one of the helpful neighbors. A fair amount of blood had been blotted up by the patch of carpet visible just inside. The smell as they forced themselves forward was a grim version of sweet.

Nick was going on three weeks inside this particular bender, with brief respites in hospitals, where he got put on hold with tranquilizers. The hospitals saw detox as helping someone make the transition from drunk to sober. But Nick was never sincerely on their program. He only went to the hospital when he ran out of the money he needed in order to stay high. When he came out of the tranquilizers they gave him to get through, it was hard for him to stabilize enough to get back to any kind of work, and so he fell again, each time sooner than the last. Sometimes he didn't care for the hospital they brought him to, and Alice would get a call in the middle of the night from a nurse or an administration person saying he left without being discharged, sometimes without his shoes. A couple of weeks ago the middle-of-the-night call came from Nick himself.

"Listen," he said.

"Yeah?"

"Three witches came in here tonight and tied me up." His voice was slurry with whatever they were giving him to bring him down.

"Are they still there?" Alice said.

"One is."

"Put her on."

Muffle and thud, bang and clatter, a receiver being passed, dropped, retrieved.

"Yesss?"—a deep, suspicious voice, like the Cheshire Cat.

"Did you tie my brother up?"

"We tied him *real* good."

"Thanks so much." Alice crawled back into bed for some peaceful sleep. It was always a good night when Nick was tied up. But then he got out.

"Mmmm," Carmen said, putting her nose into the air, as if something delicious were baking in the oven. Alice was both looking for Nick and afraid to find him. Each time they came over here like this, she thought it would be the time they'd find him dead. Often it was hard to tell right away. Like today. He lay in bed, absolutely still, naked. The TV roared. *Cagney & Lacey*—Alice spotted a boxed set of DVDs on the floor—were sharing an emotional moment that belied their tough exteriors.

His head was pretty badly banged up, a couple of deep cuts on his forehead, probably from a day or two ago, the blood now black and caked over. His body was stained with large, wine-colored bruises, his chest dotted with small, black rubber suction stickers left over from whatever monitoring machine he was hooked up to in the last hospital, which he left in an impromptu way. That was a week ago. The other thing that was hard to not notice was his penis, which was dark purple and, even folded up, huge. They had noticed this on previous visits. Also in the Polaroids that were usually lying around, souvenirs of festive activities between him and one or another of the hookers. Startling the first time, by now his dick was just another aspect of him that seemed beside the point. Carmen pulled the comforter over him, picked up a handful of Polaroids and started humming *Memories . . . light the corners of my mind,* then bent down over him and shouted "Hey!" into his ear.

Alice started to get scared. "Boocs?" she said, taking his hand, which was deadweight, but not cold. "Come on and get up." He finally stirred—slowly, carefully, as though he were in quicksand. He rolled over to the edge of the bed and started feeling around the carpet until he found a beer bottle with something left in it, drained it, then started looking for another.

Carmen grabbed him by one arm and pulled him up again.

"Not so fast, mister."

This time he grinned, impersonating sociability. His teeth were yellow and disturbingly furry. "You know—" he said, waggling his index finger at her, then lost the thought.

"You want to go to the hospital?" Alice said in a sparkly tone, as if he had a wealth of options and this was just the first one up for consideration.

A long wait, and then, "Maybe."

"See if you can get ready then," Carmen said.

He peered at her, then at Alice. As though neither of them was to be trusted, and he was coming up with a code for them to decipher, a password to stump them.

"Do you think you can manage a shower?" Carmen asked.

He got out of bed and wove toward the john, then turned around, and headed back to them.

"Hugs," he said, opening his arms.

"Uh—" Carmen said.

"We'll get back to you on that," Alice said. "We'll have our people call your people."

He turned toward the bathroom again. His butt hung like a small, empty sack behind him as he negotiated the hallway by bumping off its walls.

Alice looked into one of the pulled-out drawers of Nick's dresser. "Well, at least it's not total chaos. He does have systems of organization. Like, this would be the socks, pencil, and vomit drawer." What she was thinking was how will she be able to do this alone when Carmen drops out? Coming in here by herself would be a new level of aloneness, like falling out of a boat and being left to the sea.

Alice wandered out of the bedroom and into the kitchen. Inside the refrigerator a half-eaten (gnaw marks along one side), congealed steak was draped over one of the wire shelves. She did a quick scan of the apartment. A small end table had been toppled and smashed. She recognized this as one of the pieces of furniture Nick refinished so long ago, for when Olivia would get out of jail and come to him. A hundred bottles' worth of broken glass was strewn like sparkly green and brown gravel across the carpet. Two of her paintings from the prostitute series hung askew but didn't appear damaged. Even though the show was unpopular, the paintings were by now worth a fair amount. It was as she thought this that she noticed a blank space where a third one used to hang.

Each wave of destruction had further depleted the apartment. Stuff got broken or soiled beyond saving, or stolen by whoever came around while he was like this. This time she noticed his old telescope was gone. Nothing ever got replaced or fixed in here—just tossed out or set upright, wiped down maybe. Here and there were little swatches of his life, or of their childhood in common. Today Alice recognized a dishtowel on the kitchen counter that had drifted in from Loretta's kitchen, from that kitchen as it was thirty years ago. In the living room, maple bookcases he had made himself still held physics texts and astronomy journals, some with articles written by an earlier version of himself. His music was mostly "Best Of" compilations from the mainstream rock of his adolescence. Bad Company. Bob Seger. Earth, Wind & Fire.

On the top shelf of the bookcase was a framed photo of Nick and Olivia in shorts and polo shirts, laughing, standing in front of their Teardrop trailer—an image from the period when Nick seemed almost regular, close to happy. He had since moved so far from regular that the photo might as well be one of those old carnival tourist boards where you stick your head through and show up as a mermaid or hula dancer.

Maybe half an hour later, they had him out of the tub, where he had fallen. Dried and into some clothes—grimy khakis, a clean T-shirt and penny loafers, a parka. No socks, forget socks; his feet were too swollen. In the car he leaned against the passenger door like a sack of ball bearings.

"We need better equipment for this," Alice said, making a left turn to head south. "A winch. A tarp. A couple of burly helper guys."

"No," Carmen said from the backseat. "We need to stop doing this." From there she went into silent, full hard-ass mode.

"Do you want to try to get well?" Alice asked Nick.

"YES I DO," Nick said in a super-loud, robotic voice, then took the half can of flat Coke from her drink caddy and chugged most of it. "HERE," he shouted. He apparently hadn't got around to brushing his teeth; they were still encased in the yellow fur. "YOU CAN HAVE THE REST."

"Hey. Thanks," Alice said, putting the can back in its socket.

"This time," Carmen piped up from the backseat, "just try to go with the program, whatever it is."

It was easy to get a bad attitude at the hospital, though. Alice and Carmen both knew this. Triage did not favor drunks and addicts.

First, they took the guy with the ax in his head, then the baby with the fever, then the old man with the shooting pain in his arm, then the teenage girl having a psychotic break. Then, about ten more cases down the line, they took Nick. At Northwestern, if the wait got too long, he went across the street to Benihana and had a few beers to tide him over. Alice thought they must be really happy over there to see him come through the door.

In the past, Alice and Carmen used to go into the emergency room with him. More recently, they at least waited until he was admitted. By now, though, he had worn out his welcome at the nearby hospitals, and so tonight Alice pulled up in front of Haymarket, which wasn't a hospital; it was the hoboes' detox, the detox of last resort. This was the only place Carmen could find that would take him, and only because they took anyone. This time the sisters just stayed in the car and watched him teeter through the door.

"This makes me feel like such a terrible person," Alice said as they drove away.

"Hey," Carmen said. "Give us credit. We stopped the car. We didn't roll him out while we were driving by."

Their night wasn't over yet. They went back to where his car was parked. They came up with an alternative to locking his steering wheel with the Club. They would hide the car. Alice followed in her car as Carmen drove Nick's, its passenger-side mirror hanging by a wire and bouncing against the door as she went, its backseat littered with empties. Also the battered manila folders of X-rays he used to get pain pills out of sketchy doctors. They drove up to Carmen's neighborhood and parked Nick's car at the end of a street by a small factory.

By the time Alice dropped Carmen off, then got back to her own place, it was near four in the morning. The phone was ringing. It was Nick, of course. He was back at his apartment.

"No drugs. No Valium," he told her, no longer shouting. "Nothing at all at that crap-ass place. It's a punishment place. You're supposed to tough it out. Bite on a stick." In the background was the click and fizz of a beer can being opened, followed by what sounded like a water bubbler. Then another click and fizz.

"Do you think you could stop? Just for a while? You know, just give it a break?"

"Not really," he said.

port difficulties

The small pop of a cork being worked out of yet another bottle of wine sank Carmen's spirits. She and Rob were having dinner at the home of some friends, a meal that was going on forever. Actually, it had hit the forever mark about an hour ago. By now they had entered some further zone on the space/time continuum. Carmen wished these were friends of Rob's. That way she could enjoy how ridiculous they were instead of being mortified that they were friends of hers. Carmen had gone to Jane Addams for her MSW with Abby, now a grant writer, successful in a hands-off corner of social work where she would never have to touch a poor or crazy person. (Carmen had tried this herself, spending two years as the liaison for the homeless out of the mayor's office, but she'd hated the endless meetings with clean, fresh-smelling people, and the avalanche of paperwork, so she was back running a shelter, this time on the West Side, in a neighborhood that scared her anew every single day.) Abby's husband, Jeff, had recently become majorly rich in the PVC pipe business—innovative materials, rebuilding the infrastructure, blahblahblah, Carmen eventually ran out to the end of actually listening. She got away with a certain amount of inattention on account of her partial deafness. She didn't let everyone know that she now wore an in-ear, digital aid that had retrieved a bit of hearing in her bad ear that she'd assumed was dead and gone. Technology had jumped a little ahead of her in a nice way. When she tuned back in, she saw the subject had shifted, onto the sufferings Abby and Jeff endured in the cause of remodeling their kitchen and bathroom. Abby seemed a little embarrassed about this line of complaint, but Jeff was into it. He talked about it as though they were bombed, or victims of a landslide.

"Everything that could have gone wrong, did," he said.

Fortunately, their courage had seen them through the grim weeks when the granite for the counters was held up in Forti dei Marmi, the wood for the cabinets stuck in some port difficulties in Africa. Then the bread drawer arrived two inches too short to accommodate the particular baguette Abby gets in Wicker Park (at a small bakery that has no sign; you just have to know where it is). Then the carpenters disappeared completely on an unscheduled Florida vacation. But now, finally, the dust had settled and the drawer was remade and the unbearable standard chrome knobs were replaced with nickel.

Now that all was said and done, though, they were pleased, Abby told them, trying to bring the subject to a close. But there was no stopping Jeff. Abby eventually gave up, like a sufferer of Stockholm syndrome, in thrall to her captor. Jeff moved on to the artisans who were able to find time for Abby and Jeff in their busy schedules. These were specialists who were booked solid; no one could get them. Abby and Jeff got them, though. Jeff subscribed to a merit-badge view of life. His sash was filling up.

Carmen felt shackled to the evening. (*Back on the chain gang!* Chrissie Hynde sang in her head.) They hadn't even gotten to dessert. She had noticed a built-in espresso maker so there would surely be an elaborate cappuccino ceremony. As it turned out there was also a dessert ceremony. A soufflé was slowly on its way. Carmen had been tired coming into this social evening. She was phone banking for John Kerry in a ghostly town in western Michigan. Buchanan. Spirits ran high there. They already had their Kerry re-election voter list. She told

Jeff and Abby a little about the hard-working, small-town effort. The continuous transfusion of doughnuts and coffee, the separate room for the smoking volunteers.

"Too bad he listened to some image enhancer or whatever. Saluting off the prow of that boat," Jeff said. "That was where he lost my vote."

Until this moment, Carmen thought she didn't personally know anyone who was voting for Bush. Not to mention voting for him for a second term. The table talk hit a vacuum, like the startling thwup made by a hurtling train as it enters a tunnel. Abby turned the conversation toward the two years they recently spent in Guatemala, which PVC piping was bringing into the modern age.

"It must've been something," Carmen tried, "having all that voluptuous nature everywhere you turned."

And of course it was. Also the fruit was magnificent. And the two of them took up snorkeling, which changed their lives. And on and on in such a lulling way that Carmen was snapped to by Jeff's reference to a slowdown in pipe-laying on account of the lassitude of the "teeth-sucking natives." She felt chilled by this piece of code. She understood that if she or Rob picked up on this complaint, they would fall into a soft conversational circle of shared assumptions. She felt like Eddie Murphy in the old sketch from *Saturday Night Live* where he disguises himself as a white man to see what happens when the last black person gets off the bus, and finds they start mixing martinis and fox trotting.

Carmen looked to Rob, but he sat silent as a monk. At first she flared a little with anger, then saw that he wasn't being indifferent or cowardly, he was just totally tuned out. She could read him by now, the way he could sit and smile and nod, even inject little prompts into the conversation while he was in fact totally absorbed in his own thoughts. Sometimes she could even make a pretty good guess at what these thoughts were. In this particular moment she was almost certain he was thinking about a new promotion at MarcAntony—Revision—a section at the front of every salon where no appointment was necessary, only the impulse for immediate change.

Without backup, Carmen was on her own in the task of stopping Jeff in his tracks.

"What were you paying the workers?" she asked. "I'm just wondering if it might be easier to stop sucking your teeth and find your inner ambition if you're being paid something that might get you out of the hole of your life."

His expression lost its social composition as he saw the enemy approach.

"Right," he said. Slowly, as though the word had a dozen syllables.

"Free, free, good God Almighty—free at last!" She clutched Rob's arm to her side when they were out on the sidewalk, walking to the car through the pungent, wet-metal night air of autumn.

"Oh, he's not so bad." Rob avoided summary judgments. She usually counted this as one of his best qualities, but tonight it just made her feel totally alone. "I mean, I've heard worse. You hear everything in beauty shops. You learn to turn a deaf ear."

Then, "Oh, I'm sorry." His expression was so sincerely pained she had to laugh.

"Oh honey," she said. "Oh honey."

The night had been long and arduous. And pointless. She had not moved Jeff to think in a larger way about the world. She only pissed him off and put some final punctuation on an already run-on friendship. She was losing her belief in the possibility of changing people. It wasn't so much that they were in opposition to her, or that they held their own beliefs so strongly. Rather, they appeared to have lost interest in belief itself, as though belief were tennis, or French film. And this was so discouraging Carmen had to put a lid over the abyss or risk falling in.

"Hey," Rob said later, slipping under the covers next to her, trying to lift her spirits. "Tomorrow let's have big sex when we wake up. Read the paper in bed. Make pancakes. Not answer the phone. Let the rest of the world get along without us." He brushed her cheek with his knuckles, then sat her up, got her out of her bra and into one of his T-shirts.

"Alice called. Before. You were in the shower. I forgot to tell you. You were supposed to call her back. About your mother. I'm a terrible secretary." He turned out the light. "You should fire me."

touch and go

Loretta was not going without a fight, or at least a small scuffle. In her living will, she had checked the box saying she wanted all those extreme and heroic measures everyone else forgoes. She did not, she made clear, want her plug pulled.

And so Alice used connections and did some research and was trying to give her mother a death that was state-of-the-art. She had her hooked up with the best oncology department in the city. She had three specialists, was on a protocol so experimental that so far it had only been tried on mice and Loretta. Something like that. In the hospital, she had a private room with mahogany furniture, indirect lighting, maroon drapes, a window seat striped like a rep tie, the window itself affording a view of the lake.

Bags of thick, transparent plastic hung above the bed, also dangled beneath it. There was an industrial cast to this, as though Loretta was part of some manufacturing process, filtering the plentiful clear and pastel fluids dripping from the bags above the bed into the meager, viscous yellow and dark-green liquids filling the bags below. While she was at work in this way, resisting the firm pull of death, her progress and regress were chronicled by the orange numbers on one small black screen next to her bed, the blipping green line on another, accompanied by a thin, high-pitched beeping. Alice and Nick watched the numbers and the lines, listened to the beeps. They were waiting this out together.

When Loretta surfaced a little from the fog of drugs she began singing, softly but with jazzy, piano-bar inflections, *Do you know the muffin man?*

This prompted Nick to his feet to inspect today's IV bags, which were different from yesterday's.

"Excellent upgrade. Self-regulated morphine drip," he reported. Then tapped the control clutched in Loretta's hand. "A person could get a little trigger-happy."

"How's she doing?" Alice asked when Dr. Pryzbicki came into the room, pulled Loretta's folder out of the rack on the room door, then read the latest notes.

"It's pretty much touch and go at this point," the doctor said.

Dr. Pryzbicki then checked the bags and the orange readout and peered at the green line and listened with a stethoscope to their mother's breathing. In conclusion, she wrote something impressively detailed on a fresh page, then by way of leaving, patted Loretta's hand and told them all, "Just hang in there."

She turned in the doorway to say to Alice, "Of course, if you have any other questions—"

Alice unfolded herself from one of the visitor armchairs, left behind the book she was reading, and followed the doctor out of the room. They didn't talk the rest of the way down the hall to the small room where Dr. Pryzbicki—Diane—who was the resident on this floor on the overnight shift, slept when she got any free patch of time at all. They didn't talk once they were inside the room, which was over-air-conditioned and contained only a single cot. So far they hadn't used this. So far they'd only made out pressed hard against the door, which did not have a lock.

Technically Alice wasn't even attracted to Dr. Pryzbicki, who was too young, also overweight but not in any interesting way, and whose doctor coat was cheap and shiny and pilled, its pockets stuffed with pens, note pads, the translucent yellow tubing of the stethoscope coiling out. If this were a fantasy, Dr. Pryzbicki would be a little older and more sophisticated, tall and lean and dark and brooding. But even just the fact of her being a doctor, specifically the doctor in charge of these long nights of Loretta's death, eroticized her and impelled Alice to follow her to the little staff sleep room for these rushed necking sessions. She was disappointed to find out that Dr. Pryzbicki had a first name, although of course she would have to. Since that revelation, though, Alice had been trying to keep further confessions at bay. If she found out that Diane had a hobby or a vacation time-share, the fantasy would collapse in on itself.

"You are so hot," Dr. Pryzbicki said, dragging her lips down Alice's neck.

"Sometimes," Alice said, "and even in my hot moments, the heat hasn't always worked to my advantage. Sometimes it just jumps me a few squares into somewhere I really shouldn't be."

When Alice came back into Loretta's room, Nick was reading an astronomy journal, but with his free hand covering one of Loretta's.

"I got caught up in a discussion with the doctor. About success rates with this new infusion." She was lying just for the fun of it. "I lost track of time."

Nick waved off her excuse with a flippy hand. "You can lose track of it all you want. No problem. Time may just be a way we have of ordering events, a human construct. Some guys—some of the important guys—think everything may actually be happening simultaneously. We may have just put in time ourselves, so we don't get confused."

He had another subject he wanted to bring up for discussion. He had been throwing money at a couple of tough hookers, both named Mandy. Now he told Alice he had fallen in love with one of them.

"I'm just guessing," Alice said. "It's Mandy, isn't it?"

He pulled a folded snapshot from his wallet and handed it to Alice. "What do you think?"

"She wears an awful lot of makeup for someone in her underwear."

Loretta's illness had brought Alice and Nick into a closeness that, for once, didn't have anything to do with his troubles. It was a free, floating sort of intimacy, as though they were sitting inside one of the rainy-day card table tents of their childhood. Once they started shuffling through shared memories, though, they found they had quite different versions. Tonight, Nick went into a long rhapsody about his days on a little league team called the Boilermakers, playing shortstop in games to which Horace never came. Apparently it was Carmen who helped him, tossing sock balls to teach him to catch without fear.

Alice was surprised at being unable to retrieve this memory. Back in those days, she kept a close watch on her siblings, the three of them partners in a buddy system critical to getting them through Horace's despotic reign. Loretta's part in this only required her to sacrifice her children to her marriage.

What Alice and Nick and Carmen held on to from the long days before they were allowed to leave their bad childhoods was different for each of them. Alice's own indelible moment didn't even belong to her. It was watching Horace cuff Nick, who was maybe seven or eight, on the side of the head, hard but under the guise of genial roughhousing.

"That's for nothing," he said. "Wait until you see what happens when you actually do something." The smooth way he said this made Alice sure he had heard the line somewhere, and was trying out the joke at home, for a little extra fun. Like when he would suggest to one or the other of them, "Why don't you go outside and play in traffic?"

The cuffing moment still came to mind from time to time. A few weeks ago she read a terrible news item about hunting resorts stocked with bears drugged to make them slower, goofier, easier to shoot. And the story, of course, made her think about the bears, but it also made her think about that capricious whack, and the moment immediately following when Nick stood cupping his reddening ear with one hand, his fear stained with confusion. He didn't get it yet, that he had already been designated by Horace as the family fuckup. She could also see clearly the next moment in which Loretta looked up vaguely from the fat paperback she'd been reading to say, "You listen to your father now. Next time there's going to be real trouble."

And now Horace was in the end stages of dementia. He lived in a nursing home on Fullerton. He confused the shows on TV with the commercials. He had moved beyond the reach of their hatred.

Their mother, they had forgiven more or less—Alice more, Nick a little less. Carmen not at all. Carmen thought there was a point to not forgiving. Alice was more romantic. Her belief system still included changes of heart, overdue apologies, dramatic reconciliations, resolved misunderstandings. For her, hanging around at the hospital was mostly waiting for her mother to come up with something last-minute and significant, something that would explain her distracted, casually irresponsible version of parenting and reveal a hidden devotion to her children, particularly to Alice. Carmen, of course, would never allow herself this sort of cheesy fantasy. She had given up on Loretta long ago, had absolutely no expectations of her anymore. If she came to visit, she would be doing this for Alice. She both envied and pitied Carmen—traveling always on firm, flat ground, breathing in the fresh, gusting air of reality. Power walking through life.

"I was thinking of asking Mandy to come here to the hospital with me," Nick said to Alice after a long while of silent consideration. "To kind of bring her more into my life."

Alice didn't bother to address this.

Nick and Alice were only alone in the hospital room at night. During the day, Loretta had a brisk traffic of visitors. Agents from her Re/Max days. In these past few years of being no longer really a wife, but not actually widowed either, Loretta had blossomed in unexpected ways and had acquired a surprising new circle of acquaintances. Once Horace, a strenuous atheist, was no longer around to be withering about her religious impulses, she joined a Presbyterian congregation, which turned out to be a high-yield community in terms of corporal works of mercy. These women took "visit the sick" seriously. They showed up with soft pillowcases and verbena water they misted around Loretta's head. They read to her from religious novels, books she would have ridiculed at any previous point in her life.

Another surprise: Despite all the years spent at the center of a hipster crowd, Loretta had belatedly taken up the corniest possible interest—ballroom dancing. Two dapper guys—one old, one disconcertingly only in his forties—had turned up as frequent bedside visitors these past days. From them Alice and Nick had learned of their mother's reputation on the dance floor, particularly with the tango and West Coast swing. Alice thought this was kind of sweet, but it bugged the hell out of Carmen—Loretta having moved on, not to an old age filled with sorrow and regret, but rather to catching a second wind—twirling and dipping in God's grace, and a little limelight.

Alice had come to Diane's apartment. She'd brought along a video of *Lianna,* the old John Sayles movie. She thought this would come off as touching and innocent, that she could show Diane something of what it was like to come out when she, Alice, did. That this would serve as a bridge between them. Instead, she saw maybe twenty minutes in, that it was way too late to watch *Lianna.* When it got to a hideously embarrassing scene in a dingy dyke bar, everyone lurking and leering, Diane, like a good student, said, "This is kind of like Colonial Williamsburg. You know—pioneer folkways."

Alice did not want Diane to be the appreciative tourist. She did not herself want to be the docent in the dirndl skirt. She flipped *Lianna* off with the remote and they got down to business.

* * *

A few afternoons later, Diane was naked on a creamy leather sofa, where she had been quite commanding and masterful for the past hour or so. Initially Alice had hoped to keep this affair absolutely superficial, but everything had moved rapidly in an unexpected direction. She had no understanding of her attraction to Dr. Pryzbicki. It seemed, by this late-ish point, that she should have a type or at least some guidelines for whom she would get into bed with. Instead she still wound up in situations like this one. Not as often as when she was younger, but still.

"I'd better get back to the hospital," she said, pulling herself up against the arm of the sofa, dragging Diane, who was on top, along with her, the air around them thick with sex and sofa leather. "How do you think my mother's doing?"

Diane cocked her head. "Oh boy. I'd say at this point, your mother is kind of beyond *doing*. We're taking her off the protocol. How can I put this? You know those old doctor-patient jokes? Like the patient asks his doctor, 'How am I doing?' and the doctor says, 'Well, I'm sorry but you only have ten to live.' And the patient says, 'Ten what?' And the doctor says, 'Nine. Eight. Seven—'" Diane looked at Alice earnestly with squinty eyes and said, "I hope I'm not speaking too frankly."

Loretta slipped in and out of consciousness—back and forth between the uninteresting world of this hospital room and a pageant of scenes from her earliest years. She called out to her own mother, dead now for decades. It wasn't a cry of distress, rather a joyous shout, as though she was asking her to watch how high she could make herself go on a swing set.

"She's way back there," Alice said to Carmen, who had finally come to the hospital. She was just back from three days in New Orleans. She had gotten pissed off watching Katrina on TV, and rallied Jean to rent a bread truck with her. They went to Costco and filled the truck with all the bottled water it could hold. Then they just drove down.

"It's not an island in the Pacific, for Christ's sake," Carmen said. "It's like two states away."

And apparently they were able to get through and unload the water someplace where it did some good. Rob was really upset. Carmen did this without telling him in advance, just left a note. He said you couldn't be married and be a unilateral operator. Carmen said her political and social work were part of who she was. "I can't see something so wrong and not do anything about it. I'd start not liking myself."

She had come to the hospital for Alice. Through the revelations of Jungian analysis and studying the texts of her dreams, Carmen had dispatched Loretta to a place where she didn't have to expend energy hating her. Her way of talking about Loretta now was to damn her lightly with the faintest praise possible. "Well, she didn't drown us in the bathtub. She didn't leave us on the median strip on the highway," she would say. Or, "She didn't sell us on the black market for parts like that Russian woman with her grandson."

Alice gave it her best shot. "Look, I know she could have done better. But she was trapped under Horace's thumb. Women in her generation had to hitch their wagon to a guy they thought would take them someplace. You know about her childhood. They didn't have enough chairs for everyone at dinner. Some of the kids had to stand. She slept in the basement, by the furnace for warmth; she and Aunt Ella."

But Carmen was not impressed with the lack of chairs or the basement sleeping. She didn't find these extenuating circumstances. "She looks so harmless. Imagine that," Carmen said now, as they watched Loretta wave across the backyard of her girlhood.

Alice was in the shower with Diane. They'd been there awhile, since Alice followed Diane home in the morning when her shift was over. The water had run down from hot to lukewarm. They were by now well beyond frolicsome lathering and rinsing.

"Don't stop," Alice said.

"I might have to, though," Diane said. "Stopping might be the best thing for you."

"No," Alice said in a voice so small and distant she could hear it echo vaguely off the shower tiles. Alice was falling into something soft-focus and emotion-bearing with Dr. Pryzbicki, something she could not have predicted. She had been toppled by kindness. Outside of bed, or the shower, where Diane withheld to put a little spin on things, she was generous in a bounding way. It had only been two weeks, but already there had been small presents—unusual cut flowers from a Japanese shop on Belmont, a book of poetry. *Autobiography of Red.* But also a whole new category of sideswiping gesture. Like yesterday, on her day off, she asked to borrow Alice's car and brought it back washed, waxed, oil changed, tires rotated.

Diane wasn't any sort of person Alice ever thought she'd be interested in. Alice had spent most of her adulthood longing for Maude or falling for and recovering from adventures with Maude surrogates—good-looking, lightly cruel, mercurial women, all of whom seemed initially different from one another, movies in a darkened theater, opening against the backdrop of this or that exotic locale, stories so filled with potential she could become euphoric imagining herself into them. By their endings, though, these stories turned out to just be slightly different versions of the same story—an essentially dull tale pumped up with bursts of emotional squandering. Still, all along this bumpy way, the idea of Diane had never occurred to Alice. She hadn't considered someone serious and constant, someone who wouldn't make her nervous.

Diane knew nothing about art. Her apartment was decorated with pre-framed prints from Bed, Bath & Beyond. Parisian boulevard in the living room, water lilies over the bed, giant radish in the kitchen. When they met, she had no idea who Alice was. When Alice said "painter," Diane at first thought roller and scaffold. Even now she didn't really understand that in another—albeit small—part of the universe, Alice was famous. And, if she did understand, she wouldn't care. She would just be happy Alice gets to do what she likes.

Diane wasn't an oncologist, only rotating through on her way to becoming an emergency room doctor. She liked the frontline aspect of doing good. She also wanted to take care of Alice. If you'd asked Alice a couple of weeks ago, this wouldn't have sounded appealing. Now, she wasn't so sure.

When Loretta died, she did it so quickly no one could get there in time. Alice, who had gone home to get a night of something better than chair sleep, got a call at 3:30 in the morning from Diane, who was on duty and had just signed the death certificate. Alice called Nick but there was no answer, then tried Carmen, but just got voicemail. Rob battled insomnia with a white noise machine set to Tropical Rain Forest; once the machine was on it was raining like crazy in Brazil and you couldn't reach them. Which left Alice heading down to the hospital alone. She expected to find Loretta in some grim basement morgue, slid by an attendant from a wall cabinet on a steel body tray, her skin gray eliding into blue. In fact, her mother was still in her deluxe room, in the bed with the mahogany headboard. The machines and bags of fluids were gone, though, there being nothing left to monitor or measure. Loretta's face held no expression at all. She didn't look peaceful or angelic, only as though she was off somewhere else and had left herself behind.

Alice took her mother's cooling hand and waited for something significant and terrifying to open up around them. What she saw instead was that death wasn't going to offer much of anything, just reshape the longing for Loretta that Alice had always carried. She would remain as elusive in death as she had been in life; missing her would just seem more appropriate. Maybe Alice had been looking for the wrong person, maybe the mother she had sought for so long had turned a corner in the supermarket when Alice was small and the person she caught up with in produce was a woman who was willing to pitch in a little, but would always remain a stranger.

◆ ◆ ◆

Alice went over to Nick's apartment, buzzed twice, then let herself in with her key. It was always a little scary going in. Today a familiar bayberry aroma filled the place, the product of a large candle on the scarred Formica counter that separated the living room from the kitchen. The ceiling above the designated candle-burning spot was black with thick, furry soot.

Nick was sitting on the sofa in front of his TV, which was even larger than his old one, its picture gigantic and blurry in an aquatic way. Nick had bought it off QVC. "I was lucky to get it," he'd told her. "They only had twelve left by the time I got through."

He looked over his shoulder at Alice from a vast painless place.

"This, by the way, is a great movie." He nodded toward the TV, although the DVD—she recognized it as *Bound*—was skipping, breaking down from Gina Gershon into a thousand pieces of confetti, then reassembling once again into Gina Gershon. Her lips, magnified on the large screen, were nearly the size of throw pillows.

"Listen. Mom died."

"I know. Your friend the doctor called. She is a very persistent ringer." And then he went silent for so long Alice began to think he was preparing to offer something important. But when he finally spoke, it was to say, "Do you want an ice cream treat? I have tons in the freezer."

She got a Nutty Buddy and took the chair across from him. "I love these," she said when she was halfway through. She didn't realize she was crying until her face was completely wet.

Loretta wanted to be sent off from a funeral home in Old Town. She left instructions about everything. She wanted to be laid out in an open casket, which was disturbing to Carmen.

"Who does this anymore?" she said to Alice as they sat in Chapel Number Two. "I mean outside of Sicily?"

"Who cares, though, really?" Alice countered. "All her chums can see her one last time. And she looks pretty good. I mean, they did a nice job. The makeup and all."

"What are you even saying?" Carmen said. "She looks dead. I don't even know what to say about her now." And then all of a sudden, Carmen was weeping, then grabbing tissues from one of the many boxes set out all around the room to manage exactly this sort of flaring and unbidden emotion. She had clearly surprised herself.

"Well," Alice said, borrowing Carmen's part, "I guess we could say she didn't lock us in the cellar and make us eat dirt."

They looked around the room, which was decorated to resemble a small church.

"Where's you-know-who?" Carmen said. Nick's absence had just occurred to her.

"Indisposed. And for once, I don't have any emotion to spare for his relapse."

"You couldn't get him to come over?"

"I tried. You could try if you want. Go over there. I don't think he'll straighten out, but you could have an ice cream treat."

The funeral home asked for photos of the deceased, which had been slipped into frames and now cozily cluttered the tables in the foyer of the chapel. The one Alice had them put on the prayer cards was a shot of Loretta in her fifties, her deep-tanning years. Her teeth and the whites of her eyes popped out, as though electrically illuminated.

The first of the mourners began to drift in. The Old Town bohemian crowd from the early days of her marriage was present in faint outline—a man in a beret and a wispy ponytail, a woman in black chaps and a bolero jacket, a wide hat with a heavy veil. Alice recognized her; it was Cindy Beecham. Larry and Giselle Zorn arrived, natty and stylish, although the style was thirty years out of date. Their glasses were huge. Others of the old gang were absent because of illness, or due to being already dead themselves. Horace wasn't invited; he no longer remembered who Loretta was so her death would mean nothing to him.

The largest contingent of those in attendance was Loretta's new replacement friends—women from her church as well as the snappy dance partners. Behind them Alice spotted an aunt and windbag uncle she would just as soon duck.

"Look," Carmen said, putting a hand on Alice's arm, directing her attention to the other entrance. "Isn't that Mom's doctor? From the hospital? She must be so dedicated. To follow through like this."

At the funeral, the front pew was filled with Rob and Heather, Gabe, then Carmen and Alice, who sat with Nick between them. Carmen had gone over to his apartment, got him to put on a sport jacket, and drove him over. He looked as though he was about to come out of his skin. He muttered something about having to leave for an appointment. Carmen clamped a hand on his thigh.

"I'm sorry. You're going to have to do this. We're all doing this and then we'll be done."

On Tuesday, Alice invited Dr. Pryzbicki over. She fixed a little dinner, or rather picked up a carton of duck tortilla soup from a pricey new restaurant across the street. She poured the soup into a pot, then chopped up an avocado and left the chunks out on a cutting board so they'd look like a last step she hadn't taken yet. Alice was an inspired faux cook. She had a small repertoire of these tricks up her sleeve. For potlucks, which used to be such a cornerstone of lesbian social life, she would line an old pie plate with waxed paper (her touch of genius), arrange a boxful of KFC pieces inside, then cover the whole thing with a checkered napkin.

Diane said "Mmm. Smells good in here." She probably needed to be put into the girlfriend category. Alice was being forced to abandon the initial plan (so perfect in a small way) to have a sleazy affair with her. She worried she was following Diane down some path just because it was easy. No stones or sharp inclines. Like what Carmen had with Rob. She feared she had traded passion for this, lost something intrinsic to herself. To make this case, though, she would have to ignore how poorly passion had served her.

Diane had brought along Ed, a short black dog her neighbor found in a garbage can behind her building and she had been keeping in a temporary way that seemed to be turning into permanent. The dog was an indeterminate mix with a luxuriously plush coat, a sweet lab head, a stocky body set on spaniel legs.

A purely wonderful moment gathered up. Alice could see it forming—the new dog and Diane, Etta James on the stereo, the avocado chunks still vibrantly green on the counter, ready to garnish—everything full of small promise and beginning. She tried to stare hard past all this, down the road to the patch where this would end badly. But the view was obscured by hope and distance, and by the mist that always lies over the new. They would get there, though, Alice tried to reassure herself. They just needed a little time.

Diane shouted, "Watch out! Here he comes."

Ed the dog was high on his new life outside the trashcan. Set loose in Alice's loft, he immediately disappeared into the shadows of her studio. Now he reappeared and was trying to work up some speed despite his shortness of leg. He ran in a rocking horse canter across the vast old wood floor of the loft, put on the brakes as he skidded to a stop in front of Alice and Diane, then looked up at them, super-ready for whatever came next. The usual fog hanging over Alice's future lifted a bit.

the excellent sandwich

Nick sailed through a pocket of industrial haze south of the city. Astronauts described the smell of the universe as something like this—sparks off metal, and why not, it was a forge, all about creation and destruction. He was on his way to the exurbia of St. Louis.

He stopped at a 7-Eleven. They had a little sandwich he liked—peanut butter and jelly, but with the crusts cut off, the edges of the white bread pinched together to make a little square pad of delicious. He got two of these and a Coke, then, still in the parking lot, smashed two OxyContins on the dash with the can.

Shanna Redman lived in an apartment in a bare-basics building in a nondescript development near nothing. Sometimes he tried to figure who else lived here and why. The developers tried to liven things up with a Parisian motif. Shanna lived on rue Jacob, just off the Boulevard St-Germain. He had been visiting her for more than twenty years now. She used to live in a mobile-home community, so this was a step up. Until recently she had an office manager job at a factory that manufactured something crucial to something else. He forgot what either of these things was.

But she didn't work anymore. She had cancer of everything. She called him yesterday. She had something for him.

"Hey," he said when she answered the door. Always skinny, she was scary thin now, and traveled with an oxygen tank on a small set of wheels behind her. From the smell of things, though, she was still a smoker.

"Boy, you look terrible," she pre-empted him. "Have you been sick?"

"Just a little flu."

"Well, I'm sorry you had to drive down on such short notice. I'll make some coffee."

"No, let me."

They talked about her son, who now drove a truck for Budweiser.

"Good money," she said. "Although you couldn't pay me a million a year to wind around through the city in that huge thing, backing up into alleys with everyone honking." She paused to catch her breath, then, "They tell me I don't have long, and I wanted to give you something, you know, before—. She has never left me, you know. She's kept in touch. Sometimes she whispers to me. Sometimes she's in my dreams."

"She's in everybody's dreams. She's the star of all our dreams."

"In mine, she's running down a street of bricks, or stones. It's a hot place, and it's night and raining and the stones are slippery, but she's a little lighter than air, or there's less gravity in this place, and so she doesn't fall, she only slides along, laughing all the way. I don't know. Maybe she's giving me this dream from wherever she is now. So I can see something besides her running in front of that car."

"No one saw her," he lied. He also did not mention that they were driving with only the fog lamps on.

"She was such a careless kid. Played on construction sites, climbed high into trees. Never looked both ways like I told her to. You can tell them that. The others. Not that it was her fault. But it wasn't all theirs either."

"I will. I'll tell them." With a superior painkiller surging through him, he suddenly felt like a winged messenger. He would bring this dispensation back with him.

She had to stop talking to cough into a paper towel. She kept a roll by her side on the sofa, a wastebasket on the floor nearby. "Sorry."

"You have the cancer. You don't have to be sorry." He took advantage of her revelatory mood. "Why do you think she was heading home in the middle of the night?"

"Oh, I'm sure she just got fed up with the racket over there at her friend Summer's house. They fought something terrible, Summer's folks. The cops were always going out there to break things up. But they were decent to their kids. At home Casey was always getting on Terry's last nerve. And I catered to him in those days. That is my lasting shame, that's why I think she was taken away from me. I didn't defend her against him. The best I could do was let her go out whenever she wanted, wherever. Wait here a minute."

She got up and wheeled the small tank behind her into the bedroom. When she came back, without the tank, she sat down next to Nick, heavily for someone who was really just a sack of bones, as if she had landed in a parachute. She set on his lap a pair of beaded Indian moccasins atop a small square of folded clothing. Blue jean shorts and a madras shirt; he remembered the pink and green plaid so clearly it shocked him, as though the accident had happened last night.

"I couldn't part with these. Couldn't even wash them, so it's all still there, the blood and dirt. Anyway I want you to have them." She lit up a cigarette. "I just wanted you to know how much it's meant to me. That you never forgot."

"No one's forgotten," he told her.

And then Shanna wasn't talking, just smoking. Smoking and peering hard at him.

"You're high as a kite, aren't you?"

"Sorry."

"No, it's all right. I know you're a junkie. And I know you've lied to me, so we could keep talking, so I wouldn't blame you. But the thing is, I've moved beyond blaming anyone. And she's beyond it, too. I got that from her. What happened that night was what was going to happen. It's done. You're forgiven. She's forgiven all of us. She's let us go."

He understood what she was saying, but got lost in trying to find an emotional response. For once he wanted to feel something. He sat for a long time with the girl's clothes and shoes on his lap, waiting for this to happen. But the drugs obscured the way, both hiding the thing itself while turning up all the colors around it. And then everything disintegrated, and he was floating way above the accident and the mother and the girl.

the joke about the complaining monk

So little had come through with his body on the flight from California. Alice was told there was a wallet, but only its contents had arrived, in an envelope, and they were meager. She opened the envelope and shook the lot onto Carmen's kitchen table. A WorldPerks Visa card. (Later they would see the statement for the three-week free fall between his departure from the last-ditch rehab place in San Diego and his arrival at the alley behind the flower shop. They would make a calendar and a map. Alice's gallerist in L.A. would drive down and take photos of the Dumpster he hid behind to die.) A jail release slip. A plastic keycard from Arnold's Motel. A receipt for a $60 cab ride.

"He was really going to need a receipt," Alice said, then, "He liked Southern California. I think because of how close it was to Tijuana. Once he told me you could get anything down there. I didn't want to ask what that included. For the first time I was frightened to know."

"His watch isn't here," Carmen said. The thinnest lozenge of gold, its leather band soft as skin at the inside of the wrist. Horace's watch. Nick always wore it.

"I think when your lifestyle includes evenings spent unconscious in alleys, you can't really expect that your jewelry collection won't suffer."

Stuck inside the envelope so Alice had to reach in and pull them out were two identical passport photos. Headshots. In them he looked as if he had either been badly beaten, or taken a dead fall from the ankles. His high, narrow forehead was covered with raked scrapes and scabs. One eye was swollen nearly shut, puffy and blue and yellow. Although he was staring straight at the camera, his nose—broken and reset—had this time been dislodged into profile; it sat a little sideways on his face. It was a scary picture. You would be frightened of this person, also frightened for him.

It was hard to stop looking at the photos. They hadn't seen his body yet. The funeral home was making him as presentable as possible.

"Maybe," Carmen said, "he was trying to get together some new ID after they took his license away." She tapped a fingertip on one photo, then the other.

"I showed them to Diane before I came over," Alice said. "She said she's seen this stuff in the ER. Drunks and junkies in a bad way get a picture taken and keep it on them. In case they're not recognizable when they're found."

"Well, that's considerate of them," Carmen said. "He was circling the drain for so long. I think I started thinking the circling was the important part, not the drain. But it turns out he was just ordinarily mortal after all. I really believe letting him fall was the right thing to do, all the literature supports that. It's just a little tough sitting with my decision."

"It was hard to know how far down he was. He was such a hilarious optimist. The first time he called me from the bad motel, he said he was suicidal, but that it was a really nice room, considering. The next time I asked him what he was doing and he said he was just watching a movie, but it was a pretty good movie actually."

Carmen said, "Remember that time he wound up in the Salvation Army detox? Up in Minneapolis? And afterward I asked him how it was and he told me, 'weird people, but incredibly good cheesy eggs.'" After a long silence, she added, "There should be a word for us. Some variant of 'orphans.'"

* * *

When they had given up on making each other feel less lonely, Alice left Carmen's house and sat out front inside her car. A Metra train rushed by, heading north. She put the heat on high and fished her cell from her jacket pocket and speed dialed Nick's number. It rang in a gutter somewhere in San Diego, long since out of juice, but his voice-mail was still taking messages. She listened to his voice, then waited for the beep, then told him an old joke he loved, the one about the complaining monk.

addison stop

Gabe finished his call to Donna, telling her he was on his way home, then put his cell in his pocket, took off his shades—a new pair he'd found in Florence, with frames the exact color of Scotch tape—and exchanged them for untinted glasses. He put his earbuds in and waited for a train north. A crowd had accumulated on the other side. It was election day and in anticipation of the Chicagoan winning, much of the city was heading down to the giant rally. Although it was the first Tuesday in November, the weather was pure September, as though God were providing congenial weather for the event.

Gabe was going in the opposite direction, north toward his wife and small son. He listened, through the buds, to Rufus Wainwright. His thoughts were on home; he had disengaged from the annoyances of public transport. And so he didn't see, until just as his train was pulling up, that his mother stood in the small crowd across the tracks, on the southbound platform. She was holding a pole wound up in blue cloth. Unfurled—he knew without seeing that its message was HOPE. After all her disappointments, she had been rewarded with this man she thought would turn things around. We'll see, he thought.

He moved behind a pillar and a fat teenager. He never saw her from a distance like this, when she was unaware of being observed. She was wearing black pants and shirt, her demonstration uniform. Sneakers. A ball cap. She was reading a book. He could see the cover, which was a photograph of an old woman—for sure a woman who struggled up some steep ladder, or against all odds led an important movement, or organized a union. Carmen was still so earnest, so totally ridiculous.

His train pulled up. He boarded, noticing how humid it was inside the El car, how thick the air was. He stood watching her out the window; he saw that she was looking up, her thoughts broken by the noise. She looked down the track on her side to see if anything was coming, then went back to her book. If she had looked instead through the window of the train, she might have glimpsed his huge, crazy love for her, before he recalibrated his expression, turning down the volume to what was bearable in the give and take between them.

an opposite of iceland

"Have you always lived here?" the client asked, over the music Olivia kept at a medium-high volume, to discourage conversation. Plus she liked this song, "Cigarettes and Chocolate Milk."

But this client, a tourist, was aggressively chatty. Chatty clients posed a problem for Olivia.

"No." Olivia tried to pronounce this so the period was audible.

"You have an accent. I'm trying to pin it down."

Olivia knew the woman meant the wide-open Midwestern sprawl that still inhabited the corners of her speech.

"Actually, originally," Olivia said, "I'm from Iceland." This was usually a reliable closer. Either the client understood that Olivia wasn't interested in opening up. Or she knew nothing about Iceland, except maybe the airline, maybe Björk.

Iceland was an opposite of this place.

Olivia survived in the over-congenial atmosphere of the salon by steering toward impersonal topics. Movies. Local restaurants. Celebrity marriages and divorces and ridiculous baby names. She had chosen to work in a tourist destination where her clients wouldn't be regulars, where social adhesion was minimal.

She gave this woman a really great haircut. She looked twice as good as she did coming in here, and she saw this, which was nice. On her way out, she folded a bill, an extremely generous tip, and slipped it into the pocket of Olivia's jacket.

This was her last appointment of the day. She went around the shop shutting windows. A strong, salted breeze was coming in off the sea, washing through the palms and hibiscus.

Her right foot dragged a little as she tidied up the shop, swept clippings into a neat pile. A small neurological problem; it only came up at the end of long days. Most of the time she could counter it. This was a very upscale salon, and no one wanted to see Igor slogging around, rattling his chains. She had worked hard at creating a professional persona of cool efficiency. She wore only dark clothing—black and subtly different shades of navy. Her hair, which had gone to gray, was bleached up to white and cropped. She had changed her name, Google-proofed herself. She was now Olivia Li.

She saw a documentary a few years back about a couple of the Manson girls. They were old ladies now, still in prison. They'd never get out. Sharon Tate's sister came to all their parole hearings. One of the Manson chicks said to the interviewer that she had to, at this point, consider the possibility that her life had been a waste.

Olivia was not in that psychological place. Prisons took all sorts of shapes, and she understood she lived in a self-delineated confinement. But this was not punishment, was not about guilt. Guilt, she discovered early on, was the easiest, the simplest response. Much more complicated was living past guilt, bearing the permanence, accommodating the weight of having done something terrible and completely undoable.

Her circumscription was more drawing an invisible line around herself and staying inside that small circle. There was comfort in this.

At the moment, she wasn't thinking about any of this. Her mind was nearly empty, drained by the hectic day. She was tired and had no plans for the evening beyond fixing a salad, hanging out with her cats.

She shut off the remaining lights, grabbed her bag and her rain poncho and headed out, locking the door behind her. It had rained off and on all day, typical in this place, this season. The rain had stopped for the moment, but it would start again soon. Dark night clouds were just barely holding it back, and the plants and flowers and air were luridly enlivened, as if in apprehension of the whooshing storm to come.

Someone was sitting on the steps, a woman—maybe a girl, Olivia couldn't tell from behind—talking softly on her cell phone, laughing, picking at little beads on her shoes, beat-up moccasins. In trying to step around her, Olivia slipped a little where the old stone was slick with moss.

Righting herself, she grabbed the girl's shoulder, clutched the thin, pink and green plaid fabric of her shirt. "Oh. Sorry," she said.

The girl turned slightly and reached up, held Olivia's forearm to steady her.

"There. You're okay now," she said, then into the phone, "No, I was just talking to someone here."

acknowledgments

My gratitude:

to Peter Cieply, Sheila Daley, Lyn DelliQuadri, Janet Desaulniers, Mary Kay Kammer, Sara Levine, Judy Markey, Steve McCauley, Ellen McGarrahan, Barbara Mulvanny, Mike Ramsburg, Sarah Terez Rosenblum, and Sharon Sheehe Stark for their sharp readings and excellent criticism

to the Illinois Arts Council for its generous support

to Larry Geni for casting an astronomer's gaze on the manuscript

to Joy Harris for ninja agentry

to Trish Todd for zen master editing

and to Jessie Ewing for kindness and surprise.